"The Sime stories are set in a future in which humanity has split into two sub-species, the Simes and Gens. The Gens produce 'selyn,' a form of energy the Simes need to survive and for the transfer of which they have retractable tentacles in their arms. The series chronicles the progress of the Sime-Gen relationship over the centuries from predator-prey to a more just symbiosis. This sixth book in the series concerns Laneff, a Sime scientist who wants to further that progress by finding a way to establish prenatally (rather than in adolescence) whether a child will be Gen or Sime.

"The resulting story is typical of the series and should please those who have enjoyed it thus far. The effort Lichtenberg has put into exploring the ramifications of her basic idea is impressive. . . ."

—Publishers Weekly

D1522325

ACKNOWLEDGMENTS

When Jean Lorrah saw *Raiders of the Lost Ark*, she was inspired to write a book of nonstop, breathless action: *Dragon Lord of the Savage Empire*. She also insisted that I see the movie because I needed to use the same effect in this book. Well, I think I got the "breathless," not the "action." But that's not Jean's fault. She tried.

Thanks also go to the editors and publishers of the three Sime/Gen fanzines: Karen and Bruce Litman, who put out issues of *Companion in Zeor* despite financial and physical crises; Jean Airey, who edits *Ambrov Zeor* in Ohio, far from the Executive Editor, Anne Pinzow; and Katie Filipowicz, who hated the first two drafts of *RenSime* and made me work until I got it right. Katie has culled segments from the discarded drafts for printing in *Zeor Forum* and the other zines. (For information, send a business-size self-addressed stamped envelope to *Ambrov Zeor*, Dept. RN, Box 290, Monsey, N.Y. 10952.)

And thanks also go to all the Sime/Gen readers whose letters have helped to develop individual books, and the whole series. For this book, special thanks go to Howard Wilkins and Judith Segal, who read the final draft. My personal gratitude goes to anyone who will comment on *RenSime* or any other Sime/Gen story. Please write me through *Ambrov Zeor*, address above. I'm especially eager to know which book you would like to see next in the Sime/Gen Universe.

Jacqueline Lichtenberg
Spring Valley, New York

RENSIME

Jacqueline Lichtenberg

DAW BOOKS, INC.

DONALD A. WOLLHEIM, PUBLISHER

1633 Broadway, New York, NY 10019

TO
Ray H. Block
May He Rest in Peace

First DAW Printing, December 1984

1   2   3   4   5   6   7   8   9

PRINTED IN U.S.A.

CONTENTS

1983 by Jacqueline Lichtenberg
A DAW Book, by arrangement with Doubleday & Co., Inc.
All Rights Reserved

PUBLIC DISPLAY

Even in the last moments before dawn, the flow of mourners did not slacken. The colonnaded rotunda echoed with the soft rustle of formal Householding capes, their bright colors picked out by the newscamera lights. The public filed by the open coffin to bid goodbye to an era in Sime/Gen history and to rededicate themselves to an idealistic dream.

Now, Laneff dared to hope she was about to make her own dream a part of the new era. At the private, guarded entrance to the rotunda, she presented her pass to the armed honor guard. "Laneff Farris ambrov Sat'htine," she said crisply. "Mairis Farris wishes to see me."

"He is standing vigil. He is not to be disturbed," claimed the Sime woman.

"The pass says immediately," argued Laneff, trying to keep the edge out of her voice. She was too close to need to allow herself the luxury of a temper. Nevertheless, she felt her tentacles knotting with the tension.

The guard couldn't help noticing Laneff's state, even as she examined the pass. Then she nodded. "I'll take this to him, but you'd better wait out here. The emotional nager in there is enough to take your breath away."

She turned smartly and marched between the columns,

disappearing behind the inner ranks of columns. She was not in need, as Laneff was.

Laneff threw back the Sat'htine cloak she wore and fished a pair of attenuator rings from the pocket of her jacket. She slipped them on the ring finger of each hand, tuning them up to maximum intensity and bracing herself against the sickening surge as the tiny instruments cut the shimmering waves of emotion radiating from the building before her. It was worse than stuffing cotton in ears and nose. The attenuators damped her Sime senses, leaving her feeling drugged and disoriented but protecting her need-sensitized nerves. She was glad she'd had no breakfast. *I'll never get used to these things.*

Swallowing hard, she made her way up the steps and through the screen of columns to a vantage from which she could see the dais where Digen Farris ambrov Zeor lay in state. The bier was draped in the blue of the House of Zeor, the white of the head of the House, and the black of the Farris mutation. Mairis Farris ambrov Zeor, Digen's heir and thus Sectuib-Apparent in the House of Zeor, stood vigil, also arrayed in full archaic heraldic splendor.

The honor guard was approaching the dais from the side where Shanlun ambrov Zeor stood next to Mairis, also decked in Zeor colors. He'd stationed himself close to Mairis, half turned to face him, rather than the crowd filing by the open coffin, as if he were already assuming the office of Mairis's Companion in Zeor. He seemed comfortable, as if he'd functioned at full-dress state occasions all his life, and not just since he'd pledged to Zeor to become Digen's Companion, This uncanny knack of blending into any background, such as Laneff's laboratory, Digen's sickroom, or the midst of bizarre emergencies, had originally attracted Laneff to him.

The guard delivered the pass to Mairis, and the flow of mourners, four abreast in a line that snaked back across the polished-stone floor of the Unity Gate rotunda, paused. They had all entered on the Gen Territory side of the

Gate building. The line looped around the document display case in the center of thc rotunda, housing the first Unity Proposal, purportedly written by Klyd Farris ambrov Zeor, Mairis's five times great grandfather, more than two centuries ago. Each mourner was graphically reminded that the first effort to stop the Sime/Gen wars had been made by the Householdings, led by Zeor.

As the line halted, Laneff could make out a small knot of blond-haired, pale-skinned gypsies in their ethnic bluff-and-beige costumes, reverently examining the Unity Proposal. *Blond—like Shanlun.*

Shanlun, tall as Mairis, with broad, Gen shoulders and well-sculpted muscles such as only a Gen could have, nevertheless moved with all the grace of a Sime. Against the vivid Zeor blue, Shanlun's pale-blond hair seemed even more bizarre—perhaps even akin to that of the gypsies. *Ridiculous.*

Mairis waved the waiting line into motion again and let the honor guard escort him out of the spotlights. Laneff could imagine the excited whispers of the reporters speculating on the cause of this interruption. Shanlun moved at Mairis's side as if they'd rehearsed that march hundreds of times.

"Laneff," said Mairis, waving the guards away from them. "I didn't expect you to get here until dawn."

"I couldn't sleep. I was watching the whole thing from my hotel room when your message came. I was hoping you'd made a decision."

"I have." He glanced at Shanlun. "You're right, Laneff. The time has come to make Digen's dream, the reunification of humanity, a reality. The wave of sentiment caused by his death—" He half turned toward the crowd behind him. "Zlin that nager!" He gestured expansively.

Since he had approached, he had very smoothly taken control of the ambient nager in their vicinity. This was the channel's talent, and Mairis was known as one of the best channels in the world. As he dropped his blanketing of the crowd's emotions, Laneff felt the weight of collective grief wash over her anew, despite the attenuators.

Tears rushed to her eyes again, and she said, "I don't require them to remind me what a good man he was."

"No, that's not what I mean. Here, take those attenuators off, and really zlin them." As he spoke, he stepped closer, enveloping her in the deep silence of a channel's controlling nager.

She divested herself of the tiny machines and slipped them into a pocket. Then, gradually, Mairis let up on his grip of the fields, and she was zlinning the ambient with her own senses.

"Focus on those nearest the casket," said Mairis. "Zlin how the sense of bereavement and even fear for the future gives way to a vision of hope as they look at him. I've been watching this all night. They're ready, Laneff, as they've never been before. Look." He brought something from a pocket.

She followed his gesture and was gazing upon a small jewelry box which opened to expose a gleaming steel coin. "It's Digen!"

The coin bore the unmistakable profile of the age-ravaged face within the coffin: the elegant Farris forehead no longer graced by the characteristic cowlick, the aquiline nose, the sensitive lips so typically Farris, yet the whole imprinted by the dynamic personality of this unique individual. He was unmistakably Farris, yet no longer typically Farris.

This was what the public saw as they paused beside the coffin, and what they felt was reverberating through Laneff. Her breath caught in her throat, as Sime and Gen alike shared one powerful moment of true emotional unity, naked to each other without the cloaking of their fears.

It was too potent. This was what she had always imagined a channel and Donor shared during selyn transfer. For a renSime, a Sime who wasn't a channel, it was altogether too dangerous.

But Mairis gave her only a momentary glimpse and then

gently blurred and damped the fields until the three of them were standing in a bubble of privacy amid the emotional torrents. Laneff, still duoconscious, aware at one and the same time of her ordinary five senses and of the nageric fields produced by living selyn fields, living Gens and Simes, perceived Shanlun as a dizzying whirl of particolored fluorescent confetti, while Mairis blurred and shimmered as all channels did when working to control the nageric fields. Shanlun, too, was working as a Donor, his full concentration focused on Mairis, his awareness of her so dim that she hardly knew he was there.

When they were all breathing easily again, Mairis said, "Now do you understand? You knew how people would feel when Digen's death was announced, and I didn't. You were right. Now is the time to make Unity a reality. And your research is the key that makes it feasible."

"But it's so far from complete!" Laneff's research in Sime neurochemistry had led her to synthesize a compound which should provide the key to distinguishing Sime from Gen before birth.

He nodded. "You can't go any further without a fifteen- to twenty-year study, and that means government funding. At the funeral this morning, I'm going to go up on that podium and challenge the world: elect me World Controller, and I will see that this research—and other projects like it—gets the funding necessary to make Digen's dream a reality. When children no longer have to grow up wondering or fearing which they'll be, Sime or Gen; when no child unexpectedly goes through changeover becoming Sime and killing the nearest Gen in the berserk raging of First Need—as you did—then it will be possible to abolish the borders between Sime and Gen Territory, and to stop tearing families apart at the very roots. Humans cannot have peace in this world until we accomplish this. Digen knew that. He understood the importance of what you were doing. And I now know that the time is right. Laneff, will you help me?"

"What if they don't elect you?"

"Then the time isn't right. But I'll keep working all my life—as Digen did. And I'll keep asking for your help."

His dark Farris eyes bored into hers, but the nageric atmosphere was cool. She said, "I had thought I was asking for your help to find funding for my project."

He held out a hand to her, extending his handling tentacles, the two dorsals from the sheaths that lay along the tops of his forearms, and the two ventrals from the bottoms of each forearm, so that as their fingers met, his four tentacles reached for hers in a grip of mutual trust. The contact sent a pulse of slow, calm power through her, as if it came from Shanlun.

But with that skin contact, she realized that Mairis was himself on the edge of hard need. She could perceive the two separate selyn-transport nerve systems in the channel, where the renSimes such as herself had only one system. The primary system, which supplied energy to the channel's own body, was dim to Laneff's perceptions, though the secondary system, which the channel used to collect selyn from Gens and transmit it to renSimes in need, glowed brightly. Mairis was in need, but he carried a vast store of selyn which circulated throughout his body, allowing him to control the nager in his vicinity. The intense, solid power she felt at his touch was really being transmitted to her directly from Shanlun. And Shanlun, a Gen whose body was hyperdeveloped in the ability to produce selyn, seemed engorged with selyn.

Entranced with the immanence of such Gen essence, Laneff barely heard Mairis say, "It is best when partners help each other." He withdrew his touch, insulating her once again from the compelling field. "We'll announce our partnership on the podium later this morning. Digen's funeral shouldn't be an ending but a new beginning. You'll stand with Shanlun and me and explain your discovery to the world."

Laneff could feel the grinding effort Shanlun was making to keep his attention on Mairis. She tore her eyes from the Gen and said, "I'd be afraid to even try that without a prepared speech to read. All night, I've been listening to the reporters insisting I already have a safe chemical test for pregnant women to determine whether the child will be Sime or Gen. And they even interviewed two police chiefs in different cities claiming Distect terrorists threatened to bomb any lab where such tests were done."

Shanlun's nager flared, and his full attention came to focus on her. "Of course it's *Diet* terrorists."

"True. Bombings are more the Diet's style, not the Distect's," said Mairis, turning curiously toward the Gen.

But Laneff scarcely heard him. Need thrilled across her nerves in answer to the fabulously rich Gen nager that now tantalized with promise.

Mairis stepped between them and did something with the fields that blunted the effect. She drew a shaky breath. *It's only natural it should feel good to be the focus of a high-field Gen's attention*, she told herself. Her hard-won conditioning to be attracted only to the channel's field when in need couldn't be failing. It was just that Shanlun had been due to give Digen transfer, but the death had intervened, so he was exceptionally high field.

As Shanlun steadied back to his job, narrowing his attention onto Mairis alone, Mairis said, "These threats of violence make it all the more important to get you up there to convince them you don't *yet* have all the answers. I'm pledging only to fund your research *if* I'm elected World Controller—not to institute massive prenatal screening tomorrow! The majority of the people on both sides of the borders are ready for this, but it's got to be done slowly, to build trust."

Laneff nodded. The out-Territory Gens feared that with real Unity, the Simes would take over all Gen governments, and there would be nothing to prevent them from beginning again to keep Gens in pens and breed them for the kill. Most Gens had more sense than that, but even out-Territory had its own terrorist groups—such as the Diet.

Mairis asked, "You're not afraid of the terrorists?"

"No," she said, glancing about at the far-flung ring of guards. "But I can't say I'd care to live like this."

"It won't be very long. When the reporters find something more exciting, we can relax the precautions. And research, face it, is always dull."

She had to smile at that, despite the thrumming anxiety of prematurely roused need. Her awareness of Shanlun was heightened now, despite all Mairis could do. The ronaplin hormones and selyn-conducting fluids were seeping into the sheaths of her lateral tentacles, that normally lay quiescent and all but invisible along the sides of each arm. Mairis, she was sure, was acutely aware of her condition. *I've got to think of a way out of this. I can't stand next to Shanlun for hours, in public.*

"I'm sorry, Laneff," whispered Shanlun forlornly.

Their eyes met and locked. His shame flooded hotly through her, shame that he had failed to protect her from his nager. His yearning to touch her, to ease her need, was as sharp as her own. For a split instant, she felt englobed by the shell of scintillating nageric fragments that seemed to fluoresce in every color. It cut off awareness of Mairis and the whole world. They were alone in featureless space, and though they never touched, Laneff could feel Shanlun's expressive fingers resting on her sensitive lateral sheaths, turning her whole forearm to golden fire.

Shanlun's nager sank deeply into her body, making her feel as if her own cells produced selyn as a Gen's did, instead of merely using it to stay alive. Her laterals strained to emerge, to seek Gen skin and take the selyn her body now craved, though she knew it was too early in her cycle. It would only leave her discontent now.

Mairis, showing a bright and powerful field, intervened,

denying her urge, shattering the bubble of privacy with his intrusion. Laneff's heart thundered in her ears.

Long ago she'd given up the kill—given up all hope of ever taking selyn directly from a Gen again. To be tempted, even mildly, was to risk losing control during need and killing the nearest Gen. Only channels were allowed to assuage need directly from Gens—specially trained Donors such as Shanlun who could not be killed—because channels couldn't function otherwise.

"Are you all right, Shanlun?" asked Mairis, and simultaneously, Laneff was aware of Mairis's attention focused on her, soothing the jangle of her nerves.

In the space of two breaths, Shanlun had steadied down to a particolored fluorescent shell, neutral in its effect on her. "My apologies, Sectuib," said Shanlun, his voice schooled to a colorless, emotionless distance.

Mairis waved that aside. "My fault. I hadn't realized just how much of a strain you were under." He glanced at Laneff. "Your personal relationship doesn't make it any easier."

Zeor doesn't marry out of Zeor. The words echoed in Laneff's mind as Shanlun stood with balanced poise under the scrutiny of his Sectuib. Here was the only man who'd understood what she was doing and who, from the first moment they'd met, had truly believed she could do it. Taking her moments of despair in stride, he had grown to cherish her as she loved him. Yet now, he didn't dare even look at her. *If I had any sense, I'd cut him out of my life. But I can't.* She didn't think she could walk away from Shanlun now, even if she didn't have to work with his Sectuib. *How can I tell Mairis I dare not stand with him and Shanlun today?*

Catching Mairis's attention, Shanlun said, "There is another consideration. All the other Householding cloaks on that podium this morning will be Zeor. The other Householdings might be jealous if you favor Sat'htine with the entire world watching."

"I hadn't thought of that!" said Mairis.

"You're going to offer to lead the world into a step as big as Klyd's Unity Proposal or the signing of the First Contract between Sime and Gen governments. Either Zeor leads—alone—or *all* Householdings lead together," said Shanlun.

Mairis nodded. "And even Klyd could never get them *all* to agree." He was zlinning Laneff carefully.

"I wouldn't want to create jealousy among the Householdings," said Laneff. "Certainly not now, when we are trying to create a Unity." *It really would be best if I weren't there.*

As if echoing her very thought, Shanlun said, "It really would be best if Laneff could speak from some other location."

"It might be more dramatically effective—more visually interesting if Laneff is in the guest box. There will be all kinds of Householding colors among the guests, and there is a low-field zone established there for the renSimes in need. I'll have them rig a microphone. Get Kadi to let the camera crews know they'll have a reason to cover that area closely—but don't tell them what it is."

Mairis was off making plans, mentally rewriting his speech and shaping his campaign. Laneff felt a weight lift from her spirit. She could accomplish everything she had to in order to get the funding for her project—and not suffer.

As Mairis talked, Laneff noticed that out on the rotunda floor the small knot of gypsies had reached the bier, directly in the beam of the brightest lights, and at a point closest to where she was standing. Four gypsy Gens and a gypsy channel created a hole in the ambient nager, a pale hole of ghostly stillness that shimmered. Despite the lack of similarity to Shanlun's fluorescent effect, there seemed some indefinable kinship there.

As she watched, the gypsy channel paused over Digen's casket and gazed fixedly at Shanlun. Shanlun had his back turned to the bier, but he raised one eyebrow as if he'd heard a curious noise, and then he turned.

The gypsy channel was an old man with startlingly dark blond hair, abundant and cut short and stiff. A thin weatherbeaten face, bushy eyebrows, long vertical laugh lines, and no frown lines bespoke an innate good humor.

Mairis followed Shanlun's gaze. "Someone you know? Come greet them. We must get back there now, anyway."

The gypsy channel's attention seemed to be calling to Shanlun, and he wavered. Laneff felt that call, while at the same time a wash of cold needles raised the hairs all over her body. Despite that warning, though, she knew she'd fight to get assigned to that channel for a transfer. *But gypsies aren't on the rotation rolls.*

Shanlun turned back to Mairis, wrapping himself again in the impenetrable cloak of his nager. "I—have no business with them."

As he said that, the gypsies turned and left, but Laneff sensed a throbbing of regret in them—and in Shanlun.

Mairis assigned Laneff a security guard and told them where to wait as he and Shanlun were escorted back to the bier. Laneff had to put the attenuator rings back on when the powerful channel and Donor left her. Before long, there was a booming clang as temporary barricades cut off the flow of mourners. The end of the line snaked toward the bier.

She had seen Digen die and knew in her heart that he was gone. But she was impelled to grab this last chance—before it was too late.

She drew her hood up around her face, trying to become just another Householder, and, trailed by the guard, she joined the end of the line beside the glass case of the Unity Proposal. *Only if we know which children will be Sime can we bring Klyd's—and Digen's—dream into reality.*

She had known that in her very bones ever since she'd visited the prematurely erected Monument to the Last Berserker during her first year after changeover. She'd cried during the ceremony when her name had been added to the end of the list carved there and a prayer had been said that she should indeed be the Last Berserker—the last child to go through changeover unexpectedly and kill in First Need. Silently, she'd vowed to be the one to put an end to berserkers. But Digen Farris had to die under her care to make it possible for her to succeed.

Ridiculous.

Yet as she gazed into Digen's face, young in repose, she recalled all he'd suffered to bring the world this far. As she drank in the last moments of the sight of his face, they lowered the coffin lid.

In some odd way, under the hushed shadows and echoing vaults of the Unity Gate, it really seemed to her that he'd sacrificed his life to give her the chance to keep her vow. The weight of that responsibility came over her, and her heart cried, *I can do it, Digen. I can give up anything I have to, even Shanlun. We're going to make your dream come true.*

2

FUNERAL

From her vantage in the visitors' box, Laneff watched Simes and Gens throng into Householding Square. Most of them, men and women both, wore formal capes displaying their Householding colors. All around the edges of the square, the banners of the Houses were on display, flapping in the brisk spring wind, illumined by the rising sun.

The riotous splashes of colors divided around the granite statue of the legendary Rimon Farris, mounted on his horse. For this occasion, a Zeor-blue cloak had been draped around his shoulders and over the flanks of the horse. Rimon, as father of the first Householdings, was claimed as member by all Houses, so no one was offended by the blue today.

Laneff's place was to the right of the podium which barred the gate to the old Householding Cemetery. Elaborate displays of flowers hid the raw wood of the stage. Mairis and Shanlun were already taking their place at the center of the podium, surrounded by blue-cloaked dignitaries of the House of Zeor, those who ran the vast corporate network of businesses owned by Zeor, those who administered the education of Zeor's children, and those who held rank by virtue of skill as channels or Donors.

Across from Laneff, on the other side of the podium, a

roped-off area held the children and attending members of Zeor, a blindingly brilliant field of blue cloaks. Beside and behind Laneff, there was a sprinkling of blue, renSimes who were members of Zeor but now in need.

The guards stationed at short intervals around Laneff's end of the visitors' box were all high-order Donors or channels, most of them members of Zeor. But one Gen in particular, who seemed intent on Laneff alone, was not wearing any Householding affiliation. He paced and paused with an awkward self-consciousness before the front-center seat that had been assigned to Laneff.

When Digen's coffin was brought through the Gate behind the Zeor member's box and solemnly installed among the flowers on the podium, Laneff had to adjust the attenuators she wore to maximum, despite the horrid sensory distortion. Again, she was glad she hadn't eaten. Her peculiarly sensitive nervous system never would be able to accept the attenuators. The renSimes on either side of her were wearing attenuator rings tuned to maximum and seemed perfectly comfortable.

At last Mairis was handed a microphone wand and took his place beside a table on which various items were laid out. The public address system came to life with a drum roll, and the bell-like twang of a shiltpron plucked in the call to mourn. The crowd silenced, but the nager intensified with gut-wrenching bereavement. Many of them had known Digen personally, taken transfer from him when he was channeling, or worked with him when he was World Controller. *We were all sure he'd recover this time, too. He seemed immortal.*

Mairis, braced by Shanlun's nager, spoke calmly into the microphone. "Digen Ryan Farris, Sectuib in Zeor for the last one hundred sixteen years, is dead."

The inchoate emotions focused to a piercing sense of permanent loss. *I hate funerals!* thought Laneff, struggling to keep her awareness hypoconscious, to block out her Sime senses so she wouldn't drown in the emotions of others when her own tears were blocked by the deadening pall of need.

"My great grandfather," said Mairis, his voice low and intimate, "who held the office of World Controller a record six times in his life, is dead. An era has come to an end."

Beyond the far end of the podium, ranks of television cameras scanned the crowd for grieving faces. She knew some of them would be focusing on her, and she fought not to let her rising nausea distort her expression. The renSimes beside her sensed her discomfort and edged as far away as they could to give her breathing room.

She tried to concentrate on the nager of the Donor who paced before her. From the massive pull of his nager, she deduced he had to be a First Order Donor like Shanlun, but he was otherwise unremarkable. Reddish-blond hair framed his unweathered face. Gingery eyebrows and mustache matched his pale freckles. He wore a floppy-brimmed hat as sun protection, and a serviceable gray suit.

As he turned, his ever wandering eyes chanced to meet hers, and he smiled. His face lit and his nager glowed with an instant friendliness that wiped all trace of self-consciousness away. She inched forward in her chair and said, "Could you stop pacing? It's making me nauseated."

Chagrined, he nodded and planted his feet firmly, positioning himself between Laneff and her neighbor, a woman wearing a Householding Frihill cloak.

With the rippling in the fields tamed, Laneff turned her attention back to Mairis. ". . . and in the last hundred years, under the leadership of Digen Farris, the world has started to move once again toward the dream of our ancestors who founded the Householdings, the union of the two halves of the human race, Sime and Gen. Never again will there be a nation in which only Simes are citizens and Gens are bred and raised in pens like cattle."

On the periphery of Laneff's awareness, to her right and out in the sea of now-still bodies, there was a movement. A large silver-painted van with a broadcast camera on its roof was creeping toward the visitors' box, parting the crowd by inexorable force. Two Gens on the roof wrestled with a huge old camera, panning the long snout of a sunshade from Mairis to where Laneff sat. *Why aren't they confined to the press zone?* Most of the cameras in the press zone which was carved out of the crowd in front of the statue were aimed at Mairis now.

"Seven hundred years ago," Mairis continued, "Rimon Farris discovered he could take selyn from any Gen and give it to a Sime in need so the Sime didn't have to kill to live. He became the first channel. Two hundred thirty-two years ago, Klyd Farris founded the Modern Tecton, built on the foundations provided by the Householdings and their channels and Companions, but designed to encompass every living Sime. That was a mere beginning. Over the last century, the face of civilization has changed.

"When Digen Farris was a child, the world controllership was just being created. When he took over as Sectuib in Zeor, nobody could place a telephone call across a Territory border. He was the first Sime ever to go to school out-Territory. When he was a young man, all the Tecton's Donors were trained by channels, a method so inefficient it caused the infamous Donor Shortage.

"That was in the year one thirty-two, a full century ago. Is there anyone here who remembers that time?"

The anguish of the crowd began to give way to a sense of wonder at all that had been accomplished during one man's lifetime. The blond Gen guard, too, was caught up in it, and that drew Laneff duoconscious, aware of the full range of Sime senses as well as her ordinary senses. The blond Gen's nager paled to insignificance beside Shanlun's pyrotechnic vibrancy, a shell of positive energy that Shanlun threw around Mairis to protect him from the ambient of the crowd.

Mairis put one arm around Shanlun's shoulders. Despite attenuators and the wall of trained Donors who surrounded the low-field box with protection, she perceived how the two nagers blended in harmony. She tried to force herself to breathe evenly. But even from this distance, every nerve in her body remembered that moment in the rotunda and resonated to the barest hint of it that seeped through to her now, activating need again.

It wasn't the magnitude of Shanlun's nager that was his strongest attraction to her. It was the quality. *I'd love that man even if he was Sime*.

". . . and channels still depend on our Donors. But now there are enough such Donors. It's a profession entered not just by Companions from the Householdings but by many children raised by Simes in-Territory, and also by Gens raised by Gens out-Territory."

Mairis continued guiding the crowd through history and up to an awareness of how Digen Farris had molded their world. Laneff swallowed against throat muscles and diaphragm that insisted she was about to vomit. She scanned the crowd, knowing she couldn't speak to them feeling like this. If she tried to articulate, she knew she'd double over and retch.

Off to one side, and nearly level with the visitors' box, the silver van was still creeping through the crowd. She could make out the expressions on the faces of the camera crew. One of them, a redheaded Gen woman who seemed as young as Laneff herself, leaned over the edge of the van roof to call something to the driver, a dark-brown-skinned Gen with kinky black hair. Laneff felt the Simes in proximity to the van tense, preparing for the shock if the Gen should fall off that roof and be hurt. Gen pain could trigger a Sime to kill, even against the Sime's own will.

Two or three Gens glanced up at the van, noting the tension in the Simes around them. In the general movement to get out of the van's way, the Gens rearranged themselves to protect the renSimes in the crowd. The slow creep of the van seemed to arrow toward Laneff. And the shuffling movement of the crowd only added to her nausea. Her skin was crawling with a prickling sensation, and she couldn't breathe. The other Simes about her, protected by their attenuators, never noticed.

But the blond Gen turned as a muted gasp escaped her. "You're right," he muttered, "that van could be trouble." And he moved closer to her, firmly planting a good segment of his attention on her as if she were a channel to be supported in some channeling effort. It should have felt good, but instead it only increased her nausea.

In desperation, Laneff tuned her attenuators down to minimum. The ambient nager blasted through her nerves, raising the throbbing of need to a new height, but relieving the paralyzing sense of imminent nausea.

As the silver van crawled toward them, the redheaded Gen woman on top of it held her balance by a very precarious hold on the camera rigging and gestured to her assistant with her free hand. Another Gen—a Donor wearing a Keon red cape—began to climb up onto the van's roof, but the driver opened his door and yelled at the intruder, meanwhile letting the van creep ahead into the crowd. Laneff couldn't hear his words, but his anger came through the spellbound collective nager of the crowd. The Keon Gen desisted and went to warn Simes away.

Now the van was close enough that Laneff could read something of the redheaded Gen's nager, and she didn't like it. It was as if that woman were aiming shafts of calculated malice directly at Laneff. *Nonsense! Need-inspired paranoia!*

The tall blond Gen guarding her leaned down to say, "That's an out-Territory station. I hope there isn't going to be an incident."

Laneff replied softly, "Those Gens are nervous, and the redhead is tense, even grim. I doubt if any of them have worked in-Territory before."

He eyed her attenuator rings, unable to discern the setting she was using, of course. "They told me you were extraordinarily sensitive. Just relax and listen to the speech." He intensified the shaft of his attention relegated to her, working to her as if she were a channel and he a Donor fully prepared to give her transfer. She melted into the luxury, stealing a moment to bask in the spice of its sheer potency.

She opened her mouth to tell him that she was too far into need for this to be safe, but at that moment the audience fell into a rapt silence.

Mairis was holding up an object he'd taken from the table beside him. ". . . feel this is the most suitable tribute to the achievements of Digen Farris. I know you can't all see it, so let me describe it. It's a steel coin with the right profile of my great grandfather on one side and the epitaph that will appear on his memorial, 'Born from Death, he lived for Unity!' The obverse shows the starred-cross shape of the Monument to the Last Berserker.

"This is the very first one struck. It was delivered to me only hours ago. Soon the coin will be in general circulation, the first coin accepted at face value both in- and out-Territory, all over the world. I wish Digen had lived to see it."

For the first time emotion choked Mairis's voice and he paused. Shanlun took a step closer to his Sectuib, and it was as if Mairis disappeared into Shanlun's nager, so massive a nager that he seemed painted onto the background of the podium in glowing iridescent colors.

Meanwhile, the silver van had reached a point so close that Laneff could smell the heat of oil and paint and feel the screech of tense Gen nerves. She, too, was tense, knowing that her cue to speak would come soon, and despite having tuned the attenuators to minimum, she still felt queasy at every shift in the nageric fields about her.

A woman in dun-colored coveralls squatted next to the microphone that had been set up near Laneff. Its snout poked over the rope pedestals that marked the box, and the technician began testing it. Seeing this, Mairis waved Shanlun back with a negligent tentacle gesture. The Gens on the silver van reacted as out-Territory Gens usually did to the sight of a Sime's tentacles; a spark of nageric paralysis. Their tension increased, and Laneff again fought nausea. *Shen these shidoni attenuators!* She wrenched the offending instruments off, knowing that she'd only double over in a fit of retching if she tried to walk to the microphone while wearing them. The worse her need, the more offensive the things became. *Why couldn't I have been born normal!*

The big blond Gen turned to her, noticing her move. "Feeling better? Good, you'll be on soon." He left his hand trailing on the rope in front of her, and his smile was like a caress, his nager a palpable beat protecting her as Shanlun so often had. *He thinks I don't feel need at all now.* She drew breath to contradict that impression, but just then she heard Mairis mention her name, and she realized he had been describing the distant promise inherent in her discoveries, and how they had helped Digen survive several crises before the one that finally took him.

The big blond Gen touched her fingers, most of his attention on her, steady as if she were a channel preparing to work. "Listen! Your cue."

"Therefore, at this time of ending, I am announcing my candidacy for World Controller and a new beginning. For if I am elected, I will see to it that Laneff Farris's research will be completed all the way through the fifteen-year study necessary to determine if she can indeed predict changeover. And if she can, then within your grandchildren's lifetimes, the ultimate reunification of mankind can take place, Digen's dream can become a reality. Listen now to Laneff Farris describe how her discovery works."

The blond stood aside as Laneff rose to her feet. Her breath came easily, though her head felt light. She walked to the microphone as a circle cleared around her, and all the cameras in the press zone swerved to focus on her.

"Go ahead," muttered the squatting technician and vacated the area, scrambling under the line of sight of the cameras.

Laneff knew that part of Mairis's plan was to present her in public so that Simes could zlin her nager, read her sincerity and her certainty for themselves, before the press could round up all the neurochemistry experts whose skepticism had prevented her results from being published. So she wasn't startled when the blond guard stood well back so his nager wouldn't obscure hers. But she was dismayed at how naked it made her feel as all attention focused on her. *At least I'm not going to vomit.*

She took a deep breath and got through the formal salutations by rote, and then she began to describe the simple amniocentesis method she envisioned for her test, and how her synthetic chemical could then be used to determine the nature of the fetus.

She had no sooner begun than screams erupted around the silver van which hovered only strides away. Simultaneously, the ambient nager became a blinding sheet of white-hot Gen pain.

The cameraman on top of the van had caught his hand in the camera's aiming mechanism, and his pain was beating through every Sime around the van—Simes wide open to it because they'd been zlinning her. The redheaded Gen ground the camera mechanism back across the man's hand—Laneff could sense bones breaking—and the man yanked himself free, blood spraying in every direction. He slipped and fell off the van screaming in pain and terror.

Against her will, Laneff was thrown hyperconscious, the world dissolving into a shifting miasma of selyn fields laced with jagged slices of pain. Islands of damped-down calm identified channels working to control the ambient. Dead spots represented renSimes wearing attenuators tuned to maximum. The massive nager of the big blond Gen blazing shock moved toward the source of the ineffable pain.

But even that nager could not damp the shrieking Gen terror that dominated the ambient. That terror wakened her like nothing else since the experience of her First Need, the time she had killed.

Gens interposed themselves between renSimes and the pain-terror source that was triggering off the most basic hunting instincts in the Simes. But to Laneff, those Gens seemed to be holding off her competitors. Hardly aware that she moved, Laneff leaped the rope barricade and streaked for her prey, just as the redhead swung down from the van roof, also radiating delicious fear.

In one flashfire perception, Laneff knew the fallen Gen had not only a mashed hand, but also a broken ankle. She ignored the startlement in the massive Donor's nager she passed. Her ronaplin glands flooded her lateral sheaths with selyn-conducting hormone, and her whole body was tuned to killing pitch.

As she secured her prey, renewed terror took him when he knew the feral hunter was upon him. That promise of imminent satisfaction was too much.

Her hands seized the bloody forearm and the other clean one. Her handling tentacles lashed securely—bruisingly—into place. And her laterals flicked into position on the Gen's skin while she fastened her lips to his in a relentless demand for selyn.

She drew to her full speed, seeking the moment of egobliss she only half remembered and had renounced forever. He resisted, his nerves responding to her draw with a burst of that peculiar pain only Gens could feel—and junct Simes craved like nothing else. Lured by that hint of killbliss, she abandoned herself to the draw, increasing the Gen's pain by her swift demand.

In one crying burst of resonant triumph, the quintessence of killbliss overcame her. Too soon, the living vibration damped out of the selyn field. The brightness of soul-essence dopplered away. The pulsing surges of new selyn created in Gen tissue ceased.

The warm, pliant corpse slid from her grasp.

And as at her first kill, the amount of selyn she had been able to glean during the split instant of her attack was not enough. Need still growled within her.

She turned, unaware of the turquoise hem of her cloak trailing in the Gen's blood. The world had stopped.

I—killed . . .

The vocalization of that fact rang through the emptiness of her mind. *I—killed. Rejuncted.*

Spectators had formed a wide ring about the scene at the side of the van. On the podium stairs, Mairis and Shanlun seemed suspended in the act of racing toward her. Beside her, the big blond Donor fought back his shock. The redheaded Gen woman had reached the ground and stood near the driver's door as the other camera crew swarmed down from the van roof.

And Laneff found herself zeroing in on the redheaded woman as her next victim.

With a strangled choking noise that was hardly a cry, Laneff threw herself into the Donor's arms, knowing that her selyn draw could never produce pain in him. His nager, though enticingly Gen and replete with more selyn than she could use in a year, held no hint of promise of killbliss. With all her will, she forced herself to cling to him—not to kill again.

As if that were a signal, pandemonium erupted. Mairis and Shanlun raced down the stairs, shouting orders to the guards right and left. Simultaneously, the two men climbing down from the van roof leaped onto Laneff, catching her around in her own cape and yanking her free from the arms of the Donor, who was left stunned beside the van.

Laneff was borne into the air toward the redhead and the driver while at the same time a furious wind whipped dirt and gravel into the air. The thrumming roar of a helicopter's blades beat down on them, scattering the spectators while the guards flung arms over their eyes and groped forward.

Laneff couldn't see. They'd wrapped her cloak with its black lining full around her and over her eyes, the pin of the clasp now digging into her chest. But she could zlin Mairis and Shanlun racing toward them heedless of the

flying gravel. And she sensed the moment the Donor Gen
overcame shock enough to see she was being kidnapped.

She struggled halfheartedly, a token resistance, for she
knew that if she fought she would seek to kill again. It was
the only honor she had left, for by Tecton law she was
doomed to death by attrition of selyn—death in the Last
Year House, where she would not be allowed to kill again.
She was too old to disjunct again. She would die for lack of
the kill. *A year at the most.*

Her captors set her on her feet, quickly and expertly
lashing her forearms around with a tough belt, pulled up
tight so the pressure on her laterals held at the very
threshold of unbearable pain.

Hardly daring to breathe, she stood helpless as two of
the men drew guns. One held a gun to her head while the
other waved his at the security guards converging on
them. Meanwhile, the redhead and the other man un-
furled a banner fastened to the side of the van, reading
The Diet Proves Simes Can't Be Trusted.

Before Mairis and Shanlun could quite work their way
to the fore of the guards, the chopper almost touched
down right beside Laneff's captors, and the redhead scrambled for the open hatch, shouting instructions.

Numbly, Laneff thought, *It's not the Tecton Security
chopper!*

And then the blond Gen moved.

He charged, head down, straight for Laneff, passing the
redhead and the other man. One of Laneff's captors got off
a shot at the Donor, but he kept coming. Before the
other, whose gun was pointed at Laneff's head, could
react, the Donor had swept through them, catching Laneff
below the waist and hoisting her up over his shoulders.

For several moments, the world vanished for Laneff,
pain exploding through her nerves while her arms dangled
over the huge Donor's shoulder, and then a slamming
impact against the chopper's hatchway knocked the breath
out of her. She heard the hatch bang shut behind them,

and the patter-pop of several bullets hitting the side of the chopper.

Without instructions, the chopper pilot lifted straight up and then tilted hard as he raced for speed.

Diaphragm knotted and eyes watering, Laneff fought pain and dizziness. And then the Donor had the cruel belt off her arms, sending new lances of fiery pain through her whole body. It was only coming to her now that she wasn't dead.

"Come on, Laneff, help me take that pilot, and I'll get you out of this!"

She shook her head, unable to assimilate it all.

"Come on, get up on your feet—there now . . ." Pulling her up, he worked with his nager to steady her, though how he could do that while he himself was in such a state she didn't know.

"I can't . . ." she gasped as breath came again.

"Listen!" he commanded, spearing her with his eyes as he steadied her by the shoulders. "That pilot is part of this—that shen-be-flayed Diet set you up for that kill. They came there intending to make a Sime kill—maybe targeted on you!—just to prove Digen and Mairis are out to enslave or destroy Gens! Are you going to stand here and let that man take you to the Diet headquarters—where they'll treat you like *that?*" He kicked at the belt on the deck by her foot. "Gather your wits, woman, and zlin for me. How many of them are there up there?"

She glanced around now, curious for the first time. The chopper was designed to carry cargo, and they were in a huge lower bay, with ribbed bulkheads bare around them. Above and on the forward bulkhead, stairs led to a hatch—shut now. Undoubtedly the pilot's compartment.

She went duoconscious, to zlin through that bulkhead and hatchway. Clearly, through the light construction, she zlinned the selyn nager of one Gen—scared, but grim.

"There's only one—the pilot. But there's room up there for three." And now that she was zlinning, she noticed the

pursuing copters. "Behind us—way behind—three choppers. Must be the Tecton."

"Must be," he echoed abstractedly as he studied the
hatch. "Do you think the pilot knows what happened
down there?"

"Do you think I can read minds?" she countered.

But he was already at the hatch. "Come here. Force
this lock bar for me, and I'll take care of the pilot."

"Can you fly one of these things?"

"Sure." He grinned pure Gen male vigor and a peculiar
Gen ferocity. "How high are we?"

There were no ports in the cargo bay. Zlinning, she
estimated, "Higher than the Vermilion Tower restaurant
over there," she said, pointing, "but there are hills right in
front of us."

"Good; we'll make it." As he spoke, he put his own
strength to forcing the lock bar up. "Come on—augment!"

He knew what he was asking of her: to use selyn at
many times her normal metabolic rate to strengthen her
muscles beyond Gen abilities. He was a professional Tecton
Donor. He knew she hadn't been satisfied by that one kill,
that need still lurked within her.

At her hesitation, he turned to her, his field supportive.
"What beautiful irony: use the Diet's own selyn to defeat
them. Come on, Laneff. We don't have much time."

"Yes," she agreed, and set herself to the bar. She had to
nudge the huge male Gen hands aside to get a good
tentacle and finger grip on it, but then she summoned her
full augmentation capacity, closed her eyes to concentrate,
not caring if she injured her back or gave herself a hernia.
She let loose all her strength, and the bar tore loose, the
hatch slamming open before them, the muted noise of the
rotors bursting into a storm of sound while pure daylight
streamed through the wrapped bubble windshield.

Before she recovered her balance, the Donor was through
the hatch and onto the pilot. One huge male fist slammed
into male jaw, and the pain both of them felt ratchetted

through Laneff renewing her killust. She fought it down as the Donor extracted the unconscious Gen pilot from the control seat and threw himself into place, grabbing the controls with fair expertise. Then his nager steadied around her, and all trace of killust faded.

Over his shoulder, he shouted above the noise, "Laneff, get that belt and secure that man's hands before he comes to."

"I don't think he'll come to very soon. He hit his head on something hard when you felled him." Her voice sounded small in her ears, though she yelled the words.

The chopper had leveled and steadied under the Donor's hands. Now he turned to gaze at her, and she was aware that he was as surprised they were alive as she was.

"Please, just tie him up. Then come sit here and tell me what's going on behind us. They'll be shooting at us soon as they get close enough. You get me out of this, Laneff, and I'll take care of you. I promise."

3

STIGMA

Laneff regarded the unconscious Gen pilot. He was wearing dark-gray coveralls over tough charcoal work clothes. There was a massive ring on his right hand and a wristband on his left bearing a watch. Perhaps twenty-five years old, he showed well-developed muscles. His nager, dimmed with unconsciousness and disorganized around the head injury, was still strong for a nondonor of selyn.

"I don't suppose it would do him any harm," she shouted over the noise, "if I tie him up."

The Donor turned, grinning. "Ambrov Sat'htine!"

"Yes," replied Laneff choking back a bitter tear, "even junct, ambrov Sat'htine." Her House was dedicated to health and healing. *But it can't heal me now*. She got the belt and secured the Gen pilot, using his shoelaces on his ankles.

"How close are they now?" shouted the Donor.

She zlinned arear. "Gaining, uh—what's your name?"

"Yuan."

"Well, Yuan," she said, perching in the copilot's seat, "why don't you just land here and let them catch up. It's only Tecton security back there now." *Last Year House*. She had toured a Last Year House once, seen the ghastly death that awaited any Sime who became junct after their first year as an adult. That vision was with her now. *Why didn't it stop me then?*

Below them, rolling hills and steep water canyons peeled away one after another. "Laneff—is that what you really want?"

"Is there any choice?"

His silence drew her attention. Their eyes met. "Yes, I'm offering you a choice." He yanked down a set of earphones with attached microphone and twisted them onto his head, then reached over to pluck down the copilot's set. "Put this on so we can talk over the noise."

She complied. "Not that there's anything to say. You've got to get me to a Last Year House before I kill again."

He eyed her sideways. "In a Tecton Last Year House, you'd live maybe ten months or a year. You'd be too sick to work after maybe six months. What of your research?"

Stricken, she met his gaze silently. *All for nothing.*

"Come with me and live—maybe eighteen months, two years—maybe more. And have a laboratory where you can complete your work, refine your synthesis so others can duplicate it, set up protocols for your fifteen-year project, and maybe even publish. In two years, you could do all that!"

"And who would I have to kill to do it?" Her rejection of temptation was visceral, but the temptation beckoned like that Gen's sweet terror. Her body had first known selyn satisfaction coupled to that peculiar kind of Gen fear, and, disjunction aside, that touch of fear would always be the measure of quality in her satisfaction. *Why did I have to be renSime!*

A heavy rumble shook the chopper. Yuan clutched the controls, glancing futilely behind. "They're shooting at us! They think we're Diet!" He grabbed for the radio microphone, and fighting the controls, reached to dial across the frequencies.

Laneff couldn't help thinking how ludicrous he seemed as he tried to do everything with fingers. Lacking tentacles,

Gens had no easy life of it. As she reached to adjust the radio for him, she thought, *They were sure I'd establish as a Gen, not change over at all. And if I'd been Gen, I wouldn't now be condemned to death.* Savagely, she heard herself add, *If it would add a year to my life now, I'd cut off every one of my tentacles!*

She found their signal. " . . . unmarked Straight-Riser, you are assisting a junct to flee the scene of a kill. You will be shot down if you do not land immediately. Tecton law requires that any fleeing junct be summarily executed. You have been warned. Repeat . . ."

Yuan cut in over their signal. "This is Yuan Sirat Tiernan, TN-1. I can't land this thing! The pilot is unconscious. Help!"

"You can't?" asked Laneff, surprised at her own panic.

"Of course I can. Playing for time." And he tried again, then twice more. But the Tecton voice kept on repeating. Frustrated, he searched the maze of dials around him until he grunted, "Shidoni-be-flayed Diet! We can't get out on the Tecton frequencies! Just like them not to trust their own pilots!" Disgust and contempt vied for nageric prominence with hatred of the Diet.

Another boom jolted them, and Yuan tilted them into a tight turn, righted, and then swept around a looming butte, skimming low to the rolling hills below.

"There they come!" said Laneff. "It's no use."

He ran one finger over the gauges, tapped one triumphantly. "Those choppers won't give up until they run out of selyn in their fuel cells, but we've got to lose them before they call in reinforcements." He shot a frown back over his shoulder in the direction of their own fuel cells. "Another glorious irony!" The frown vanished into a grin of boyish delight. "The shen-be-dunked Diet depended on a selyn-powered chopper for their escape!"

"Terrorists don't have to be sane. Their van was selyn-powered, too. After all, it's cheapest." Zlinning her death creeping up on her from behind, Laneff wondered how she could be so calm. Then she realized it was Yuan who was calm—tense like the eye of a storm, but nagerically still. "You act as if you do this every day. You're not—not a terrorist, are you?" *Or worse?*

"No," he answered as another rumble tossed them about.

He's a great pilot for a Gen, she thought. Where would a Tecton Donor get such a skill?

"Shen!" swore the Gen. "I've lost track of the compass bearing. Laneff, you've got to guide us. Listen," he said, his nager vibrating pure sincerity. "The Tecton and its Last Year Houses, murdering juncts on sight, isn't all there is in the world. I know a place where you can live—*and not kill*. Eighteen months—maybe two years, or more, with your wits about you. Help get us there, and I promise you won't regret it."

The deck rocked under them again, and a tiny hole appeared in the bulkhead near Laneff's knee, air whistling shrilly. *No matter who he is, it's a better chance than trying to surrender now!*

For the next two hours, she talked at the Gen, spotting the pursuers and keeping them oriented as they dodged up and down canyons. Then she sensed a concentration of nageric fields that whispered into nonexistence as they approached. "As if a number of Gens had dived into a deep cave."

"Diet hideout for sure! Knew it was here somewhere! There! That one?" When she nodded, his nager flared fiercely, and he gritted through compressed lips, "Hang on!"

He swooped high, turning so the pursuers got a fix on them, and then he dived straight toward that cave mouth until the Tecton craft had surely lost them from their instruments and their Sime spotters would be unable to zlin them through the intervening hills. At the very last second, he gunned the motors and pulled the chopper around into a low curve that set them skimming along the course of a stream, their downwash lashing the rain-swelled water to foam.

The river gorge twisted and turned, putting solid hills between them and the cave mouth—and the Tecton choppers. Yuan kept low, nearly on the water so the rising edges of the canyon hid them. "I don't believe this; we're really going to make it!"

The boyish delight glowed once again in his nager, as if life and death were all a game to him. Laneff began to like this crazy Gen who was always so surprised at his "good luck"—the result of incredible skill and daring. Zlinning behind, she said, "No trace of the Tecton choppers."

"Unless Mairis himself was with them, we've lost them!"

"He wasn't." That nager, she'd always recognize. As the canyon turned, they both spotted a column of rich black smoke billowing into the breeze far behind them—too far for Laneff to zlin anything more than a dim haze of selyn field against the empty landscape.

"They've attacked the shenoni-be-dunked Diet hideout! Laneff—the Tecton owes you for that one. That base has been a launching pad for Diet escapades in Garby, Peroa, and Zyfnild. At least fifty people have been murdered just that I know of, from that rathole."

"What *are* you? Some kind of antiterrorist task force?"

He laughed. It was a merry laugh, lacing his nager with sheer delight. "I guess some people might say so. But if so, you're looking at one thoroughly lost task force!"

They had come out onto a valley floor, where spring flowers turned a meadow into a riot of color reminiscent of the Household Square decked out for Digen's funeral. The stream widened into a shallow lake, a few shade trees overhanging it. Yuan worked at the controls until he produced a map on the screen in front of Laneff. "Can you place us on that?"

Map reading had never been one of Laneff's strong points, but a graph was a graph. Matching her innate Sime sense of position with the Gen-drawn map, she said, "North of that section."

He showed her how to scroll the display. They were

still flying low, but with reduced speed. Without looking at the gauge, Laneff knew the fuel cells were depleted. Her vast relief at their escape faded. It would be terrible to be left on foot in this wilderness.

"Here!" She set the autocursor onto their position and watched it track them.

Working with the compass, he veered onto a new heading. "We've got fuel enough to get pretty close!"

"Where?"

"Safety."

His certainty made her bones believe it, and tension melted out of her. She buried her face in her hands, scrubbing her tentacles over her forehead and scalp, feeling the tremor in every muscle. And she just noticed she had to urinate.

"What kind of safety?" she asked miserably.

"From Gens who tempt Simes to kill; from Simes who'll murder you for yielding to that temptation." He reached over to grip her wrist, just around the tentacle orifices. He, too, was trembling from the prolonged strain, but his nager was steady. "First thing, I'll give you the selyn you still need. Then, we'll talk—make plans. By the day after tomorrow, you'll be far from here—and you'll have a lab you can stock and design yourself. I promise."

Promises! But despite the painful cynicism, Laneff felt reassured. An hour passed in which they watched the dwindling fuel supply and the unconscious pilot. Laneff endured the backwash of shock and the lingering ache of unsatisfied need. She had been days away from her scheduled transfer. She kept telling herself she wasn't really in need, but it didn't help. It wouldn't take much to make her go for another kill. But Yuan steadied her with his nager.

And then the rotors chugged into a descending rhythm, each individual beat audible. "We're going down!" said Yuan. "Not too bad, though."

Before them was a highland meadow, thickly wooded

except for a flat rock outcropping near a cliff face that blocked the eastern approach. They came in from the west and with the very last beats of the rotors bounced to a landing on the flat rock.

Gasping, they laughed together to have survived once more. Then Laneff noticed a wooden cabin built against the cliff. It was old, weathered to a bare gray, the roof beam swaybacked, but the windows were glazed, and new wood shone here and there. A curl of smoke rose from the chimney.

As they scrabbled out of the cockpit to open the cargo bay door, an elderly Sime emerged from the cabin, whipcord slender and tough, weathered to a leathery brown startling against white hair.

Yuan jumped down first and went to the Sime, yelling his greeting, "Callen! Callen! You've got company!"

"What's all this?" called the old man back.

"Excitement—adventure—and challenge. We're going to change the course of history!" As Yuan announced that, the two men met. Yuan scooped the smaller Sime into a quick embrace and walked him toward Laneff, who was sitting on the deck of the chopper, her legs dangling high above the ground. "Let me introduce Laneff Farris ambrov Sat'htine, the most important person in the world today."

"Ambrov Sat'htine?" The old man scrutinized her duoconsciously. "Ain't no one sick here! But if Yuan says you're welcome—then you're welcome!" He turned to Yuan. "Back room is ready—like always. You go on in. I'll fetch some more wood and find something for you to eat." He gave her one more appraising glance.

He'd certainly perceived her junct condition. It was a nageric stigma that felt to Laneff like a deformity. But maybe he didn't recognize it. How many people these days had ever zlinned a junct up close? And there was something odd about his nager, too.

Yuan said, "A meal would be nice, but let's get this chopper covered. And we've got to haul out the transmitter and arrange to get us out of here before the Tecton net closes on us. Maybe— Callen, maybe you should go with us?"

"Nope. This's my place. Picked out my dyin' spot already. Get you on inside before you freeze!"

A brisk wind was blowing dark clouds over the sun, and here the air was somehow thinner—colder than in the city. Flower-tipped ground cover whipped in the wind, and a pond at the far side of the meadow rippled with waves on which ducks and geese bobbed contentedly.

Yuan helped Laneff down, saying, "We've got a Diet prisoner inside. Unconscious. Probable concussion. Make him comfortable in the side room, and let me know when he comes to."

"Leave it to me," said the Sime, waving them away.

Again Laneff wondered what kind of people she'd fallen in with: people who casually harbored Tecton fugitives, took Diet prisoners, and maintained secret hideouts. But the wind gusted sharply and big pats of rain hammered into them. "Come on!" said Yuan, scooping her along in the crook of his arm.

They dashed under the roof of the wooden porch, and clattered inside. Here it was warm, with a cheery fire going in an open hearth in the center of the room. Nearby, some books were spread on a rough table, a pair of wire-frame glasses tossed on top of them. An oil lamp gave reading light. The walls were lined with shelves of books, making them almost a selyn-insulated density. She could barely zlin the outside.

One end of the room held a deep-red couch and a couple of high-backed chairs that could swallow a person whole. The other end was a kitchen, with a sink rigged with a hand pump for water, and a foam-and-plastic cooler chest. Herbs hung from the rafters in dry bundles, and racks held a myriad sacks and bottles. Near the hearth, a crockery teapot steamed trin aroma into the air.

Under Yuan's touch, a section of bookcase swung out

revealing a heavy door behind which opened a tunnel leading back into the living rock of the hillside; something one only read about in storybooks, a place Gens could hide from Simes come raiding. The cabin *could* be that old.

"Come on," coaxed Yuan. He lit an oil lamp and closed both doors behind them. Then he stopped at a door on their left, went into a dark room sparsely appointed with rough-hewn furniture, and turned on a heater. "Callen will bring blankets to keep the prisoner warm. Come!"

At the end of the tunnel, a room opened—a natural cave that had been nicely wood-paneled and -floored. There were two large beds, a studio couch, and two chairs around a small table. A selyn-powered heater started at Yuan's touch, and then he had regular selyn-powered lights going. In one corner, an opulent antique transfer lounge was surrounded by a heavy drape of modern insulating fabric. The carved-wood scrollwork made it worth a fortune, but Laneff liked the sensuous emerald-velvet upholstery.

"Like it?" asked Yuan, warming his hands at the heater. "You can't zlin this from outside!"

"Even Mairis couldn't zlin us if he were right outside!"

"But does it have facilities?"

"Of course, but not too glamorous." He gestured to a door framed by knotty pine cabinetry, enough storage for five people.

She opened the door and found a short tunnel, chill with underground humidity. At the end, a door opened into a dank chamber lit by a bare lamp. The toilet was a raised platform with a hole in it, set over the wash of an underground stream. A pitcher and basin on a washstand and a bathtub ripped from some old hotel, rigged with a selyn-powered heater—fully charged.

When she returned to the room, flinging her grimy and tattered cloak over a chair, Yuan said, "Someday we'll get around to decorating in there, too!"

"You like this place, don't you?"

He was seated on the transfer lounge, one hand smoothing the soft velvet. He beckoned her. "It's safe—and comfortable." When she didn't move, he added, "And necessary."

The half-finished feeling she had fought down after the kill was returning. "Yuan—I have to know more about you."

The relentless pull of his nager let up. "I did promise you transfer—as soon as we were safe. How could you trust my other promises if I renege on this one?"

Somehow, the very easing of that pull sent a renewed shiver of need through her. She couldn't suppress a sound that verged on a whimper. "You mean—you meant everything?"

"Zlin me. I don't promise rashly. We're safe now—"

"No. They'll divert the agrosatellite to photosearch for the chopper. They'll find us—"

"That'll take time. We won't be here by then."

"Where could we go? How?"

"First let's complete what you started this morning. Then we'll get something hot to eat and plan the future." She still held back, and he added, "How can you make rational plans while your whole body is screaming in agony?"

"It isn't *that* bad."

"Fretting in misery?"

"Well . . ."

In a different tone, he suggested, "Yearning in hope."

If it hadn't been for the need he was coaxing to the surface in her, she'd have laughed at his search for the right inflection on the Simelan noun "need." The tension had drained out of her. *What harm could it do me now?*

She joined him on the lounge. In a perfectly rehearsed maneuver, he had her reclining, her knees bent over the contoured rest and her shoulders raised comfortably against the back of the lounge. He sat at her side, on the curved projection, as if he were a channel about to give her transfer. But he was Gen. It was her most secret—and forbidden—dream come true. The future and the past fell away, and she gave herself to the moment.

His field narrowed to focus wholly on her. It wasn't anything like Shanlun's attention, yet it wakened echoes of the power she'd often felt in him. With firm control, he drew her hyperconscious. The Gen body hovering over her pulsed with an ever brighter selyn field as each cell in him produced selyn. It was a brightness that lit the room to her Sime senses. The furniture wisped into transparency, the clothes in the closets became perceptible and dissolved into nothing. They were encased in a private bubble of reality. She could not zlin outside, and so there was no world outside.

Her tentacles slid naturally into place on his bare arms, feeling each cord of muscle under the curly hair on his skin, outlined by the richly coursing selyn pulsing through his tissues. In a flash of peak need, she yanked the big Gen down until his weight was almost crushing her slight frame, and their lips met.

Brilliant selyn burst into the dark pockets of her brain. The first abundant gush choked off to a mere trickle. Suffocating, she struggled to draw selyn against that immense resistance. She could sense the limitless supply in him, but not the mechanism whereby he denied her. Furious at betrayal, she redoubled her effort and was rewarded with a tiny increase in flow rate.

But the Gen felt no pain, no fear. No killbliss promise was carried on that current of selyn. Yet the struggle itself was exhilarating. The knotting, cramping tensions of need melted. The sense of cold darkness within evaporated. Strength came back. He made it last long enough despite the shallowness of her need.

She came up out of it gasping, exultant, having won selyn from a Gen despite his resistance. She grinned up into his face, feeling now his body heat against her. "You never learned that from the Tecton!"

"Actually, Therapists sometimes have to do such things for channels in trouble."

Shanlun. She remembered Shanlun working over Digen, coaxing and tempting him. And Digen lax against the fluffed white pillows, dead. All the grief she'd been unable to experience during the last few days welled up, choking her. In two breaths, she was sobbing against the sharp knives of loss and failure, of ending. Clutching Yuan's huge shoulders, she sat up to bury her face in his chest.

He gave a relieved sigh. "So I got you post, anyway."

Between sobs, she gasped, "I've never had it like this."

Reaching into a drawer under the lounge, he produced a box of tissues. "Don't resist. Cry it out."

She could imagine him saying that to the channels he'd given transfer to, encouraging their posttransfer reactions. During need, a Sime was unable to experience the powerful personal emotions because of the interfering jangle of need gearing the whole organism to fight for life. Once need was assuaged, however, the human mind regurgitated all the suppressed emotions in a flood.

Laneff cried for Digen now, as she had not been able to before. And she wept for the life she had known when Digen was rallying strongly and all was well. But as she grieved over the death of that old self, buried that self in a tomb of false expectations, she found a new self emerging, fed on hope.

She wadded up the pile of soggy tissues. "I'm all right now."

"You've always been all right."

She blinked burning eyes. "What a peculiar thing to say."

"Laneff, nothing you've done has been pathological. Any one of the renSimes in that box would have gone for that Gen if they weren't wearing attenuators."

"And why wasn't I wearing mine?" She asked his unspoken question, but her voice crackled with a belligerence that shamed her.

"They told me only that you were suffering from prematurely raised intil, that you had a full five days until your transfer schedule. I assumed you'd taken them off because you felt better."

"No. I took them off *to* feel better." And she explained how the perfectly miraculous devices only made her feel sick. "I was afraid I'd actually vomit at the microphone."

"I know something about the Farris channels, but that's a new one on me. I didn't have time to study up on you. All I know about you is what I've read in the papers."

"It wasn't your fault."

He shook his head. "If I'd thought it through, I'd have stayed by you as I was charged to."

"Logically, it made better sense for you to get in close to the Gen and work with the channels to shield everyone, not just me."

"But I was set to guard you, not 'everyone.' Mairis will undoubtedly bring charges against me if I ever show my nose in the Tecton again. Laneff, they were after *you!*"

"Why?"

I could have stopped them if I'd—and because I didn't, they've wrecked Mairis's plans. Oh, I really blew it this time!"

He rested his forehead in his palm, a gesture so reminiscent of Mairis feeling the weight of his responsibilities that she had to ask again, "Yuan, just *who* are you?"

He froze. Then he jerked to his feet, paused a moment with his back to her, and turned, shoulders thrown back, head high. "Yuan Sirat Tiernan, First Order Donor in the Tecton's scale, and erstwhile Sosectu in Rior in the Distect."

"Rior!" she breathed. For months, the peripheral presses had been carrying rumors of a revived Distect movement headed by a self-styled Sosectu trying to reconstitute the House of Rior of legend, the Tecton's traditional adversary.

But within hours of Digen's death, Mairis had received a crisp document purporting to be from this elusive modern Distect, pledging to support him in any move he might make toward Unity. The legitimate press had plastered that news all over the world until rumors of Mairis's next move had begun to fling Laneff into the spotlight.

Laneff's hand went to her mouth, scrubbing as if to erase the whisper of Yuan's touch. The Distect philosophy held that in any transfer situation, the Gen, not the Sime, was fully responsible for the results: the complete opposite of the Tecton attitude she had been raised to. It was said that one taste of Distect-style transfer was sure to lead any Sime into going junct.

What difference does it make? For me it's too late. But it did make a difference. She went to pick up her cloak from the chair where she'd tossed it. It was all she had left of Sat'htine, and all she believed in. "I can see why you didn't tell me that before—transfer."

"In the chopper, running from Tecton guns, would you have helped me if I'd told you my identity?"

She zlinned him. His nager was calm, steady, barely diminished by her selyn draw. She remembered the ferocious snarl on his lips as he lowered his head and charged straight at the terrorists holding her. "When you attacked those men who held me hostage, what did you plan? Why did you do it? Didn't you realize you'd probably be shot along with me?"

"Laneff, I'm not the heroic type. I wasn't calculating odds, or even planning. I just saw the shendi-flamin' Diet destroying humanity's last chance at Unity in my lifetime. No matter what, I couldn't let them get out of there with you prisoner. I've been fighting them for a couple of years. They've held some of my Simes prisoner—and what they returned to me was hardly worth burying!"

Laneff dropped the cloak and rubbed the welts on her tentacle sheaths where the Diet's belt had lashed her arms together. If she'd struggled any harder against that confinement, she'd have injured her lateral tentacles and have been unable to take the finishing transfer from Yuan, which had left her more clearheaded than she'd been in days.

A pattern stood out starkly in her mind. She'd ended up in Yuan's care because she didn't want to risk exposure to Shanlun's overripe nager. She'd shed the attenuators because she didn't want to risk vomiting in public. And she'd killed—and then refused to risk injuring her laterals. *Augmenting, I could have gotten away—and I'd probably have died before my laterals healed enough so they could get selyn into me.*

Chuckling at the grotesque irony, she explained the sequence of her decisions to Yuan. "At each point I've done the right thing, and matters have gotten worse!"

He savored the irony, too, and said, "I've always thought that God has an intricate sense of humor. If we can just go along with the joke, we can often come out with the last laugh. You game to try it?"

"What do you mean?" His oddball point of view made a queer sense to her now.

"I promised you a lab and time enough to do some significant work. I don't pretend to understand neurochemistry or the big project you have to launch, but with us, you can expect eighteen months—"

"No!" she interrupted. "I told you I won't kill—"

He cut her off. "You didn't kill me, and you feel better. Laneff, in the Tecton, the most they've ever sustained a junct's life without permitting a kill is thirteen months. In the Neo-Distect, we have people who have lived three years after rejuncting, have lived without killing, and feel no real need to kill."

"They're the exception, not the rule, aren't they?"

"True. It seems to have a lot to do with finding the right transfer partner." He smiled ruefully. "I'm not the right one for you."

She couldn't deny that. All her daydreams had always centered on the most powerful Donors, trained to serve the Farris channels. Now that she'd experienced such a Donor, she could see it wasn't ideal at all. Her minuscule selyn draw could never evoke any sensation in such a Donor.

"I do have someone in mind for you, Laneff. And there are others who can be asked. We don't assign donors. We let people choose each other."

"What if no one chooses me?"

"Someone will. You are—attractive."

And you're a very attractive man. She leashed back the surge of pure sexual awareness that hit her then, knowing its power was a measure of how good a transfer she'd had from Yuan.

"Yuan, would I have access to the latest journals in your laboratory?"

"*Your* laboratory," he corrected, nodding. "Certainly."

"And if by some long-shot chance I produce a breakthrough, and I put into your hands the ability to distinguish Sime from Gen early in life, what would you do with that knowledge?"

She zlinned him keenly now, using all her sensitivity to discern if he was lying.

"We'd give the knowledge to the world."

"Immediately?"

"If not instantly. Certainly within the month."

She could find no note of falseness in him.

"Are you *really* Sosectu? Do you have the authority to make such a decision? Will the others follow you?"

"They'd follow me into death. Some have."

The grave vibration of that shook Laneff's bones. "Why are you trying to convince me to side with you? I'm as much your prisoner here as I'd be prisoner of the Diet."

"No!"

His indignation was like a nageric slap. He paced. "Laneff, the shidoni-be-flayed Diet lorshes would have forced you to do—whatever they could think of to benefit them. If they could get your research, they'd use it to abort every Sime fetus. If they couldn't get you to cooperate, they'd force you to kill for them and litter the world with corpses marked with your peculiar signature. Their propaganda people could build that into an embarrassment for Mairis that could cost us the whole Unity movement."

True, any competent channel could identify the burn pattern she left on a kill: the searing of nerves before the selyn reserves were barely depleted. "And you won't do the same?"

"No, Laneff. You have your freedom. Say the word, and my organization will deliver you up safe and sound inside the walls of any Last Year House you name."

He'd made her many promises. He'd delivered on two impossible ones: safety and transfer. He really didn't promise what he couldn't deliver. And she was afraid to challenge him on this one. And that told her just how much she rejected the option of giving herself up to the Tecton. So where else did she have to go?

"All right, I'll go with you." But she made up her mind right there to keep a very close score on his promises. At the least suspicion, she'd do her utmost to see to it that Yuan and his people never got their hands on any of her results until Mairis had them safely in his.

He greeted her concession with one of those fresh grins that radiated vitality. "Good, that's settled. Now, I'm starved, and we do have a prisoner to see to. Then it'll be time to get on the radio and make some travel arrangements. This time tomorrow, you'll be halfway around the world."

4

CONFIDENCE
RESERVED

The Neo-Distect's headquarters lay outside the ancient capital, P'ris. From the air, approaching, Laneff could see the city, bisected by the broad, flat river that gleamed in the moonlight. A rainbow of artificial light outlined the Monument to the Last Berserker, huge chunks of stone shaped into a starred cross and dedicated to the ending of the kill.

It seemed like centuries since that day when she'd stood there to have her name engraved on that monument signifying her disjunction. *And now I've betrayed that vow*.

Flying low, the silent craft skimmed fields freshly plowed for the spring planting. The ancient checkerboard of the countryside seemed painted rather than real. Nothing could be so perfect. Heading away from the city, they crossed vineyards, the gnarled old vines like rows of gnomes dancing through moonshadow. Patches of virgin woods sliced by gleaming streams housed cleared areas carved out by stubborn farmers.

Beside her, Yuan said, "Once, in Ancient times, before humanity mutated into Sime and Gen, all this was city. Farmers are still digging relics out of the ground."

"How do you keep the Tecton Air Traffic plotters from tracking this plane so close to the city?"

"Well, let us say that a new organization has to use novel methods."

She'd been zlinning the plane, trying to detect any equipment that might bedazzle the Traffic Towers or prevent the Simes in the towers from noticing the plane. But it carried all the usual beacons and seemed utterly normal.

"I guess you don't trust me yet," she commented.

"If you were in my place, would you trust any new Sime who could abandon Tecton values so quickly?"

"No." *I haven't abandoned them. I just can't live them.*

"When you know more about us, you can choose freely. Then we'll trust you with all our secrets."

Laneff couldn't fault him for that. After all, there were still things she wouldn't trust him with—such as the Endowment.

"Yuan," she asked as the plane circled for landing, "what prevents the Tecton from tracing me here?"

"Only my most trusted people know where you are. We've left the Tecton no clue about you. Rest secure, Laneff."

His nager was so powerful she couldn't help but believe him. But she also knew that Mairis and Shanlun had other ways of getting information. Lore out of all the fantasy stories she'd ever read led her to suspect that the Endowment could be used to locate a missing person. And the Endowment was no fantasy. Digen had been able to set fires by some trick of nageric focus, which Shanlun was trained to deal with. Mairis, she was sure, could do equally exotic tricks.

She shut off that line of thought as they bumped down onto a fragment of Ancient roadbed that started in the midst of a field and ended at a ramshackle farmhouse and barn shaded by a grove of trees.

They were in Gen Territory. The farmyard, spilling off to one side of the house, held chickens, goats, and an old cow. A handworked pump stood in the yard, while the air held a taint of outhouse.

As they climbed out of the tiny plane, the pilot and copilot helped a nurse move the stretcher their prisoner was strapped to. They were the only occupants of the plane. Zlinning as well as looking about her, Laneff observed, "A little primitive, but then your bolt-hole in the mountains seemed primitive from outside, too."

"Can you detect any selyn batteries in use?"

"Except for the plane, no. But then I'm no channel."

"You have the sensitivity of one, though."

She shrugged. "In a renSime, it's a handicap." It was, in fact, what had condemned her to an ugly death, no matter what Yuan promised. It was her sensitivity that made her react badly to attenuators. And her sensitivity left her open to enticement by Gens—whether she was disjunct or not. *A channel's sensitivity without a channel's control.*

They followed the stretcher into the farmhouse, where a Gen woman met them with two toddlers clinging to her slacks. She was holding a bowl, kneading bread dough as she talked. "Sosectu, you're running late," she said in heavily accented Simelan. "Everybody's been so anxious. You better get on downstairs right away."

"I'm going, Tithra. Tell Becket to set the dogs tonight."

"He would anyway, with you here."

The plane's pilot manipulated something on the mantel of the fireplace, and the whole façade swung out to reveal a stairwell lit by a single candle. Yuan followed the stretcher, calling over his shoulder, "And save me a slice of that bread! It smells great!"

The woman swore in some dialect Laneff couldn't identify except that it sounded P'risian. "It had better," she added in Simelan, "I'm working hard enough at this flacked-out business!"

At her show of temper, Yuan paused. "Tithra—trust me. Your bread baking and barnyard mucking are going to reunite all mankind. I know it!"

"I don't really resent it, Sosectu," she responded in a

kinder voice. "I volunteered. And—the transfers are worth it all!"

Yuan grinned one of his bright, satisfied grins. Then he led Laneff down into candlelit dimness, his red-blond hair like burnished copper. The door whumped shut behind them. By candlelight, they followed a dank corridor lined with Ancient brick. Down a ramp and around a corner, down more stairs, they found another door. The plane's pilot and copilot were already returning without the stretcher.

"Get that plane back before dawn," ordered Yuan, "then go to ground for a few weeks."

The Sime pilot answered, "We've got our instructions, Sosectu." And the Gen copilot added a grin of adoration to the Sime's nageric respect for Yuan.

Yuan waved them along. "On with it, then!"

Beyond the massive door, Laneff found clean, white-tiled corridors leading in several directions from a wide foyer. Fresh, machine-scrubbed air, brilliant selyn-powered lighting, computerized offices, and a staff of crisp, alert young Simes and Gens behaving as if they worked for one of the far-flung House of Keon corporations confirmed Laneff's expectations.

Everywhere they passed, Yuan was hailed as Sosectu, deferred to, consulted, and respected, just as if he were Sectuib of this secret Householding. Rior had coined the word, Sosectu, to mean a Gen Head of Householding, and here it had become a reality once again, the past brought alive.

Laneff was given an ID tag keyed so she wouldn't set off alarms wherever she walked, a passkey chip to her new lab, sleeping quarters, and other low-security areas, just as if she were employed by any big research corporation. Then Yuan guided her through a maze of corridors into a sleek new section. At the very end of the newest hallway, only half lined with white ceramic tile and mosaic patterns, they came to a door painted with the lighthouse symbol of Rior. Yuan commanded, "Use your key."

She slid the disk into its slot, and the door purred open. Instantly, a Gen's nager blushed the ambient rose-pink. "You said this was an empty lab!"

He smiled. "Your assistant, Jarmi ambrov Rior!"

The Gen woman bent over a packing case in the midst of the empty floor straightened and turned, her nager flooded with guilelessness. But Laneff went cold inside. Now she knew how Yuan meant to keep tabs on her work and make sure she didn't sneak her results out to Mairis. A spy.

"Jarmi, this is Laneff Farris ambrov Sat'htine. I'm hoping you two will hit it off. She has the draw speed to match you and the renSime capacity you've been hoping for."

Laneff turned her back on the Gen, confronting Yuan. "I don't want an assistant. I work alone."

Yuan circled Laneff. "Jarmi volunteered to help you set this place up." He gestured to the bare tile floor littered with debris from construction. Plumbing lines and power cables plumed up out of the tiles. Along the walls, modern vent chambers with manufacturers' labels still stuck to the glass windows gaped darkly at them. "She's the closest to a neurochemist I have here. This was to be her lab."

"Sosectu," complained Jarmi, "I'd much rather see this lab and budget going on Laneff's project than on the microwave patterns on the skin of mice and rats!"

Yuan's movement brought Laneff to face Jarmi again. The Gen woman was not much taller than Laneff, but plump as only a Gen could be. She had a fringe of dark hair, and a short nose that supported black wire eyeglass frames.

"You mean," asked Laneff, "*you're* developing that new diagnostic microwave detector? The one that was abandoned by Paidridge Labs?"

"Of course," replied Jarmi. "Our House is mostly Gen. We have Gen healers. Channels shouldn't have to be overtrained just so we can use them as diagnosticians! That's no way to treat a vulnerable minority like channels."

Laneff had never before heard channels referred to as a vulnerable minority. To most people, they were powerful authority figures. Bemused, she said, "It sounds like a worthwhile project. Sat'htine was toying with the idea of funding it last year."

"But your project is so much more worthwhile!" Jarmi was looking up at Laneff, squatting next to the packing box, her pale-green lab coat spread on the dirty floor around her. Her nager, nearly blanked out by Yuan's, held a wistful enchantment laced with sparks of excitement. But then it dimmed, and with sadness she added, "But if you don't want help . . ."

Laneff felt the objections caught in the back of Yaun's throat, nearly choking him. But he kept silent as Jarmi finished repacking the instrument and closed the box. "There, now my things are out of your way. You can start requisitioning." She rose. "I'll send someone for that."

"Wait!" called Laneff, stopping her halfway to the door. "You know, it won't be long until you can have this lab back. I probably won't survive the year." She kept talking over the Gens' combined objections. "If my work is ever to be completed, somebody has to work with me who can carry on after I die. Yuan says you're the best he's got; why should I pick anybody else?" A thousand years from now, would it matter if the Neo-Distect or the Tecton had the first method of distinguishing Sime from Gen before birth?

Jarmi smiled tentatively. "I'll do my best. . . ."

And she did, exceeding all Laneff's expectations because Jarmi really wanted to work on this project. Within three days, they had the bare lab furnished with wet benches, cabinetry, standard glassware, reagents, and computer terminals. Work crews labored around the clock until every drain, power outlet, fan, and water tap worked perfectly.

On the fourth morning, when Laneff came back from breakfast, she found Jarmi had set up two partitioned office areas. One was surrounded by light-orange fabric-covered partitions, not quite the Sat'htine hue. The other partitions were the sickly green color Jarmi seemed to prefer.

"This will be your desk," said Jarmi in greeting. "I bribed a friend of mine to give up his new terminal so you can have it. We're short this month, with all this expanding."

"I wish I knew where you get the money for all this!"

"Legally," assured Jarmi. "But by the time you're cleared to learn all the details, you won't have time. See," she proffered a stack of shiny magazines, "your first mail."

"But—" She'd never gotten a subscription started in under two months.

"You have to know who to ask," explained Jarmi brightly.

The Gen's happiness was too soothing to Laneff's nerves for her to want to tarnish it with suspicious questions. She sat down at the desk; the chair wasn't new and creaked in a friendly way. "May I clip these magazines for file?"

"Certainly. They're yours."

And Laneff dug in, catching up on all she'd missed since Digen had died. Specifically, she searched for articles on his death. The autopsy results would surely be published, and so would her treatment notes, and those of Shanlun and Digen's other physicians.

Around noon, Jarmi came back with two Simes pushing a wheeled platform stacked with electrical equipment. While they unloaded, Jarmi came to the office. "Here! Top-priority requisition forms for the NMR machine and the big mass spectrometer!" She thumbed the stack onto the desk. "Key to the balance room." The chip went on top of the stack. "We're set. Now, what do I do next?"

Laneff had found the articles she wanted, but only part of the information was there. "Have you read any of my papers?"

"Sure, not that I understand much of it. It seems to me it's a long, long way from identifying receptor sites on nerve sheaths to distinguishing Sime from Gen *in utero!*"

"Well, I haven't been able to publish my synthesis because nobody else has ever been able to duplicate it. Without that, there's no hope of making this commercial!"

Laneff took a sheet of paper and began to lecture. "I call this compound K/A because it's the eleventh compound I tried when looking for a reaction distinctly different between Sime and Gen placental material. Now, please never forget that this has not been field-tested. My evidence is entirely statistical. I tested five hundred specimens taken from Sime women with Sime husbands—and I assumed that two thirds of those placentas had to be from Sime children, while about one third would be from Gen children."

"Reasonable enough."

"But not conclusive, even though K/A bonds to receptors on two thirds of those placentas, and not at all on the other third. Dissecting out the nerve fibers, I found that the bonding takes place on the selyn transport nerve sheath in the placenta that supplies the fetus with selyn from the mother. Further, a nerve saturated with K/A will not transport selyn. I tried it on selyn transport nerves from other parts of the body and got the same effect.

"My theory is that this substance I've synthesized is naturally present in all Simes, but especially abundant in channels, and is responsible for regulating selyn flow. I have no idea how its level in the blood would be regulated. And I've never done any experiments to isolate it from blood. I was about to try that when Digen was brought into the Center suffering from hypersensitivity to selyn flow causing transfer abort."

Laneff told a highly censored version of that story to Jarmi, leaving out everything to do with the Endowment. But she now felt close enough to the Gen woman to tell all the rest of the story of Shanlun.

The first time she'd met Shanlun, she'd been wandering the corridors of the university hospital/Sime Center where her lab was. Frustration had driven her from the lab that evening, and despair had once more set in when she checked her mailbox and found yet another rejection by a major journal. It was close to midnight, the hallway lights dimmed. She wandered into her favorite waiting alcove, where huge windows overlooked the far-flung lights of the city. She was halfway through the door before she even noticed the muted nager.

She recognized Shanlun as the Companion-Therapist to the world-famous elder statesman housed in the security wing. She'd heard the Gen's nager was distinctive, but she'd never imagined anything like this.

"Jarmi, it seemed as if he'd wrapped his nager about him like a cloak, defining his personal space so that he literally didn't exist beyond it. I could zlin the compressed intensity of his selyn field, but you know how when a Gen is paying attention to something, it's as if a shaft of nageric light beams out of them and sets the object of attention glowing? Awake, any Gen is aware of *something*, and things around them—*glow*. The First Order Gens, when they're high-field, set the whole room on fire. Shanlun does that, but he can also *not* do it. He can pay attention to *nothing*. It's as if he just becomes invisible or unzlinnable, rather. I've never heard of anyone who can do such a thing, but he was doing it that night when I first saw him."

He seemed to be staring out the window, unaware of her. His nager was composed of tiny flakes of particolored light that blended to an iridescent silver. Knowing it was impolite to zlin a Gen so fixedly, she blurted the first thing that came to mind. "Beautiful view, isn't it?"

After a long silence in which his nager didn't react, he said in the deep voice of a working Companion, "Yes, it is beautiful. It's a beauty which is easy to perceive. There are others which are much harder."

"Beauty comes in grades of difficulty?"

His nager relaxed, spreading to suffuse the room with an even glow of his attention. This, too, was an effect Laneff had never zlinned before, even in other First Order Donors. "Is there anything," he asked in a rhetorical tone, "that is not beautiful when viewed from the center of its own moment?"

"What?" Yet the words made an odd echo of sense.

He turned, his eyes raking her as if astonished to find someone there. "I'm sorry, that must sound like nonsense." He shrugged ingenuously, like a gypsy. "I'm just feeling terribly frustrated, and I don't want to splatter that on every Sime around me. Excuse me, Hajene."

He left before she could deny the title "hajene," given only to channels. She brooded, aware that she should have realized the First Companion in Zeor would not be feeling talkative while his Sectuib was so ill. She couldn't get image, nager and flesh, out of her mind, and so the next night, she pinned her Householding signet to her lab coat conspicuously, and sought the same waiting-room alcove just before midnight. He was there, gazing at the last quarter moon rising over the city.

Silently, she joined him. They shared the alcove without a word for nearly half an hour and parted with only a nod. Five nights she joined him in that silent midnight vigil, aware for the first time in her life of the way the moon shifted phase and time day by day. Finally, on the sixth night they gazed on a moonless sky over a multicolored city of jewels, a visual effect parallel to his nageric effect.

As he turned to leave the alcove, she dared to speak again. "I think I see now how beauty comes in grades of difficulty. Sometimes, a model of a molecule can seem ugly on first sight. But understand how its bonds imbue it with special character—how they strike a chord and sing together—and the sight of the model can make you cry. But people think you're crazy if you sit over a reaction pot and cry for joy. Especially if the reaction won't go!"

His nageric astonishment melted into an avid hunger that even her sensitivity might have missed, it was folded away so quickly. His eye lit on her Householding signet. "You're not Perrin Farris, are you?"

"Laneff Farris ambrov Sat'htine. Hajene Perrin's my cousin. I'm just a renSime."

"Shanlun ambrov Zeor." He added, "Just a Gen."

They had talked for another hour. She found that Shanlun had pledged Zeor, to Digen, expecting to be his last Companion, but accepting that in order to be part of Zeor. "I hadn't expected, though, to come to admire him so much, Laneff. I don't want him to die so soon. He's come to be the definition of Sectuib to me. I suppose that sounds odd from someone who was never even a Householder before."

"No," Laneff replied. "I've never met Digen; he's not even a relative of mine; not all Farrises are related, you know. But I've heard Digen can make people understand what creates and sustains a Householding. It's the ideals of Zeor that have touched your heart. You're as much Zeor as I am Sat'htine."

"I hope so," he sighed. On subsequent nights, he began to talk of the intricate medical problems Digen was enduring. She was a researcher, not a clinician, so all she could offer at first was Sat'htine philosophy: "Shanlun, a physician can never win the battle against death, for death is a part of nature. A physician's job is to enhance the quality—and length—of life, or perhaps to ease death."

Astonishment whirled through his nager in dizzying sparks that left her as breathless as his smile did. "Thank you!" As he hurried away, she thought that never had anyone learned one of Sat'htine's hardest lessons so quickly. *Or maybe I just reminded him*.

She wished that her own spirits could be lifted so easily. Her grant money was running out, she couldn't figure why nobody else was able to reproduce her synthesis of K/A, and she couldn't find a cheap enough way to extract and purify it from Sime blood—if it was even there. Every time she heard the news or read a newspaper and encountered a report of a berserker, she ground her teeth in frustration, for she knew from intimate personal experience what they were suffering. She couldn't give up, yet she couldn't go on, and as hard as she prayed, there was no answer in sight.

The moments around midnight she spent with Shanlun became the focus of her days, the rest a dull endurance trial. One night, he turned from the rain-sheeted windows and sat heavily in one of the padded green chairs. He admitted, "It wouldn't be so bad if it weren't for the abort seizures. He's dying, Laneff, and I can't even make him comfortable."

Earlier that day, she'd dutifully plowed through an article on the mechanism of transfer-abort seizures in elderly channels. It had been a hopeless, heartless article, and she had pondered how her synthetic compound reduced selyn flow and thus nervous sensitivity to selyn flow. She began explaining this to Shanlun before she had it all thought out herself. "But, no! You don't use the Sectuib in Zeor as a human experiment! Especially not on a wild theory."

But he wouldn't listen to that. He made her repeat her explanation three times until he understood.

"I call it olquenolone, though I'm not at all sure of the stereochemistry; my synthesis produces a messy mixture. The fraction I purify out of it I call K/A because it's the first fraction of the eleventh compound I've tried. But I'll bet olquenolone will be a good name for it."

"And this molecule could be the key to transport nerve irritability."

"Maybe, but it's never been tried on living tissue!"

Pacing, Shanlun decided, "I have to tell Mairis—and Digen—about this. Remember, Digen once submitted to Rindaleo ambrov Zeor's experiments, and that led to the end of the Donor shortage. He might go for this, too."

She had learned about the great Rindaleo ambrov Zeor in school, but she was hardly his equal.

The next day Shanlun brought Mairis to her lab. She spent the entire day with them, between their trips to check on Digen. They grilled her on her every experiment more closely than any doctoral committee ever had.

Every time she successfully fielded a challenge, she noticed Shanlun's attention on her, and there was more than just hope in his nager. It was admiration that was gradually becoming intensely personal.

The following day, Mairis brought in two top experts, one a member of Zeor and another a nonHouseholder. She was halfway through the entire reprise of her experiments before the nickname introductions finally sank in, and she realized these men were behind two of the most exalted names in her profession.

The Householder, a Sime, stayed in her lab all night checking her benchwork. She sweated that out torn by a mixture of hope that he'd find her mistake, and a perverse conviction that there *was* no mistake to find.

At dawn, when Mairis and Shanlun rejoined them, the Householder zlinned her sharply, and said, "Her theory could even be right. The compound does work as described, but I'd like a few weeks to check—"

"We don't have a few weeks," interrupted Shanlun, seeming haggard. "We've got to get a transfer into the Sectuib—or he'll be dead in *hours*."

Mairis elaborated gravely, "My top four channels have been working with him around the clock, and we can't do anything. This, at least, is worth a try—and he's for it. So tell us what you want set up to capture all the data possible out of this test. And let's get started."

They took all the K/A she had left and set her to synthesizing more under the watchful eyes of their experts. She had to shut her mind to the experiment going on in the security wing in order to stop her hands from shaking. To focus her concentration, she always visualized the reacting molecules tumbling through their gyrations, stage by stage, turning themselves inside out like contortionists or adagio dancers around a gypsy campfire. When she failed to concentrate like this, on each step of the reaction precisely executed, some untraceable error crept in and she often got no yield of her desired product.

She knew she'd put on a proud display of her bench technique when, nine hours later, she weighed out her yield of K/A, pure. She was beaming radiantly when Shanlun and Mairis returned.

"He's alive! We did it!" announced Mairis, and the Householder observing her beamed radiantly.

Shanlun was weary, but still fluorescent. "Here's the record and a printout from the vital signs display. I think it shows the effect of the drug; I know *I* felt it when it hit Digen. It was—a miracle."

His hand brushed hers as she took the strip of paper, and he caught at one of her handling tentacles with a finger. "I would have given up if it hadn't been for you. Thank you, Laneff." The tremor of sensuality in his touch kindled a like response in her. His nager was depleted of selyn though its usual pyrotechnic whirling still dizzied her. *He's post*, she thought, and knew she could have him in bed if she chose. As delightful as the thought was, she found she didn't want to take advantage of him that way. *Not this man*.

She put on her best clinical façade and examined the recordings. She could see how blood pressure, heartbeat, respiration, and ronaplin secretion had varied as the drug was introduced. The graphs jittered at the transfer point, trembling at the brink of abort for several moments, but then steadied through the transfer. "There's no way," said Laneff regretfully, "to rule out the placebo effect."

"I know," answered Shanlun, but she could tell his agreement was only intellectual. "The important thing is that it did work. And now Digen wants to meet you!"

Her first view of the living legend was in the ruddy light of a stormy dawn. He was propped up slightly in the white-sheeted bed, watching the sunrise while his withered old hands plucked aimlessly at the covers. He turned when she approached, and his eyes were fully alive in a way that belied the bruised throb of his nager.

"So you're the one responsible for letting me see yet

another dawn." He paused to slide laboriously hyperconscious and zlin her. Then he said, "You remind me of
Ercy—my daughter. I loved her, you know."

"With good reason," Laneff replied, recalling the story
of how Ercy had returned from a self-imposed exile and
died giving birth to an heir to Zeor, Mairis's mother. "But
I'm not a channel like Ercy was."

"So I noticed. I'm not that old and feeble yet, young lady.
And with your help, I may be out of this bed again soon."

Laneff glanced about the bare room. For a Sectuib's
hospital room, it was singularly bare and depressing. Even
the curtains had been removed leaving only shutters. On a
rolling tray at the bedside stood a lone cup of water. The
absence of flowers she could understand. Farrises tended
to be allergic. But usually the rooms in this hospital had
some cheerful pictures on the walls, a television, brightly
colored curtains, lamps, dresser scarves. This room had
been stripped bare except for the yellow fire extinguisher
on the wall near the door. The whole place echoed sharply.

"Sectuib Farris, is there anything I might bring you to
make your stay more enjoyable?"

"Oh, no. They'll be bringing me in some food in a few
minutes. Not much that I'm allowed to eat lately, but they
insist. A Sat'htine knows about such things . . .'

She nodded, and he asked that she stay and eat with
him. Over the bland diet, which she tried to pretend
wasn't so dismal, they discussed everything from how
the weather had changed from his youth to the moderniza-
tion of the Householdings.

Weeks passed during which she became increasingly
intimate with Shanlun. He nursed her patiently through
pretransfer depression as if it were a malady he himself
suffered from. And after her transfer, he quietly let her
seduce him into a physical culmination of the growing
emotional closeness between them. She had made love to
many First Order Donors, but never had there been
anything like this.

Shortly after that, she dared to offer the old Sectuib a present. "I made this for your wall," she said, showing him a knotted yarn hanging in shades of deep orange, brown and yellow. "I thought it would cheer this place up. And you can take it home with you later."

Shanlun's nager melted into a tenderness toward her that made Laneff shiver. She hadn't done it to please Shanlun; she'd done it for Digen. But she suddenly realized she couldn't have found a more direct way to Shanlun's heart. Digen, suffering through the woes of turnover, hitched himself a bit higher in the bed and gestured with two dry, wrinkled tentacles. "Shanlun, see if it will go on the wall over there. Just what we ought to have to brighten this room!"

Shanlun hesitated, about to argue as second thoughts brought an odd tension to his nager. In this moment of alertness, Digen glanced from her to his Companion, and said, "Shanlun, you mustn't be too cautious—especially in matters of the heart."

With severe reluctance, Shanlun hung her creation, but she knew then that something was very wrong—very odd in that room. It wasn't until two weeks later that she found out what it was. That day, Digen had demanded that she join him and Shanlun for lunch, and she did, though she was at turnover and lacked appetite.

Digen was approaching need on a twenty-eight-day cycle, while they kept her on a twenty-five-day cycle like most renSimes, so that she'd never experience the true depths of hard need. And she was glad of that, for even at turnover, the first cold inklings of need brought reminders of her disjunction crisis. Shanlun had little patience with her now, for as Digen approached need, his nager became monumentally unwieldy and he experienced the high-order Donor's equivalent of need. His appetite fell off, and his interest in sex declined. With Digen's precarious condition, Shanlun's anxiety about his Sectuib grew to dominate his conversation again. It had become central to

her life, too, and she was glad of the chance to observe
him in person again.

When she arrived at Digen's room, Shanlun was bending over the bed, preparing to help the old Sectuib into
the chair where he was lately permitted to sit up for
meals. "No, wait," fretted Digen. "I don't feel right."

Immediately, Shanlun's fluorescent particolored confetti
nager flared to an even, brilliant gold, fastened wholly on
Digen. Laneff was drawn hyperconscious by that unexpectedly alluring promise of every pleasure her body now
craved. Never before had she zlinned Shanlun working
as a Donor, and never had she zlinned any Donor so
enticing.

Sternly, she shook herself out of it. She wasn't really in
need. She only felt that way. But it scared her.

Duoconscious, she heard Shanlun mutter, "Tertiary
entran, again, Digen." He added some even less intelligible instruction. Entran was a disorder of the channel's
secondary selyn-storage system, the system used to draw
selyn from untrained Gens at controlled speeds so they
felt no pain or fear, and then to give that selyn to renSimes
in need. She'd read in Digen's charts that he'd once
experienced an episode of a bizarre malady dubbed primary entran, where his own personal selyn-using system
had been involved. But there was no such thing as a
tertiary selyn system.

Telling herself it was professional curiosity, she floated
hyperconscious again, zlinning the blurring and shifting
fields between the channel and his vibrant young Donor.
Her scientific detachment vanished at the impact of
Shanlun's fully unleashed field.

The Donor's concentration on his patient never wavered,
but he produced a brown vial of medication from an inside
pocket of his smock and coaxed Digen to swallow. Slowly,
the golden aura of the Gen became brighter and paler,
intensifying until Laneff was drawn despite herself.

She reached out to caress the core of the Gen promise,

as it tugged at her memory of the one total satisfaction she'd ever had in her life—the kill in First Need.

Chaos erupted.

Tongues of flame seemed to shoot from Digen's inner fields, white-gold flame. A moment, and she thought she herself would be engulfed in jagged spikes of whirling selyn, *solid* selyn! It was as if zlinning and seeing had become one and the same thing, a nightmare vision. Unreal. Yet she knew the touch of that selyn bolt was death.

Suddenly, the lances of searing energies converged on a spot just past her right shoulder. She flung herself left, falling to the floor as she went duoconscious, the world fading into view solidly about her, her shoulder bruised where she hit the floor, and Shanlun's voice, deep and commanding, shouting, "Digen, no!"

The sound of his voice reverberated into that plane of nightmare where the flashing bolts of solid selyn lashed all around her, and she saw the voice etching cracks in the bolts.

Behind her, the wall hanging she'd made burst into flame, sending sparks flying outward in a shower of real flame, hot air searing her face.

Shanlun grabbed the yellow fire extinguisher off the wall beside the door and sprayed the flames, his whole manner bespeaking a routine bedside drill. His attitude seemed to be the same as hers might be at dropping a beaker and causing a fire in a lab. That, more than anything, convinced her that what had happened was in fact real.

When the loud rush of the extinguisher subsided, char-stained foam ran down the immaculate wall. Shanlun turned to Laneff. "Are you all right?"

She forced her muscles to gather her legs under her. "I'm not hurt."

Without another glance at her, he set the extinguisher aside and returned to his patient. She saw the dark-brown vial discarded on the white blanket. Digen was limp against the pillows, panting, an expression of anguish on his face to match the sore throb in his nager.

Pocketing the vial, Shanlun sat beside the channel. "It's over now, Digen. Let me—"

"No." His head rolled against the pillow as if he was trying to escape. "No, it'll just happen again—"

"No. I just didn't realize she was there—"

But Digen's eyes focused on Laneff. "I knew I shouldn't have accepted your gift—"

"Actually," contradicted Shanlun, "I think it saved her life. You had another target associated with her to—"

Digen turned back to his Companion. "Yes—go on. She has a right to know—now. And she *is* Farris."

Shanlun sighed, glancing from Digen to Laneff, his nager once again neutralized by the particolored effect. He went to snap a lock on the door and flip on the privacy light. "You're a Farris—and daughter of a Sectuib. All the others who know of this are First Order channels and Donors, all sworn by their Oath of Firsts not to reveal it to anyone not so sworn."

"The secret originated with my daughter," said Digen, "and I was the first one sworn. I'll accept your oath, Laneff, if you make it Unto Sat'htine." He glanced at Shanlun with a knowing significance as he added, "Her children may be involved. It's dangerous for her not to know."

Amid the firm nageric presence of the working Donor, Laneff could detect no response to that. But she knew Shanlun was thinking of her children as his own, and at war with himself because Zeor does not marry out of Zeor. His commitment to Zeor gave him an understanding of her feeling for Sat'htine. He could not believe she could leave Sat'htine for him, any more than he could leave Zeor for her.

Shanlun said, "In the last few weeks, I've come to know the strength she brings to her dedications. I would trust her with more than my life." From inside his shirt, he fished a tiny silver medallion in the form of a starred cross, which he wore on a gold chain. Looping the chain over his head, he held the medallion out to her. "Hold this, and remember the Monument to the Last Berserker, swear Unto Sat'htine, and I will accept that seal as binding as my own."

The warmth of his body made the emblem seem to tingle against her palm, and she was transported back to that moment when she'd watched her name going onto the Monument plate, and the feeling that had never wholly left her: *I can't rest while others are lost in suffering.* The pain and anguish of each and every berserker was her own pain. She had explained that to Shanlun, and he had understood instantly—as no other ever had—how that moment at the Monument was the most sacred moment in her life, rivaling her Householding Pledge.

"I swear to keep this confidence sealed and hold it only for my children, Unto Sat'htine, Forever."

Digen sank back into his pillows with a sigh. Then he pulled himself together. "Laneff, you've always been taught that 'junct' means 'joined to the kill'—a Sime addicted to killing Gens for selyn. But for the second time in my life, I'm junct, Laneff, yet *I* have never killed—or even badly harmed—a Gen. Being junct and killing are really two completely different things. They are related in that being junct makes life—brighter, more keenly experienced, more *beautiful* even in its ugly moments, and thus ever so much more worth fighting for. A junct *will* go after the selyn necessary to live, regardless of the Gen's opinion in the matter. If the wrong Gen gets in the way, the result is a dead Gen."

"This is true of a nonjunct who has never killed."

"Yes, but it takes a whole lot more to push a nonjunct into disregarding the Gen's opinion. My point is that junctedness and the kill are two opposite things. Junctedness enhances the quality of life; the kill ruins all of that enhancement and more. Junctedness is not a pathology, not an unnatural condition as most of my physicians seem to think. The kill, on the other hand, is unnatural."

"There is a truth hidden by the word 'kill,' " said Shanlun.

"The kill isn't something the Sime does. It's something the Gen does. To himself, most of the time. Perhaps nature intended the Gen's reflex to waken the Sime to the junct condition. But unfortunately, it only works in the rare instance where Sime and Gen are well and truly matched. A junct Sime can often be a dreadful danger to any other Gen but his own."

"The great question," said Digen heavily, "is whether it is worthwhile to humanity to unleash such a dreadful danger among us."

"But it's not a fruitless danger," answered Shanlun. "Laneff, what you just witnessed here," he said gesturing to the blackened foam oozing down the white wall, "was a full and proper functioning of a channel's systems in what the Tecton terms the junct condition. You're at turnover now. I must have seemed—irresistible. And Digen has been hurt so often he can't tolerate any other Sime even zlinning his Donor at such moments."

"I think I'm begining to understand," said Laneff.

Shanlun turned to Digen. "I think this may have been the first really positive sign we've had that you'll recover. You were able to deflect your focus from Laneff to a symbol for Laneff. You did that on purpose, didn't you?"

Digen nodded. "No matter what—I *won't* harm anyone."

"But you've never had any directional control at all before Laneff's presence made you *find* your own controls."

For the first time since she'd come in, Laneff saw real hope in the old Sectuib's eyes. "Ha! You're right! I knew from the first she'd be important!"

Shanlun caught her eye with his. "A few of the First Order, four-plus channels like Digen have developed the ability to utilize selyn as energy that can do work at a distance—without any physical contact with the object being manipulated; to move objects, to kindle materials, to transform materials . . . but usually these talents show during the first year after changeover, and the Tecton has developed trust in these aberrant channels because so far they're all Farrises—and they *never* kill. But Digen's Endowment has only erupted now, too late in life for his body to adjust easily, and *that* is what's causing the abort problems your compound alleviates."

This supported her theory that K/A was produced naturally in the Sime body to control selyn transport rates. During First Year, the plasticity of the young body would allow glands to develop the capability of producing large amounts of K/A, and the governors to control that amount precisely. An endowed channel would require especially abundant K/A and very precise control of the levels of it. "Then what you're saying is that even renSimes are endowed."

"No, it's not that simple," said Shanlun. "We don't fully understand the theory of junctedness or the Endowment, let alone the exact nature of their relationship. We simply have to live with the fact of all of this and struggle to develop a philosophy that can handle it. One of the facts is that we have never recorded the existence of an endowed renSime."

At that point, Digen moaned, and simultaneously Laneff became aware of another channel's presence—outside the heavily insulated door. A Farris? She moved closer to the door as Shanlun focused wholly on Digen, who seemed to be suffering hallucinations. She identified the channel. *Mairis!* At once she flipped off the privacy seal and opened the door.

Mairis glanced unsurprised at the charred wall and oozing foam, zlinned Digen and Shanlun, then commanded, "Laneff, go bring a hefty dose of your K/A. We've got to get a transfer into the Sectuib—now!"

She sped down the hall to her lab knowing that Mairis had not come expecting such a scene. His swift acceptance told her more about how routine it was than all of Shanlun's theory. When she returned with her new supply, fresh from her drying oven, Mairis cupped the jar of white powder in one hand.

"That's his third abort, Laneff. Shanlun can't control it. We're going to have to try your miracle drug again."

"Here's the analysis," she answered, handing over a long sheet of graph paper on which a single tall peak was sketched with only a few tiny peaks to either side of it. "It's the same stuff, and pure."

Shanlun took the jar and rotated it while Mairis eyed the graph. Shanlun nodded, and Laneff handed him a folded envelope of the compound. "This is the same dosage we used last time."

The Gen conferred with Mairis, and then introduced the entire contents of the envelope into the intravenous bottle they had prepared, feeding into Digen's ankle.

The old man now seemed frail and withered, unconscious against the smooth linens. His skin was pale, and the animated *presence* had disappeared. But still he breathed.

They waited while the drips rolled down the tubing. Mairis held the shape of the selyn fields around Digen so steady that Laneff knew she could stay and watch without danger of her causing another of Digen's fits. She leaned against the medications cart, duoconscious, and waited.

Presently, Mairis said, "Try it again. He's weakening."

"I'd rather wait for Yanine," said Shanlun. "You said she'd be right along."

"I can work without my Companion," argued Mairis. "We don't have time."

As if to verify that, Digen tossed restlessly as he came to partial consciousness. He was in hard need, but Laneff couldn't tell how close to attrition. A renSime couldn't zlin such detail in a channel's nager.

Sitting on the edge of the bed, Shanlun captured Digen's hands in his own—Gen muscles straining even against the enfeebled old channel. Once again, the Gen's field flowered into a peculiarly compelling gold—blunted for Laneff by Mairis.

As Shanlun made the fifth contact point, Laneff was

sure it would work this time. And then, with a surge of thrashing, Digen sent Shanlun flying across the room to crash into the wall and slump senseless to the floor.

Mairis closed on his great grandfather, twisting and distorting the fields so oddly that Laneff fled to hypoconsciousness to avoid it. Able only to see, hear, feel, but not to zlin, she dashed across the room to Shanlun. *What if his neck is broken?*

She had to go duoconscious to check for broken bones before moving him, and the fields once more compelled her.

Digen, also a channel of supreme capacity, was fighting Mairis for control of the field gradients. The effect was a stomach-wrenching distortion of space about the two men. And then something changed.

Mairis grew still. Digen sat up, arms reaching out, tentacles extended, even the sensitive laterals out and searching. His face took on a glow of ecstasy, sloughing off decades. His nager twanged with an odd—*killbliss?*

Whatever it was Digen was experiencing, it spoke to Laneff. It was what she'd sought in the kill and never found. She'd trade her soul for one moment of it.

One word escaped Digen's lips. "Ilyana!"

And then the selyn fields collapsed in on themselves to a pinpoint black vortex. Attrition.

Transfixed by the gut-chilling horror, she stared as the limp old body sank into Mairis's arms.

5

COMPASSION

As she finished the story, Laneff couldn't suppress the tears she hadn't been able to shed at Digen's death. She grabbed a tissue from her lab coat pocket, and then Jarmi was hugging her, sniffling in sympathy. There was no reason to fight the upwelling emotions.

In seconds, Laneff was crying openly, her arms around the Gen woman's shoulders, her face cradled against her neck. She wasn't sure if she was crying for the valiant Sectuib of the last century, for the ineffable beauty his death had let her glimpse set forever beyond her reach this side of the grave, or for the cruel parting from Shanlun, who was as good as dead to her now because she could never—ever—return to the Tecton. The sobs renewed themselves when she thought it would be kinder for Shanlun if he thought her dead now, because in mere months she'd be dead anyway.

Jarmi cried with Laneff, resonating with the same texture of emotion. It wasn't at all like Yuan. He had been a tower of strength supporting her in weakness. Jarmi understood that weakness and shared it. Together, they overcame it.

At last, Jarmi searched out a box of tissues, and over a clenched wad of them she said, "No wonder Mairis accepted the alliance with us. Digen understood junctedness as a totally separate thing from the kill. In Digen's vision of Unity, any Sime could be junct and walk the streets safely because every Gen would understand what he was. Any Sime could have that experience you had when he died."

Laneff had only told her that they'd once discussed the theory of junctedness, not why it had been brought up. "Maybe it was that forbidden glimpse that weakened my conditioning. Maybe if I hadn't been in that room then, I wouldn't have killed."

She shrugged. "We can't do science on maybes. What I don't understand is *why* Digen died. If K/A controlled the aborts the first time, why not the second?"

"I never had a chance to discuss that with Mairis or Shanlun. They were caught up in the funeral arrangements, and the grand convocation of Zeor to elect Mairis Sectuib. Shanlun never got to give Digen that final transfer, which left Shanlun with so much selyn he couldn't really control his fields. Mairis wasn't quite due for transfer at the time, but they arranged it for just after the funeral. *Then* we were scheduled to have a meeting on the data I'd collected."

"Makes sense. Underdraw is hell on those higher-order Donors. It's a travesty, what the Tecton does to them and the channels." Before Laneff could object to the slur on the Tecton, Jarmi added, "Look at the time! No wonder I'm starved. Come on, Laneff. Let's go eat."

Laneff had never shared a meal with the woman before, an odd omission considering the time they'd spent together. Laneff had been reluctant, after the first day, to go to the cafeteria, where it seemed each Sime ate paired with a Gen, shrouded in privacy. She felt people regarding her with an odd wariness as she sat alone, and thereafter took to skipping meals or grabbing a bite at the snack bar that was always open.

Jarmi was standing by the door, watching Laneff, who rose from her desk chair and shrugged. "All right."

But Jarmi stayed put, tilting her head to one side. "You don't know what I'm talking about, do you?"

"Dinner."

"No. I'm offering you a transfer date, Laneff. It's our custom around here to take meals only with a transfer partner."

Yuan had said they didn't assign for transfer here. "Jarmi, I could—kill—you."

"I doubt it. But, if it'll make you feel better, let's go to the infirmary and see a channel who can match us. Yuan was right. I do like you."

"I like you, too, Jarmi. But I've never known that to make a difference."

"Well—it does around here. Look, it's also our custom that you can refuse my offer, and no hard feelings. There's no accounting for a Sime's taste in nageric timbre. We could still be friends."

In a wild moment, Laneff imagined what it would be to take transfer from this Gen—not kill her. Yuan had felt nothing from her draw. Jarmi—might. For just a hint of what Digen had felt—for a fractional taste of the killbliss that would stave off disjunction crisis and her own death—no. "Jarmi, we have to be absolutely sure that it's safe. You don't know anything about me—"

"I know that Yuan promised you a chance to live without killing, without going mad for lack of killbliss. And I know I'm that chance. I *didn't* know how much I was going to want to do it."

Jarmi's sincerity loosened the tough binding of Tecton law on Laneff. "Let's go see your channel."

The Gen woman bounced cheerfully out the door and along the hall. "Oh, I'm so happy! I didn't know I could feel so happy!"

Laneff was buoyed on the Gen's flaring nager, surprised at how very good it felt. "Jarmi, this channel had better be awfully good . . ."

Jarmi sobered. "We don't have any First Order channels.

They just don't seem to gravitate to our movement. But our Seconds have become keen judges of a good match. It's been years since a bad match caused a kill."

The infirmary was deserted except for the duty channel and her—Companion? The old Householding designation seemed more apt than the Tecton title Donor, because their relationship was so obviously personal. Jarmi explained what they wanted. The channel, a tall woman with curly brown hair, perhaps in her mid-twenties, had the look of a dedicated healer. Her Companion, a man with the body of a weight lifter, a silly mustache, and a nager that sparkled with pure good humor, exclaimed jovially, "So *you're* Laneff Farris! I'd never have guessed you were so small from your pictures!"

Laneff didn't consider herself overly sensitive about her height, but that rankled. She looked up at the bulging muscles, estimating his weight. "I could challenge you to two falls out of three. Don't worry, I'd be careful not to injure you."

He threw his head back and laughed. "No contest! You could easily tie me in a bow knot!"

As they bantered, the channel was scrutinizing Laneff. Now she ordered, "Come on over here so I can zlin you."

As Laneff moved over against the backdrop screen, standard equipment in any infirmary, she felt for the first time in her adult life as if there were no embarrassing stigma on her nager. She knew the channel zlinned the junct signature, a worse embarrassment than the disjunction scars had been, but this channel didn't regard it as a moral weakness.

"Jarmi," ordered the channel.

Jarmi stepped up against the screen to let the channel zlin them. "Laneff, I'm so nervous!"

"No you're not. You're riding a peak of hope. But from a peak, there's nowhere to go but down." Duoconscious, Laneff zlinned her. "But *what* are you hoping for?"

"There's a lot you don't know about me, yet. Like—I

was rejected for Third Order Donor training by the Tecton. It nearly crushed me."

The girl's accent held overtones of a Sime territory somewhere to the northwest of Householding Invor— possibly Alberta Leaf Territory. She looked as if she might have some Indian blood. "You zlin like a Third, though . . ."

The channel answered. "She doesn't zlin like a Third to a channel, because she never Qualified Third. She was rejected by the Tecton because she has extremely high internal barriers, a very low yield of selyn, yet she delivers that selyn at what any Third Order channel would consider violent speed. She has the speed of a First, and there's no way to train her to deliver the capacity of a First, or at the speed of a Third. She'd make an ideal transfer mate for you, Laneff. May I make a contact examination?"

Jarmi held her breath to keep from cheering. Laneff simply nodded and extended her tentacles to twine them about the channel's tentacles. Then, the channel twined her laterals around Laneff's laterals and made lip contact in full transfer position.

The woman's fields penetrated to Laneff's core, but without the delicate dimensionality of a First Order channel's touch. Anxiety billowed through Laneff as the channel created selyn movement throughout their linked systems. But it was slow and clumsy movement. Unable to stand it another instant, Laneff retracted her laterals and pushed the channel away, gasping.

Instantly embarrassed, Laneff apologized.

"That's all right," soothed the channel. "I'm not used to handling Farrises. But your previous transfer has left your system in prime condition, though coitally deprived. No residual killbliss need. So this is a good time for you two to start a relationship. Jarmi is high-field—as high as she ever gets. You're matched in speed and capacity. But"— she turned to Jarmi—"style may give you problems. You've never handled an active junct before. And Laneff is *fast*. I couldn't judge levels within the First range. There could be a discrepancy between you two that I can't perceive. There shouldn't be any real difficulty, though, if you handle her firmly."

Jarmi smiled, the relief she felt pulsing through her nager. "I'll handle her carefully, all right! She deserves the best!"

At that point, Yuan swung into the room, talking before his eyes focused on them. "I certainly hope you have good news for me tonight, because—Laneff! Jarmi!" He beamed. "Paired?"

Jarmi answered, shyly, "For just one transfer, but I'm hoping."

The ponderous brilliance of his field lit the whole office as he turned to the channel, hugging her spontaneously. "You see, Bianka, I was right!"

In that single moment before Yuan let her go, Laneff sensed a spear of quickly suppressed jealousy from the channel's Donor. Yuan turned from the channel and hugged both Jarmi and Laneff together, his field leaving her dizzy as he withdrew.

"I *knew* something had to go right today!" said Yuan.

The channel said, "So tell us what's gone wrong."

"First tell me, how's our prisoner?"

The channel went to a desk near an inner door and picked up a standard Sime Center file folder with a chart tacked inside it. She rattled off some numbers, then said, "I got his name out of him today. Odeah Polk. He's nearly recovered from the blow on the head, but he's in a constant state of stark terror that's wearing him out physically. I don't—like to go near him. He's convinced Simes are going to torture him."

Jarmi said, "That just shows how his people would torture any Sime they caught."

What happened to my world of law and order? Adventure novels were no fun to live in. Her arms still remembered the feel of that leather belt, the rough hands, the hard gun barrel.

Yuan hooked one knee over a corner of the desk and perched on a stack of chart folders, one of which, Laneff now noticed, had the black flashing that indicated a Farris's records. *Mine.* The channel had done her homework, and probably did know enough about her to assign Jarmi in transfer.

"Then we could release this Odeah Polk anytime now?"

"Yes, Sosectu," answered the channel. "But why?"

He eyed Laneff with that same dancing light of spontaneous enjoyment she'd seen during their escape from the Tecton choppers. "You know, Laneff, you really do look to a Gen's eyes just like Hajene Perrin—or just any Farris channel."

"What's that got to do with anything?" asked Bianka.

Yuan picked up Laneff's file and idly flipped through it. "Bianka, Nen, we could all be in imminent danger now, because of what I did rescuing Laneff."

"How?" asked Nen, the Companion. "The Tecton thinks you were captive in that chopper. They never heard your radio signal. As far as they know, you and Laneff were flown into that Diet hideout which their choppers promptly blew sky high with one of those new missiles. I saw the Tecton tapes on the news. That cave must have been a munitions dump to have gone up like that. Nobody survived. You're both officially dead."

Bianka said, "You could let yourself be found wandering dazed in those hills, survivor by a miracle."

"I don't have any explanation for why I swept Laneff *into* the Diet chopper instead of away into the crowd, letting the Tecton guards deal with the terrorists. Do you think even *I* could fool Mairis Farris in a face-to-face interrogation? Five minutes, and he'd *know* Yuan Sirat Tiernan is Sosectu ambrov Rior." His overcharged nager ached. "I could never come back here again for fear of revealing everything. I don't think I could live like that for long."

Bianka said, "You obviously can't live like this for long,

either." Her nager cried out her sympathy for the Gen's *need* for a good transfer with a First Order channel.

"You're my best channel, Bianka."

She glanced at Nen, who assented to her unspoken question with a shrug while his nager throbbed denial. She said, "I'm willing to try a transfer, Yuan, but I don't think I can help you much. You're a First."

Yuan fixed Nen with a meditative stare. Then he shook his head. "No, Nen, I won't try to take her from you. Even if it would help me, I wouldn't. What is our way of life worth if we discard it at a moment's discomfort?"

Nen smiled, a relief radiating from him that weakened Laneff's knees. "You are my Sosectu."

"Some Sosectu! I may have gotten us into more of a war with the Diet than we can handle."

"But there couldn't have been any survivors from that Diet hideout. As far as *they* know, you're as dead as the Tecton thinks you are."

He shook his head. "In an organization this size, there is no way to eliminate spies. We have to assume that they know what Sosectu ambrov Rior looks like. With Yuan Sirat Tiernan's face plastered all over the media these last few days, we have to assume the Diet now knows Yuan Sirat Tiernan *is* Sosectu ambrov Rior. Their spy or spies would know that the Sosectu is alive and well, and might also know that Laneff is here, alive and well. If they don't know it, they can deduce it from the fact that I am here. They would figure that we'll provide her with time and a place to work—and then use her results to breed Gens for our juncts to kill. And they have more bombs—and suicide volunteers."

"Yuan," said Bianka when he'd run down, "you're building a remote possibility that's been with us for years into an acute threat. Are you sure you're not suffering underdraw?"

"My governors work well enough," countered Yuan. "My selyn production will level off soon. I just feel rotten, that's all. Look, I know it's a remote chance, but I haven't built this organization by ignoring remote chances."

"You have a plan," accused Nen.

"I didn't until I walked in here and found Laneff paired already," replied Yuan grinning at Jarmi. "With that stabilizing her, I think it's safe to expose her to Odeah Polk. We'll call her Hajene Farris, avoiding first names, and let him think she's an emissary from Mairis, and that Laneff is actually in some Tecton Last Year House being treated royally, with lab facilities and the best transfers the House of Rior can provide."

Laneff objected, "Mairis would never agree to that! It would have been channel's transfer only. He couldn't afford to break the law, even if he had the power!"

"I know, but the Diet doesn't think that way. By now, they've convinced themselves that we're using your process to breed Gen babies in test tubes, to take the whole world back onto the kill. They'll try to convince Mairis and the rest of the world of that, so when they attack and destroy us, they'll be taken as heroes."

"It won't work," said Nen.

"I hope not," said Yuan. He rubbed his red-blond mustache thoughtfully. "Laneff, I just got word that Sat'htine has mourned your death, and inscribed your name with their disjuncts in their Memorial."

Logically, she had known her father would have accepted her death by now. But to have ignored her final kill? Jarmi's hand, cool and Gen, closed about her shoulder. Laneff leaned gratefully on the Gen's field, fighting tears.

"The Diet will use that small kindness to your memory to argue that the Householdings don't consider the kill immoral anymore." He let that sink in and then added, "Until now, the Diet has been a bunch of disenfranchised and bitter paranoids ranting and raving in a corner. But since Mairis's announcement that he's running for World Controller to abolish the borders within two generations, money and recruits—real professionals—have been gravitating to the Diet organization, and it's growing. *Now* is the time to put a stop to them."

"By convincing them that Laneff is in a Last Year House?" asked Bianka incredulously.

"Right," answered Yuan. He turned to Laneff. "We set them up. They self-righteously attack a facility for the helpless. Media coverage demonstrates Laneff was not there, has never been there, and no secret Gen pens are being kept to supply juncts with kills. The Diet is shown to be the hysterical paranoids they really are."

"Suppose somebody gets hurt?" asked Laneff.

"I have my spies in their organization. Mairis will be warned in plenty of time."

"All right," agreed Laneff. "I'll go along." It crossed her mind that if she didn't, Yuan might be less enthusiastic about supplying her lab with all the expensive things she'd requisitioned. Pretending she wasn't herself for a few minutes was a small price to pay for being able to do her work. The Diet represented the kind of Gens who raised their children without preparing them for changeover, and then condemned the changeover victim for killing. *That* was what she'd dedicated her life to stopping. "What do I do?"

Yuan answered, "Discernment is one channel's trick I'll bet you, with your sensitivity, can do almost as well as a channel can—at least on anyone not a trained Donor."

Discernment, the art of detecting truth in a Gen's nager, or diagnosing an ailment, was indeed one of Laneff's talents. She nodded.

"All you have to do is watch Polk's nager as I interrogate him."

Bianka interrupted. "That man's nager is vicious. I'd want to be there, too."

"Fine," he said, looking to Nen, "if you'll go along."

"Sure. I wouldn't let Bianka go in there alone."

Laneff felt that Yuan's nager alone would be enough to protect her and any army of renSimes from a non-Donor Gen, but she didn't say anything.

Yuan led the way through the infirmary offices and down a long narrow corridor lined with double-insulated doors and shiny tile walls and floors. The door at the end of the hall opened to reveal a room not unlike the one where Laneff slept.

It was plastered and painted in light pastels. The furniture was gypsy wickerwork. Polished aquamarine ceramic tile floors reflected it all, as if they were standing on water. On the hospital bed lay the pilot from the chopper, his head swathed in white bandage, one wrist chained to the bed frame. Over his lap, a standard bed tray held the remains of a meal.

Bianka took the lead. "I see you're eating at last," she said in English.

"Decided you wouldn't try to poison me after all this, even if you don't give me any real food," he answered in a heavy out-Territory accent. Then his gaze centered on Laneff.

The jangle of alarm in Polk's nager at sight of Bianka's tentacles rose to a shrill scream of panic at Laneff's. Yuan was off to one side, behind Bianka, functioning in his working Donor's mode and allowing her to zlin the prisoner. Jarmi at her side was comforting, but only the fact that Laneff wasn't in need kept her from reacting to the Gen panic.

Yuan said, "Hajene Farris, please zlin him carefully when he answers." He moved as Bianka and Nen shifted position in a feat of professional field management that left a sheltered window for Laneff to zlin Polk without suffering the full brunt of his nager. It was, of course, lost on Polk.

"What is this?" challenged the prisoner.

"Consider it your trial," replied Yuan evenly. "Do you know who I am?"

"You're the guy we figure runs this outfit."

Yuan glanced at Laneff, asking with his nager if the Gen spoke truth. She nodded as the prisoner considered Yuan from a different angle. "You're the guy that hit me!"

As if in reflex, he lunged up off the bed, swinging his right fist at Yuan's nose. But the handcuff stopped the swing, sending a screaming pain through the Gen's nerves.

Without prompting, Jarmi seized Laneff's hand and let the tentacles clutch her arm. Simultaneously, Bianka moved closer, fogging Laneff s window with a selyn field that cut the intensity of the Gen's emotions. With a free tentacle, Laneff signaled that she was all right, and everyone resumed their positions as Polk subsided to a sullen anger.

"Distect traitor!" spat the prisoner.

"Distect Loyalist," corrected Yuan mildly. "Someday, if you're reasonable about things, I'll take you into the gym and give you a fair fight. I don't like hitting a man unawares—but I don't like dying even more. To business."

The Gen's lips clamped shut, a look of grim determination on his face that didn't match the fright in his nager.

"How many Distect bases have your people identified?" Silence.

Yuan consulted Laneff with a glance, and Laneff read Polk's silence. "A few at least," she said.

Polk sat up straight, ignoring the renewed throbbing in his head. "She can read minds!"

Laneff was shocked. She'd thought *that* stupidity had died out a hundred years ago. But Yuan let a secret smile play over his features as he asked, "Where are they located?"

Again silence.

"He's afraid you'll get it out of him," supplied Laneff.

"I will," answered Yuan. "With drugs, if necessary."

"Just have that witch pluck it out of my mind!"

"Nobody could do that, you idiot. She's reading your nager. Any Farris channel could do as well."

"Farris," repeated Polk eyeing her, fear crystallizing into belligerence. "You go tell that Mairis he's not going to learn anything from me! You—and all his kind—are going to be stopped before you've made the whole world into a Genfarm!"

Laneff hadn't really believed Yuan's sketch of Diet psychology until she heard that. She recovered as Yuan glanced at her. "It's bravado," she reported.

"But how did he know?" asked Yuan, then rounded on the Gen. "How did you know Mairis sent her here!"

A cagey reserve came over the prisoner. "We know a lot more than that about your operations!"

Yuan turned on Bianka, his expression ferocious but his nager ringing with unsung laughter. "Did *you* tell him about Laneff?"

Bianka feigned fear, shrinking from Yuan. "No, not me!"

"We know all about Laneff!" claimed the prisoner.

But he was lying, and Yuan didn't require her to tell him that. He bore down on Nen. "I'm going to find the Diet spy who got in here and talked to him. You get me a list of every guard assigned to this room!"

"Yes, Sosectu," answered Nen wide-eyed.

Then Yuan stalked over to Laneff. "You told me there was no chance of a leak at that Last Year House! You don't expect me to send one of my Gens in there for Laneff if the place is swarming with Diet spies! You go back and tell Mairis—" He tossed a cautious glance over his shoulder at the prisoner. "Bianka, drug him. I don't want any slipups. I'm going to have it all out of him—now." Then to Laneff, he said with sweet deference, "Hajene Farris, would you please accompany me to my office?"

Outside, Yuan was in high spirits. "You're a great actor, Laneff. You should have been on the stage! That was glorious!"

"Yuan, he fears those drugs. Perhaps he's allergic—"

"Don't worry, Bianka's checked that. He fears drugs because he knows he'll babble out everything—and he's one of their best pilots, so he probably knows the locations of every one of our places they've found. Ha! He knows the location of *every* one of theirs! And I'll have them all!"

"What will you do with the information?"

"Set spies on them. Leak my knowledge to them and

force them to abandon and move—just to keep them from accomplishing much. Oh, there's lots to do with such information!"

He spoke as if he'd been carrying on this war for years, right in the middle of civilization and the Tecton didn't even know it. "Yuan, why do you hate the Diet so? They're only frightened."

"I don't hate them because they're afraid! Look, they worm their way into a perfectly happy Gen community, and start sowing rumors that the Sime Center harbors a Pen full of Gens used for the kill. They start talking about certain channels who take donations from the community as being junct. Soon, the Gens of the area stop coming to donate selyn. They turn perfectly happy people into suspicious paranoids, and from each destroyed community they reap a few fanatics to join their suicide corps. There is no life form lower than a Gen who'd seduce a Sime into a kill!"

"But I thought the Distect condoned junctedness?"

"Condoned? No, Laneff. We stand for the right of each Sime and Gen to choose a mode of transfer that suits them, as long as nobody gets hurt."

There was so much vivid passion emanating from him that Laneff had to ask, "How did you get into all this?"

"I was raised in a coastal island village that was one of the first the Diet took over. But I joined the Tecton's Donor classes when I established. Maybe I halfway believed the lies. I was prepared to die on my first Qualification! I found out what Sime and Gen are really about—but too late to save my sister. She joined the Diet's suicide squad, only she hadn't established yet. She went through changeover instead, and they murdered her. The same kind of thing was happening in all the families in our village. I swore to stop it, Laneff!"

"Swearing isn't enough. The Tecton—"

"Oh—I found some old books and began reading up on how the Tecton came about. It wasn't always like this, you know. And Klyd Farris never did have much more than a bare majority when founding the Tecton. There were a number of Householdings that withdrew to form the original Distect, and a lot of other ideas about how the Tecton ought to be run. The time has come for the world to reconsider some of them."

In the narrow white corridor, Laneff looked up at the huge Gen, the powerful, hurtfully brilliant nager enfolding her. Wistfully, she recalled the scintillating tingle of Shanlun's nager. But she would never see him again. *Shanlun thinks I'm dead—and it's better for him that way. He shouldn't have to go through it all twice.* "I wish I could believe in your way, Yuan."

He examined her face as if trying to zlin her nager. "I'd like a chance to show you—all of it." His hand came up to graze her jawline. "The way we finish a transfer between a man and a woman . . ."

The pure maleness of him, from scent to the little tufts of hair on the backs of his fingers, penetrated her perceptions. She knew what he meant. In the Tecton, a man and woman who shared transfer were sexually forbidden to each other for that month. *Another rule discarded.*

Jarmi had drifted down the corridor toward the exit into the infirmary proper, offering them privacy. *Do I really want to do this?* She had watched Yuan deliberately frightening a helpless prisoner, but with a peculiar measure of compassion. *In his place, Shanlun might have done the same.* "Are you really going to let him go?" she asked.

"We don't have any prison cells. I think—I'll have him transported to another facility, and on the way, he'll get an irresistible chance to escape. Then, the Diet won't know exactly where he was. I don't *think* they know about this place yet. But all that's for tomorrow. For tonight . . ." He hesitated, awaiting her permission to touch her.

"Life is a game to you, isn't it?"

"A very dangerous game."

"But it's the danger you like, isn't it?"

"How is it you know me so well?"

"Haven't you ever known a Farris before?" she teased.

"Only channels," he murmured, distracted but still holding back his touch. His nager communicated his desire very clearly, but there was no hint of coercion in him.

For all his Distect philosophy, she knew at core he was a Tecton Donor, and a nonHouseholder at that. He was inviting her for only one night, because he was attracted. *If I'd met him before I met Shanlun, I wouldn't have thought twice about saying yes. I have to try to live as if Shanlun never existed. And this man—is very special.*

"Yuan—"

"It will be good for you, too. You're not a channel. It wouldn't hurt you to go a few months without sex. But, Laneff, you're *Sime*, and that's a wonderful thing to be. There's no reason to make it less wonderful by ignoring the essence of your being."

An utterly spontaneous smile overcame her. "You make a very strong case, Sosectu ambrov Rior."

At her assent, he bent down and kissed her with delicate passion.

6

DISTECT TRANSFER

"I've always wondered what he's like in bed," said Jarmi wistfully, her eyes fixed on Laneff and her nager glowing with admiration.

Laneff was sitting with Jarmi in the cafeteria. Over the last two days, she'd overheard a number of comments about how unusual it was for Yuan to take any member of Rior to bed. Most of the women were wondering what she had that they lacked, but Jarmi seemed to know. Laneff wished she knew, too.

"He's an expert," replied Laneff, burying her nose in her trin tea glass. "I suppose, anyway."

"You mean after all that you didn't—" Jarmi whispered.

Suddenly reminding herself of her original suspicion that Jarmi had to be Yuan's spy, Laneff asked, "Should we be gossiping about the Sosectu?"

Jarmi took that rebuke meekly, but Laneff felt the burning curiosity eating at the Gen—as did every Sime in the room. "Jarmi, he's practically in underdraw. He's more interested in Simeness than sex right now."

That terse hint covered a night of frustration. As much as he'd wanted to, Yuan had been unable to show her the other side of Rior. And she, not being in need yet, had become urgently fascinated to learn that side. His fortitude in the face of their dual frustration had touched her heart as nothing else could have.

She had responded by offering undemanding physical warmth, and in the morning they'd both felt stronger. Shanlun would have understood Yuan's plight even sooner than she did, and being the consummate Tecton Donor he was, he'd have urged her to Yuan's bed.

As she dwelled on that, Laneff saw Yuan come in, going immediately to the serving line. His field seemed to have leveled off.

Staring curiously at the Sosectu, Jarmi said, "I've often wondered what underdraw feels like."

Lost in her own thoughts, Laneff answered, "I much prefer need!"

"No—I meant not wanting sex because you want transfer."

"Oh, it's a little like being a child again. Sex just doesn't exist for you, but—hunger does."

"Hard to imagine." She was working enthusiastically on a mound of mashed potatoes and turnips heaped onto some kind of cheese pie.

Yuan caught Laneff's gaze and smiled. The beam of his attention lanced across the scattering of Simes and Gens and sent a warm thrill along Laneff's nerves. He started to weave his way toward them.

Jarmi weighed Yuan's smile and Laneff's response. "I've never seen him like that about anyone. Laneff, he's falling in love with you. Be gentle with him."

Shocked by that thought, Laneff zlinned the Sosectu again as he was greeted by people. Jarmi could be right. There might be something personal in Yuan's attitude. She'd known enough Tecton Donors to have learned not to expect anything personal in a sexual relationship. But with Shanlun, it had gone from the deeply intimate to the physical, and had always been personal first and professional afterward. For her, it wasn't the same with Yuan. But for him?

And he was looming over their table. "Well, and here I

thought I'd have to eat alone," he said, putting his tray down on the square table and seating himself between them. "You don't mind, do you?"

"No," said Jarmi, glancing defiantly at Laneff. "We were just discussing the results we got today."

"Oh? Anything encouraging?"

"We've synthesized all the starting materials for Laneff's compound," answered Jarmi, "and tested them all. Purity is good and the yields were phenomenal. We're going to start the synthesis tomorrow."

"Tonight," contradicted Laneff. "I'll start while you get some sleep." She'd never done it in any other lab before, and others who had tried had failed. If they were going to debug the procedure, they couldn't afford to lose time.

"Don't push yourself too hard, Laneff," said Yuan. And his concern was overpowering.

"I want to get most of this tedious stuff done before my turnover," said Laneff. "Need always slows me down."

Jarmi added, "Once Laneff has the K/A synthesized, I'll start running the structural analyses she couldn't do in her old lab for lack of funds and equipment. That will leave her free to sit and try to figure out what it all means."

"I'm going to require a number of expensive test materials," said Laneff. "I'm designing an experiment that may tell us what went wrong when I gave K/A to Digen the last time. But I'm going to require a supply of lateral tentacles from cadavers—preferably channels."

Yuan went right on eating the cheese-and-fruit salad on his tray, ignoring the steaming bean soup. "You're right, cadavers don't come cheap. But I know a supplier. Have Stores send your requisition to my office."

The clinical detachment was real, Laneff decided. For all his Rior airs, he was still a Tecton Donor. "Yuan, what were you going to do with the pilot before you decided to let him 'escape'?"

He stopped eating to examine her. "I was very depressed over that. He's so deeply indoctrinated I had to get Bianka to take his field down while he was drugged. He'd have died of fright, or committed suicide otherwise. I don't think we could ever have persuaded him to join us. So I'm glad we hit on this solution."

"Did the drugs do him any harm?" asked Laneff.

"No. Bianka knows her job. We got a good set of map coordinates from him, too. Soon I'll arrange his escape."

Later that night, Laneff completed one stage of the synthesis and left her product drying in the oven. She'd planned to read during this time, but a thought nagged her.

Yuan's attitude was both too soft for a general fighting a war and too callous to suit her Sat'htine ethics. He shouldn't allow that pilot to escape able-bodied enough to come back and fight again. Or he could have brainwashed him into gibbering helplessness. Suddenly, she had to see for herself what his condition was. She didn't dare trust the Sosectu without concrete evidence.

The infirmary was quiet three hours before dawn, the lights dimmed. A Gen was drowsing at the desk in the outer office. Laneff decided not to wake him and just walked on through to the hospital corridor. If everything was all right, there was no reason for Yuan ever to know she'd been checking on his word.

The door at the end of the narrow, tiled corridor was bolted, but no security lock fastened to it. A sign on the door said, "TO BE OPENED ONLY IN THE PRESENCE OF A SIME."

She opened the door.

The room was dark except for a dim glow of a night-light set beside the door. Leaving the door open, she went in, zlinning. The Gen was asleep and seemed perfectly healthy. His selyn field was weak, though. She tried to judge whether Bianka had just taken the superficial levels, or had stripped him deeper than an ordinary volunteer would be stripped. But she was no channel, and couldn't be sure.

It was obvious, though, why they had done it. This place ran on selyn power, and everyone had to pay their own way. Also, it certainly made it easier to be in the man's presence.

On the bed, the Gen tossed fitfully, reacting, Laneff surmised, to the corridor lighting. And then he was sitting bolt upright. "Who's there?"

Laneff noticed the wrist shackle had been removed. *For the night, so he could sleep?* That was Yuan's compassion. And now the sign on the door made sense. "It's only me," she answered, turning a bit so he could see her by the light.

"The Farris!" Startled as he was, his hand stayed habitually near the point where it had been moored by the shackle.

"I came to ask if Bianka had done a good job taking down your field." It had been weeks since Laneff had spoken English, and the idiom now came hard.

"She never did any such thing!" charged the pilot.

So it was under drugs. "Oh. I see."

But he knew. "She did it while I was out cold?"

The lancing panic in the Gen was a mere whisper compared to what it had been during the interrogation when his emotions had been carried on a replete selyn field. Laneff stepped closer to speak more quietly. "You're a lot safer now around Simes. Bianka tried to make it easy for you." She added in a rhetorical tone, "Has anybody here tortured you?"

Wonderingly, he noticed that his hand was free. *They took off the shackle while he was asleep!*

He eyed her, puzzled. "You don't think waiting for torture is torture? You think I don't know what you came here for tonight? You go back and tell that Mairis that the Diet doesn't breed fools!"

And with that, he launched himself at the open door, in a forward rolling dive. While his body flew through the air, Laneff went into high-level augmentation and stepped forward to block the Gen. She caught his rotating body by the shoulders, tensing to absorb the momentum of the massive Gen.

His shoulders smacked into her palms and she grabbed with outspread tentacles, taking the expected weight on flexed thigh muscles as her whole body leaned into the task. But she had forgotten the slick, polished floor and her smooth soled shoes. Her feet slipped out from under her and she pitched forward, landing prone with the Gen's weight smashing down right on top of her. Her head snapped down hard against the tile floor. Pain starred her forehead, and a black curtain engulfed her.

Twenty-two minutes later, she came to with a Gen bending over her anxiously—a Donor, the one from the front desk. "Hajene Fa—I mean, you must be Laneff!" He looked up at the empty bed. He had flipped on the light—painfully bright. "The prisoner! Shenshay!" He lunged toward the door, then checked himself. "You all right?"

Laneff tried to pull her legs under her, then gave up as her head burst. "Go! Tell Yuan. Call out the guards! Polk has a twenty-three-minute head start!"

The Gen pounded away down the narrow corridor. Moments later, loudspeakers filled the compound with a raucous buzzing sound. Laneff groped her way to the door, clutching her ears to cut the aching sound. Yuan's voice came on over the alarm giving cryptic instructions. Before the booming echoes died, feet were pounding everywhere, and Laneff thought her head would fly apart.

Ten minutes later, Bianka arrived, took in Laneff's condition, and called for Jarmi. Then she helped Laneff to an examining table. "Can you walk, or should I carry you?"

"Walk! I've got to go help—" The world dissolved into a dazzle with billowing blackness on the edges.

"How long were you unconscious?"

Laneff told her, certain of the time by her Sime senses.

Bianka draped one of Laneff's arms over her shoulders and lifted her onto the hard treatment table in the emergency room. Flat on her back, Laneff actually felt better. Bianka bandaged Laneff's forehead, which had bled mightily, all the while muttering about having just cured one concussion patient and being saddled with another. Then she made a full lateral contact examination.

Nen came in with Jarmi, and the ambient nager was suffused with pure Genness. Jarmi ran to Laneff's side, taking her arms to look for bruises. "What happened?" she demanded.

At that moment, Yuan appeared in the doorway, his nageric brilliance overshadowing the other two Gens. Laneff felt instantly better and began to struggle against the restraining chest strap to sit up.

"Oh, no you don't!" warned Bianka, pushing her down. "You're not moving that head for at least twenty-four hours even if I have to sandbag it for you! Understand?"

"Will you let her answer some questions?" asked Yuan.

"Make it quick," answered Bianka from her drug cabinet.

Yuan spread his hands wide in a silent plea.

Laneff confessed why she had been there, and how she'd let the Gen get by her. Tears of shame pooling at the outer corners of her eyes, she finished, "And now I can't even help you get him back!"

"You're a scientist, Laneff, not combat-trained. And that man was willing to die in that escape attempt. I knew his state of mind when I decided to let him sleep without the shackle. Don't blame yourself too harshly. But next time you doubt me, do a little more research before trying your experiments!"

"Any chance of recapturing him?" asked Jarmi.

Yuan sighed. "Not if he's gotten outside, like we think he did. Besides—there's no point to it. One look at the sky and he'll know where he is. Let's just hope he doesn't realize how large this installation is. And—I think they'll still go for the Last Year House— Oh, no! I've got to warn Mairis!" He turned on his heel and ran from the room.

Laneff remembered the times Mairis had been called away from Digen's funeral arrangements for a supersecret phone call, the rumors that it was the self-styled Sosectu ambrov Rior urging Mairis to stand for Unification now and pledging the support of the powerful Neo-Distect in a true alliance. Now she was the cause of a call of a different kind.

They moved her into a room off the hospital corridor, and she slept holding Jarmi's hand to blunt the pain Bianka's drugs couldn't reach.

In a few days, she was back on her feet, determined to let nothing interfere with her concentration on the problem in hand: the real cause of Digen's death. With the Diet knowing of this location, she couldn't be sure how much time she'd have in this well-equipped lab.

But still, in the hours between midnight and dawn when Jarmi had gone off to sleep and she had to face the cold fingers of need gripping her guts, she found herself dwelling on getting her life in order for her own death.

Unable to work, she often sat writing letters to Shanlun, Mairis, and her father, her older brother, and others she'd known in her life. She wrote them among the notes in her bound notebooks, certain that people considered those so valuable they would see that they survived. She didn't bother disposing of her few personal possessions. As she'd already been proclaimed dead, no doubt her possessions had been disposed of. She told them how she felt about them, and what she remembered best about them.

She found herself composing a letter to Shanlun in which she tried to explain Yuan, and how much it had meant to her when Yuan had not been angry at her for what she'd done behind his back. *No! It's impossible. Just a waste of time!* Jarmi had found her slumped exhausted over the open notebook page, having accomplished little or nothing through the night.

The next night, she steadfastly refused to indulge in letter writing, but despite her good intentions, she found herself reviewing each task and her notes on it with a very real sense that someone else would be forced to finish her

job. She became so meticulous in her note taking that
each procedure took twice the time it should have.

A little over a week after her turnover, there was a raid
by the Diet on a Tecton Last Year House. Twelve people
died—eleven terrorists and a channel.

Yuan brought the newspaper to the lab personally, sitting on one corner of her desk, his nager paralyzingly
brilliant and terribly controlled. "Mairis's strategy worked.
He told me he'd triple the guard at Teeren House, and
make no changes elsewhere, so they'd attack Teeren, which
was prepared."

Teeren House was the Last Year House just off the
Rialite campus, and run mostly by the Zeor Farrises who
answered to Mairis. It was an old renovated Householding
compound, originally built to be defended against Freeband
Raiders. "They were foolish to attack Teeren," said Laneff.

"Not foolish, desperate. They believe everything they've
been saying for ten years." He handed her a more disrepu-
table newspaper.

"Do you read this thing?" she asked, taking it with the
tips of two tentacles, as if it were a noxious substance.

"There are people who believe every word of that gar-
bage just because it's in print and contradicts what the
legitimate press has verified."

This article suggested that the Diet in fact knew that
Laneff was alive and working—if not at Teeren, then
somewhere under Tecton supervision. Mairis, it said, had
staked so much of his campaign on Laneff's research that it
seemed logical he would lie about her death to protect her
remaining time for her work. And since the Distect was
his known ally, and it was known that the Distect condoned the kill and harbored real juncts, it could easily be
providing Donors and even real kills for Laneff.

The editorial took off on that article and suggested that
the only way for Mairis to clear his name was to renounce
his alliance with the Distect.

"But Mairis never publicly espoused your shenned

Distect! *You* are the only one who ever said anything about an alliance!"

Yuan laughed. "It's easy to see where your loyalties lie! Mairis is a good man. He's accepted our support privately. And I understand why he hasn't been able to make a public statement; opinions like this," he said, smacking the paper with one hand, "aren't limited to the wild fringes. But Mairis knows that some of the prominent people who are now supporting his candidacy, who have never done anything like it before, are our people. He knows how much weight we swing in modern politics. Nobody else has to know—yet."

Laneff wondered just how closely Yuan's vision matched Digen's vision of Unity. What kind of world would the Distect build? Even if her method were foolproof, and every Sime was spotted long enough before changeover to be trained to seek help, and there were no more berserkers, still there would be Gens who couldn't tolerate the sensation of selyn movement. Such Gens could be killed. And as long as they existed, a world in which each renSime was free to seek his own transfer arrangements would be a world in which the kill was common.

Other papers carried the story of the public outcry that forced an open inspection of the Teeren facility which was televised around the world, to convince people it had never harbored Laneff or permitted rejuncts to kill.

Yuan brought her a small television monitor on which to view the inspection, but she busied herself with setting up some glassware and running a calibration, only glancing at the screen.

Afterward, Yuan said, quietly, "The Diet has had spies checking every other Last Year House. There aren't so many, you know. Soon they are going to conclude that *we* have you."

"They'll raid us," said Jarmi, who had watched the televised inspection with horrified fascination. "Shouldn't we think about moving Laneff?"

"To where?" asked Yuan. "No. This is our most defensible installation. We'll stand here."

Over the next day or so, people began to arrive, transforming themselves from ordinary citizens to combat troops within hours. They had to double up in the sleeping rooms, and Laneff was asked to move in with Jarmi. They even quartered troops in the hospital. Men and women, Sime and Gen, they carried arms, field rations, and ammunition, and wore high laced boots, crash helmets, and unmarked uniforms.

Laneff had once thought such things existed only in history—or films. But these were live people with a collective nager of leashed threat and brawny eagerness.

When she told Jarmi, as they were waiting for a slow reaction to terminate, that she found them frightening, Jarmi only said, "They're all ours, and they're *good* at fighting. It's only that you're in need, now, and so anxious about—us. Afterward, you'll see. They really are friendly."

Trying to see Jarmi's point of view, Laneff zlinned many of the strangers. She found no obvious juncts among the Simes now guarding them, though many of those who lived underground all the time bore the stigma she knew glowed in her own nager.

"Yuan wouldn't ask juncts to fight Gens," assured Jarmi. "They might accidentally kill someone."

Jarmi's attitude seemed to be that any Gen who wanted to get himself killed ought to do it on purpose, and ought to get the Sime to agree first! Laneff couldn't encompass that.

In a few days, the defenders settled into a routine, melding themselves into the life of the installation, helping with construction as well as defense. The cafeteria now worked around the clock. Extra tables were set up and the rules changed to allow trays to leave the area. A schedule was instituted on flushing toilets, because sewers were overloading. And the thermostats were turned up because the air conditioners couldn't cope with all the body heat and kept burning out their condensers.

The troops trained constantly in a large underground garage area Laneff hadn't even known was there until Jarmi took her to watch the mock battles. "Some archaeologists once decided this was an old church. I don't believe it."

On the twenty-third day after her kill, Laneff found Jarmi dogging her tracks unmercifully. She rounded on the woman, letting out a bellow of frustration. "Can't I even go to pee without you looking over my shoulder!"

Jarmi grinned, shrugged, and waited in the corridor. The public room had three stalls, used by Sime and Gen women. It was an arrangement that had always made Laneff nervous. Now, as she waited her turn among noncombatants and troops, she couldn't keep the four Gens in the room from etching into her consciousness. She fidgeted and wished for Jarmi's buffering field.

Then she berated herself for that wish, horrified at how dependent she was becoming on the Gen. *And if I kill her?*

When she claimed a stall, she found it ridiculously difficult to relax enough to do her business. Having wasted almost five minutes, when others were waiting—some of them Sime and aware of her problem—she gave up, washed her hands and left.

That night, she was going over some test results at her desk in the lab—the only place that had not been invaded by troops—when a woman came hesitantly through the door. "I thought I'd find you here," she said in a Simelan dialect that sounded local.

The woman was renSime and had been here for years. She was pale, and her nager seemed to echo with the tremor of the junct stigma.

"Did I forget to file a form?"

"No—I was—it's just that I—Well, maybe it's not my place . . . it's personal of course . . ."

Laneff scrutinized the woman more closely. She was of advanced middle years, thin as any Sime, medium height, mouse-brown hair. And there was an aura of calm there that Laneff had not noticed before, despite the woman's obvious embarrassment. "Is there something I can help you with?" asked Laneff.

She beamed. "No. I just wanted to tell you that—well, *I* killed for the first and last time when I was fifteen years past changeover. And that was nearly five years ago. If you don't fight Jarmi, I'll bet she can do the same for you."

Surprised, Laneff zlinned the woman and remembered the last time she'd seen her. In the toilet room. She'd taken the stall Laneff had vacated, unsuccessful.

"Well, I've got to get back to the kitchen. We've got hungry troops to feed!" And she was gone.

Laneff decided nobody had put the woman up to this. But by the time her shock had worn off, it was too late to call her back. When Jarmi turned up, near dawn the next morning, Laneff had made peace with the idea of the Gen's solicitous and permeating *presence*.

Jarmi's attitude seemed to be a signal to the other Gens they met in halls and cafeteria. It seemed all the Distect Gens were Donors, and the ones who were high-field were dreadfully polite about it, being very careful never to tempt Laneff. Yet she couldn't help but shy from every high-field Gen except Yuan.

His field continued at that searingly brilliant level, but he seemed to be making his peace with his condition. When he was around, Laneff found she could truly relax her guard. And so she encouraged him to drop into the lab to talk about her work, not caring whether he understood or not.

The morning of the twenty-fifth day, after Yuan had left the lab, Jarmi followed Laneff to the exhaust chamber where they had set up a trin tea service using a lab flask and a sand bath. "We've got to talk, Laneff."

Laneff had been indulging in the thousandth comparison between Shanlun and Yuan. "Why?" she snapped.

"A lot of things haven't been said yet. Like—well, I

know the Tecton keeps renSimes on a twenty-five or -six-day cycle. But I don't know your cycle, exactly."

Laneff wasn't used to discussing need with Gens. Need was a medical condition treated in confidence by a channel—a fellow Sime who knew without asking what it was like. Jarmi didn't have the clinical attitude that would have made Laneff comfortable. She hitched herself onto a wickerwork lab stool and toyed with a rack of test tubes. "Do you realize, Jarmi, I know even less about you than you know about me?"

"We've both put the work above personal interests. And we've accomplished a *lot*. We'll accomplish a lot more after this transfer. You can't expect your mind to be working efficiently now!"

"It's not so bad yet—at least when you're around." She grinned and confessed her experience in the public toilet. "The Tecton had me on a twenty-five-day cycle most of the time. But I don't *feel* twenty-fifth-day right now. Even when Yuan was here—he was comfortable, not raising my intil."

Even without technical training, Jarmi knew that intil meant the appetite for transfer which was as different from need as appetite was from hunger. "If you're not high-intil, then we shouldn't push it. But you don't know when you might be taken by it."

"And this place full of Gens!"

"Yes. I'd be horribly jealous. And so would their Sime."

Laneff had meant she might kill, and she knew Jarmi had deliberately misunderstood. Yet *this* was very much the Rior attitude. "How do you manage without a Controller? What *if* somebody took the wrong Gen?"

"Sosectu would straighten it out, and of course Bianka or one of the other channels would have to find a match for the other Sime—or serve them channel's transfer."

"Don't renSimes who've taken direct Gen transfer, and carry that signature in their nagers, get caught by the channels when they turn up at Sime Centers for channel's transfer? And what about the computers? Every renSime is expected to turn up somewhere for transfer on schedule! Surely they notice?"

"The Tecton system isn't as tight as you might think. But seriously, how can I tell you our secrets when you aren't even pledged to the House?"

"I'm not likely to go back to the Tecton!" said Laneff. "I've had enough of the Diet." She rubbed the band on her arms. "Where else is there but here?"

"Well," replied Jarmi with real daring in her nager, "you could go back to the Tecton and live on channel's transfer by using K/A to control the transfer aborts that cause death in disjunction crisis. You'd live as long as you could here—maybe a good lifetime."

Laneff had never considered that, but in a moment she rejected it. "K/A *may* have been the cause of Digen's death. Not a bad way to go, actually, but I'll try everything else first. K/A might help control aborts, maybe even all the way into disjunction crisis. But it won't prevent death in disjunction for an adult."

"Why?"

The experience of her own disjunction was with her as never before. "Because if a drug stopped the aborts, and let the channels force selyn into you, you'd die of the *cause* of the aborts anyway: the craving for killbliss. *Nothing* can substitute for killbliss."

She remembered the Sime woman, looking older than her years but alive five years without killing. *How?*

"Laneff, I don't intend to substitute anything for killbliss. I intend to give it to you. And I intend to survive to give it to you again and again. I'll get better at it with practice." Her smile glowed through her nager. "If I get good enough, if you'll help me learn, then maybe you'll be like Thereda, and not even go into disjunction crisis at all."

"I wish I could believe that," said Laneff miserably.

"Listen. This is the great secret of the Distect. Killbliss is the Gen experience, not a Sime experience at all. The

Sime only shares it. The few who've learned to give real killbliss tell me it's better than the ordinary pleasure everyone takes in transfer. Do you know how that used to make me feel? With my speed/capacity profile, I couldn't even have the kind of ordinary transfer partner everybody else has. But you and I are match-on, and you're junct. We have a chance at the very best possible kind of experience. My life is finally turning around, and I'm so happy I could scream!"

Jarmi's relish for the experience eased Laneff's misgivings, letting her need progress smoothly. With each passing day, Jarmi took increasing delight in the advancing symptoms of need, patiently wanting the transfer, and thus making Laneff want it, too.

But, after the killbliss she'd had at the kill, she found the grinding ache of need slower in onset. She realized she hadn't known what she was getting into when she accepted Jarmi's offer of transfer. True, she couldn't choose channel's transfer here because Bianka, their best channel, was just too infernally slow for Laneff. That one taste of Bianka's touch was all Laneff thought she could tolerate. But she could have asked Yuan.

Perhaps it would be better if I brought him my full need? Yet the memory of the infinite depths of his nager told her that even if she were in attrition, she couldn't scratch the outermost layer of his selyn pattern. And it was the core of that pattern that she craved.

Struggling to keep at least some of the momentum of the lab work going, Laneff took to snacking and sleeping in the lab while nursing the various procedures they had in progress. In need, she could hardly sleep, but would rest on the surface of sleep, skimming shallowly into dream and nightmare.

Once, when she lay down to wait for solvent to wash out a chromatography column, she dove into a most familiar need nightmare.

The desert heat blazed down on the high-walled compound. White-painted adobe buildings with red-tile roofs and barred windows baked under the noon sun. Heat shimmered off the surface of the swimming pool and ball courts, barely shadowed by the trees. Two tall palms waved fronds in a slight breeze so high it was unfelt on the ground. Not a person moved on the grounds of the Rialite disjunction compound, Teeren.

Laneff drew the heavy drapery across her window, shutting out the hot sun and depressing scene. She turned the air conditioner up a notch. The frigid breeze chilled her, making her body want to burn selyn faster just to keep warm. Need blazed brighter than the outdoor sun.

She paced, fighting the obsession, her hands shaking. She tried the breathing exercises they'd taught her to calm the jangle of tension, but they only made her gasp breathlessly, her heart pounding even faster. She wished she could cry, but need blocked that release, too. Need would accept only one kind of release.

Time crawled as her body raced to its death with herself as a helpless passenger, until at last, two hours before her scheduled transfer with the channel, she ripped open the door to her room, and leaving it hanging by one hinge, she went in search of a Gen.

Because of what she was, there were many Gens in the compound she could kill. Even a few of the channels might be vulnerable to her if she caught them by surprise, as she had her first kill. By the time she reached the main lobby of her building, she was hyperconscious, zlinning hard for the whisper of a replete selyn field. Only the tiniest part of her mind was aware of what she was doing: giving up on her chance to disjunct and live a normal life.

In nightmare, she relived over and over again that frantic search for life, the corridors of adobe and polished tile stretching before her endlessly. In reality, it had taken only seconds to traverse the length of the building. In nightmare, it was days during which every turn led back to her room, every hall was lined with a gallery of staring faces—channels of her Householding; people from ages past who had died disjuncting rather than live on the kill.

Intense shame overcame her, but still her feet fled through the halls. In reality, the building was full of Gens. In nightmare, the world was devoid of selyn nager.

Bright fog of selyn nager suffused the insulated brick. It was a warm Gen pulse that grabbed at her body just below her neck, between her breasts. She burst through a door, and there, spread out and waiting for her were two selyn fields, two Gens beckoning tantalizingly.

In her gut, she knew one would deliver the satisfaction she craved. The other would not. Which? *Choose!* they commanded. But which?

Equally intense, two ruddy gold hearth fires vied for her favor. One was pure Genness laced with familiar overtones that told her of an understanding of her need. The other was like the Donors here, throbbing with compassion verging on pity. PureGen knew what was being asked of her, and was confident she could do it. The other, groping blind, only hoped.

A viciousness that shamed her rose. *I could make Groping Blind pity himself! I could make him give me egobliss!*

She looked at the viciousness pouring up into her, knew it for a part of herself she had never acknowledged before, and thought, *I don't have to be this way.*

PureGen knew that about her, as he knew it about himself. She chose to let the lifeline of PureGen pull her into a full contact. She took the selyn offered, clumsy with greedy haste, laving her insides with warmth and life. It came fast as she could desire, sensitive and clean, washing through her with bright delight as only a Gen could experience it. Each dynopter of selyn pulsing through her carried that bottomless Gen attitude toward life modulated by ineffable relief from the strain of need.

That modulation soaked into her own nerves, and the

shrieking alarm of need was stilled, the jangle of urgencies faded and was gone.

She found herself lip to lip with warm flesh. Her tentacles were held securely by matching tentacles. *Channel!* As it came to her that PureGen was in fact a channel, a Sime not a Gen, the woman released her, dismantling the contact gently while a ferocious grin transformed her face. A Farris face. A Farris channel she hadn't met before.

Blinking in the bright light, stunned by what had happened, Laneff heard the woman introduce herself and her Donor, the GropingBlind she had rejected. "Congratulations on your disjunction. You'll never need for a Gen again."

The horror of the nightmare returned full force as she woke, the taste of satisfaction still on her nerves and the emptiness of need cramping her guts. The dreamed satisfaction only raised intil, leaving her sweating and shaking as she remembered the lab, the Distect, and her last-ditch effort to make her life's work mean something.

She rolled on her side, curling up against the familiar craving for killbliss, wiping out the easing channel's touch had once given her. In mourning that loss, all she could produce was a sort of coughing bark halfway between a laugh and a sob. The pain of wanting to cry and being unable to swamped out the need for selyn just long enough for her to sit up and calm herself with the breathing techniques she had thought forgotten.

Jarmi arrived at dawn while Laneff was once again going over her notebook to make sure nothing had been left out. "What are you doing?" asked Jarmi. "Got a new idea?"

Laneff closed the cloth-bound book, clasped it to her chest. "Jarmi, I've got to have transfer now. I'm dangerous like this."

The smile transformed the rather plain woman's face. "At last! I thought you'd *never* be ready!"

She went with Jarmi back to the room they shared now. Laneff had been there so seldom she hardly knew the way. She paid no attention to the twists and turns, for her mind was busy reviewing her decision. Her only other choice was Yuan, and now that she'd had a new taste of the sort of need she'd suffered during disjunction and then been protected from all these years, she knew that with the infinitely imperturbable field of the higher-order Donor, she would not achieve enough satisfaction to keep her from yearning after every other passing Gen. With Jarmi, match-on to herself, there was a good chance. *This way, I'll be safe for a month.*

Her decision made finally, Laneff looked around Jarmi's room as if she'd never seen it before. Years of accumulated clutter gave the place character. Woven-reed matting, as everywhere else in the installation, provided padding from the tile floors. Handmade needlework adorned the walls. Wicker shelves held books, heaps of file folders, speakers for her sound system, and an assortment of personal-care items. Between the beds, a double pad of mats was cleared and equipped for weightlifting and exercise.

Laneff took a shower while Jarmi tidied up and gathered the laundry. In her bathrobe, Laneff came out, toweling her hair. "I had a pair of pink slacks and an ivory shirt."

"You wore that four days ago, remember? It got splashed with tomato soup."

Laneff remembered, and the realization she had nothing to wear was overwhelming. She dropped onto the bed she used, despairing.

"Never mind," said Jarmi cheerfully. "I can rinse out your cream-and-maroon skirt, and you can wear it with the ivory shirt."

"Shuven! I'd look like somebody from Householding Juanatec!"

"Nonsense. They don't have any Farrises!" chided Jarmi.

"The point is I don't have anything to go out in *now!*" With overcrowding, they had rationed laundry, too.

"Go out?" asked Jarmi, bewildered.

Exasperation lent an edge to her voice, and Laneff let

herself shout, "To wherever they do transfer around here!"

"There's no transfer suite here. Anyway, what's wrong with right here? I don't have a transfer lounge like your room did. But people did without for centuries . . . "

With that, she moved to Laneff's side and, grabbing pillows from the other bed, she edged onto the bed. The bed sagged under the plump Gen's weight. With a few deft moves, the Gen had Laneff propped against a heap of pillows, one pillow under her knees to simulate the contours of a proper lounge for complete relaxation.

By some alchemy, Jarmi seized as firm control of the selyn fields as she had done of their physical situation. She laid her hands about Laneff's wrists very lightly.

The wrist orifices, sensitized by ronaplin, seemed to feel every pore in the Gen's skin. Her tentacles ached, licking at the orifices, searching for the Gen skin. Laneff gasped, unable to deny the raging intil that seized her. But Jarmi firmly denied them emergence, with both field and grip.

Laneff hung at the peaking wave of need until Jarmi stroked Laneff's forearms, her fingers massaging the ronaplin glands that lay just under the lateral tentacles and fed the selyn-conducting hormone into the lateral sheaths. Tenderly, Jarmi massaged those four glands, sending ineffable sensation throughout Laneff's body, relaxation and intil together in wave after wave.

Laneff heard her own whispered groans, felt saliva flood her mouth, ronaplin oozing from her lateral orifices. In moments, Jarmi had Laneff's ronaplin smeared all over her arms.

Hyperconscious, zlinning only, in the Sime's hunting mode which conferred strength and speed beyond imagining, Laneff was keenly aware of everything about her, a predator primed for the kill. Yet the imperturbable Gen nager held her in thrall. Her will to *take* was swamped out by the Gen's self-absorption in pleasure.

Totally helpless, Laneff tried to convince her rioting glands that she wasn't about to die in attrition this moment. Unsuccessful, she had to wait in mounting terror of death while Jarmi slowly secured the fifth contact point. For one stretched instant, Jarmi held back the selyn flow, and Laneff had time to think in shock, *She's got my ronaplin on her lips!*

Then selyn was pouring into her at need-slaking speed. She struggled to take control, to draw selyn herself, but Jarmi wouldn't permit it. The Gen forced selyn into Laneff, selyn full of bright, bubbling laughter, sheer joy in the discovery of life. The ebullient spirit of the Gen impressed the selyn with her personality.

Irrepressible delight coursed through Laneff, warring with the roused predator's instinct that commanded, *Take life!* The riptide of emotion lasted only an instant. With so little selyn to transfer, and such a high speed, the experience was abnormally brief, abnormally intense.

Laneff came up out of it to find the sparkling Gen nager reflected in the bright grin on Jarmi's round face. "Oh, Laneff, you're magnificent! Better than anybody, ever!"

With Jarmi's selyn soaking into the roots of her being, Laneff couldn't find it in herself to spoil the moment for the Gen. She summoned a smile to cover a grimace of tears. "You've made your love of life a part of me. I've never experienced anything like it before." *But her selyn is all one color.*

Suddenly, the remembered feel of Shanlun's nager was with her, a tangible thing: the whirling colored texture spinning brightly into one throbbing sunlike golden glow. She relived the moment when Shanlun had been offering Digen transfer. *It wouldn't have been like that.* She didn't know how it would have been, but she knew the difference. *It wouldn't even have been like Yuan.*

Suddenly, she was crying, a wail of loss and abandonment that she shaped into Shanlun's name. Jarmi was there, quietly proud that she'd induced post syndrome in

Laneff, and Laneff didn't disabuse her of that notion, for in a way it was true. She mourned for the life she knew she must give up forever, for the work she would leave undone in a bare six months from now. Her need was slaked, for the present, she was indeed post, but she had felt no whisper of killbliss. That craving would blast back through her nerves redoubled all too soon. If she couldn't satisfy it, she would go into disjunction crisis. She would either kill or die.

Eventually, exhausted, she fell into a light doze as Jarmi relaxed into deep sleep. Dreams flickered through Laneff's consciousness, inconsequential pleasures that turned to mild nightmare from which she struggled to wake.

After three hours of this, she rose leaving Jarmi sound asleep. As she made her toilet, she found herself full of energy, driven to accomplish the most she could before her time ran out. She took a notebook into the bathroom and scribbled down ideas for streamlining her experiments and reordering priorities. *Six months. It can be done!*

Finished, she was all for going to the lab right then. But she remembered the fretful dreams, and was aware of her jangled state of nerves. She also knew the cure from long experience as an adult Sime. If she went to the lab now, she knew she wouldn't accomplish a thing, and would probably just break glassware and ruin experiments through inattention.

Yuan would understand. He'd be willing to help. She remembered the way he'd come into the lab to wish her a satisfying transfer. There had been a wistful invitation in his nager, though he wouldn't ask her outright since he'd failed before. *He's still feeling underdraw.*

But as far as she was concerned, there *were* no other men in the installation. And, from her own observations, she was sure Yuan's field had leveled off. The worst symptoms of underdraw might be over for him, though he might still be sterile from it.

It was only just after midnight. She took one of Jarmi's

floppy sweaters and a paint-smeared pair of pants she'd torn while they were setting up the lab. Dressed like a beachcomber, her Sat'htine signet on a chain around her neck but hidden beneath the sweater, she ventured into the corridors.

The lights were dimmed, but people bustled everywhere, excited by something. She wended her way toward the branch tunnel where Yuan lived and worked, a branch just off the entrance from the farmhouse. Here the lights were on full strength. Armed men were stationed three deep, rigidly alert.

A whole platoon guarded the stair down from the farmhouse. She was answering another in an endless sequence of challenges, trying to gain entrance to Yuan's hallway, when the door to the stair flew open admitting a puff of damp outside air.

Booted feet tromped down those stairs, revealing knees, and then torsos. Laneff had no trouble identifying Yuan's nager before his red-blond hair appeared. His field filled the entryway, then cleared it as he stepped into the corridor intersection. He surveyed the ranked troops, barked, "At ease!" and then saw Laneff. "What—!"

Simultaneously, Laneff recognized the next nager coming down the stairs. Fluorescent confetti whirled out of that stairwell like a particolored snowstorm. Laneff flung herself at the man she'd thought never to see again.

"Shanlun!"

7

TEMPTATION

Uncontrolled sobs poured from Laneff as she clung desperately to the apparition of Shanlun, trying to convince herself he was indeed real. Wrapped in the glowing core of his nager, she felt him echoing the same maelstrom of emotions, magnifying them for her, until her overloaded nerves screamed for surcease.

Then an odd thing happened. His nager shrank within her grip to a darkened point, a nonexistence, as if he'd died and pulled her along with him.

Her innards went hollow. Duoconscious, she heard herself making strangling noises. A fractional second later, the particolored snowstorm was whirling about her, isolating her within the suddenly calm core nager. She found her feet dangling in midair, Shanlun's hard, muscular arms wrapped about the small of her back, and his lips searching her own.

Peripherally, she was aware of the growing audience behind her, of Yuan's astonishment, and of a strange and powerful channel who had come down the stairs behind Shanlun. As everything in her answered to Shanlun's sudden physical hunger for her, she heard Yuan dismissing his troops, setting guards, and then marshaling all of them into his own private office. Shanlun wanted to carry her, but she squirmed down and went on her own feet, clinging with both arms to his waist as curiosity surged into her consciousness.

She hardly had patience with the formal trin tea ritual. But the warm tea helped calm her. Shanlun drew her to a wicker bench with seat cushions in crushed green velvet and sat with one arm around her shoulders. Yuan watched from behind his own reed-and-wicker desk with its milk-white ceramic top. His smile was tight—*a hint of jealousy?*

Laneff straightened away from Shanlun, feeling for Yuan in a rising tide of confusion. She dropped her gaze to the woven floor mats, here dyed a shadow purple with threads of gold and white. "Shanlun was the last person in the world I expected to find here!" offered Laneff by way of apology.

The strange channel had taken the visitor's chair directly across the desk from Yuan. He turned and flashed her a grin, and then she recognized him: the gypsy channel from the viewing of Digen's body. His grin transformed his craggy old face into grandfatherly serenity. "The truth is that none of us expected to be here with each other—now. Such surprises add the zest that makes life worth living."

He had uncannily found words to express Laneff's feelings: the renewal of the will to live frightening in its intensity because it was impossible to satisfy.

Yuan answered, "When a small army is standing to defend a homestead, any surprise is likely to be painful rather than pleasant. You took a terrible chance crossing our perimeter."

"Gypsies go where they will," answered the channel.

Shanlun raised a finger, his nager claiming attention. "Which is why I requested the escort. I had to find you."

"Why?" asked Yuan.

Shanlun darted a glance at Laneff. "Had I known she was here, that would have been enough reason. But I was ordered by my Sectuib to come to you as his emissary. He has no way of contacting you unless you call him."

"I've arranged it that way deliberately," answered Yuan. He speared the channel with a glance. "I never expected you to betray our confidence like this, Azevedo."

"Hear him out, Sosectu, and you may not consider it betrayal. If you do, I stand responsible."

Yuan turned to Shanlun. "But how did you know who to ask for escort?"

"I didn't. I was desperate. Mairis's message is urgent. He wants you to repudiate this alliance publicly, and withdraw all your support, because it is making it impossible to achieve our mutual goals."

Yuan's nager was still ultrabrilliant, untapped by channel's transfer for too many weeks. Now it filled the room with a deadly weariness. "I see. Mairis has been forced to yield to the hysterics."

On the desk before Yuan lay a copy of the paper he'd shown Laneff a few days before. Next to it was a clip filled with other, similar articles Laneff also recognized. "Shanlun, I'm certain this paper is Diet-controlled. They're trying to spook Mairis into just this move, so they can see which of his backers withdraw. Then they'll know which prominent figures are *ours*—and those will become assassins' targets, like Laneff did. I can't do that to my own people!" Yuan emphasized that by slamming his fist into the desk top, with a ferocious grimace. "Damn the shendi-fleckin' Diet! I *won't* do it!" He smacked his whole aching hand into the desk top again.

Azevedo winced, and Yuan apologized. For the first time Laneff noticed the hint of need in the channel's nager. Then it disappeared as his fields shifted into the channel's working mode, shrouding him in nageric blur.

Slumping back in his chair, Yuan said to Azevedo, "RenSimes don't affect me the way you do. I don't think I can manage this. Perhaps you'd better leave."

Now, Laneff noticed that Yuan's field had increased in just the short time they'd been talking. His whole body, trained by Tecton methods, was responding to Azevedo's need.

Shanlun had tensed, perching on the edge of the seat, his Tecton training urging him to move to reshape the ambient, while something else held him back. Azevedo turned to meet Shanlun's gaze, no more than that, and Shanlun rose to stand beside and a little in front of Azevedo. The bland confetti nager swirled to enclose Azevedo's blur, and in moments the two of them had disappeared nagerically. *Like channel and Companion*. But a House-holding Companion traditionally didn't do that with any-one but his own channel—unless the Tecton ordered it.

Yuan closed his eyes, his face softening in relief, and Laneff's heart went out to the man, remembering his delight in the twists of fortune as they'd made good their escape, and understanding now why he couldn't laugh at this one.

When he opened his eyes, Yuan glanced from Azevedo to Shanlun and back. Then he centered on Shanlun. "Rior is a daughter House to Zeor. I have returned that pledge and granted Mairis all our loyalty. He has accepted my pledge. Such a pledge transcends temporal alliances of political convenience. If Mairis yields now to Diet de-mands to repudiate my allegiance, the Diet's next move will be to demand he prove he means it by throwing all Tecton resources into a drive to wipe out Rior. He knows almost enough about us now to do that."

"Mairis wouldn't do that to a daughter House or a sworn ally," replied Shanlun. "But that allegiance is going to be strained when I report that you've got not only Laneff here, but a huge standing army as well. After the raid on Teeren, the Diet and its violent tactics are looking very bad. Mairis can't afford to be associated with similar tactics—and I'm wondering if we can afford to trust you at all."

He didn't look at Laneff, but she felt his attention dart in her direction, then return to the schooled professional-ism of a working Donor.

"Shanlun, Yuan has saved my life. And he's provided me a fully equipped lab to work in. He pledged to give Mairis all my findings."

Shanlun did look around then. "And to defend you with
an army that just begs to be attacked?" He turned back to
Yuan. "You engineered the Diet's attack on Teeren. You're
prepared here for real violence. The Sime/Gen wars were
over centuries ago. *This* isn't going to further the cause of
Unity." He gestured around him. "And someone as valuable as Laneff shouldn't be caught in the middle of it. I
don't see how Mairis could still have the same confidence
in you, knowing you've held Laneff here secretly."

Yuan's eyes narrowed, though his nager was so bright
Laneff couldn't discern anything by the Gen's anxiety.
"I'm not sure that Mairis will ever know you got through
to me. You know too much to be allowed to go back to an
enemy camp. If Mairis is weak enough to fold at a little
throat-clearing from the Diet, the next thing you know
he'll betray us into their hands."

Shanlun did not seem cowed by the threat. "Mairis is
not your enemy. Don't you realize that in order to create
real Unity, Mairis has to treat with the Diet and their
silent sympathizers just as he treats with you? You represent the extreme in-Territory attitude, and they represent
the extreme out-Territory attitude. You're both the tiniest
of minorities, but the strength of your organizations is
keeping the rest of the world from progress!"

"*We*'re keeping the world—" choked Yuan, rising to his
feet, leaning over the desk as if to throttle Shanlun.

Azevedo stepped between them, the ambient nager
flowing and shifting as he moved. Yuan's flaming anger
was blocked off from Laneff's senses, and all she could zlin
was a faint tinge of bewildered exasperation on the surface
of Shanlun's nager as it emerged from the fusion with
Azevedo.

"Enough!" commanded the channel as if rebuking small
boys. "Yuan, you can't see a tentacle in front of your
eyelashes, you're so woozy with underdraw. You're in no
condition to decide affairs of state on which the future of
all humanity may hinge."

"Well what the shidoni shenshay frayed deproda do you expect me to do? Go crawling back to the Tecton and beg for transfer?"

Laneff felt the hot sting of tears in the Gen's eyes, but his face betrayed none of the anguish he felt. Azevedo did not react to the anger. He simply said, "No, my friend," and held out his hands to the Gen, tentacles extended in invitation. Simultaneously, his field dropped its masking blur, and pure need blazed forth so powerful that it rammed Laneff's breath solid in her throat. *What kind of a channel could mask such a need!*

"Azevedo!" exclaimed Shanlun, one hand checked in midair.

Laneff, too, was on her feet now. Two heartbeats later, Yuan pulled back from the brink of surrender. His haunted eyes went to Shanlun, as if sensing a prior claim. "It would be against our ethic—if you two have an agreement?" And then, hastily, he added, "Forgive me, Shanlun, if I misread you. It makes no sense for a Tecton Donor to be involved with a gypsy channel, but—"

"You don't misread him," supplied Azevedo. He turned to the speechless Shanlun. "You can handle your condition by the training you've had which Yuan has not. And you *do* have Mairis. Yuan has nobody. If Desha can give me to you, can you not give me to Yuan?"

Shanlun met the channel's gaze. "I've no claim on you, Azevedo. I am ambrov Zeor." Straight as a rod, he turned and left, walking as if he had something precious balanced on his head.

Azevedo gazed after him, and Laneff read a tearing regret in his nager, a sharing of Shanlun's disappointment. But then he turned to Yuan, melting into a compassion that could not be overshadowed even by the bottomless need he felt. Yuan came around the desk, his whole body quivering in anticipation as he reached to take Azevedo's proffered hand. The Gen's field was rising again, but when the nageric blending took place as it had with Shanlun, Yuan steadied, then blinked and turned to Laneff.

He frowned at the door as it closed behind Shanlun. "I've taken his channel from him. I don't want to take his woman, too. Laneff, he's the one you prefer, isn't he?"

"Yuan, I—" She couldn't deny it, but she wasn't all that sure in her heart, either.

"Whatever else," said Yuan, "he and I are sworn to the Tecton's First Order. Do you know what that means?" At her nod, he urged, "Go to him. And if you never come back to me, Laneff, then do not fail him."

There was no tinge of jealousy in the Gen now, Azevedo let her discern that. Then the channel said, "*This* is the real Yuan ambrov Rior. And in the morning, he'll be able to reconsider this whole matter and create a novel solution."

Laneff didn't want the two Gens to fight over her work or herself. This was probably the best way to avoid that.

She followed the two men out of the office. In the corridor intersection, Shanlun was standing among the small knot of gypsies who had apparently come with Azevedo, two Simes and two Gens. They spoke quietly as Yuan gave orders.

"Find quarters for our guests. With careful regret, you will deny them exit. They may, however, access all the public areas. They are to be treated with respect. Any problems, refer up chain of command. Understood?"

"Understood!" snapped a Sime woman, but she was hard put not to smile at the new agreement between Yuan and Azevedo. Laneff understood that Yuan had been particularly difficult to live with lately.

"Desha," called Azevedo. A very young Gen woman separated from the gypsies and came to him.

"Shan told me, Azevedo," said the woman in a very thick accent. Her field was bright, and Laneff surmised that she had been Azevedo's scheduled Donor. *If gypsies have schedules.*

In a whirl of crisp orders, the group sorted itself out, Yuan and Azevedo disappearing down a side hallway, guards hustling the four gypsies away, and two more guards trying to spirit Shanlun off with them. But he turned to her. "Laneff, can we talk?"

Laneff stepped toward the guards, two renSimes she knew only by sight. "*Where* can you possibly quarter him? There's hardly a patch of floor to sleep on anywhere!"

"We'll put him with the gypsies, in Hyssop Corridor."

"Five people in one of those dinky rooms? And zlin his nager? Two of those gypsies are renSime! Do you think Yuan would ask that of anyone?"

The guard looked after the retreating figure of Yuan. Laneff added, "Jarmi and I have a much larger room—and I don't use my bed much. We'll take him in."

The two guards zlinned her replete nager and shrugged. One turned to Shanlun. "Is that agreeable with you?"

"Yes."

The second guard shrugged, and Laneff took Shanlun back along the main trunk corridor toward her lab. "I hope you're not sleepy yet. Jarmi is heavily out of it after our transfer, and—"

Shanlun beamed. "So you didn't kill again!" He muttered something in the odd language she'd heard him speaking with the gypsies. "I should have trusted Yuan for that. But who's Jarmi?"

She explained tersely, then opened a fire door that led off into a crisscrossed maze of tunnels. "My lab is this way—that is, if you're not hungry?"

"Breakfast is yet a couple of hours away."

In the lab, she made trin tea while he inspected the place. She explained what they had accomplished, how Jarmi had helped, and what she hoped yet to do.

"My heart told me you were still alive, Laneff, but my head wouldn't listen. Laneff—I have never been— bereaved—like that before. If Yuan hadn't forced me to stay, I think I'd have fought him for the privilege. And I don't think Mairis would fault me for that."

"No, he won't, because after I die, you'll be able somehow—maybe through your gypsy friends—to get my work back to him. I've been praying for someone I could trust—"

He wasn't listening. With one huge, cool Gen hand, he reached behind her neck and cradled her head, forcing her to face him. His eyes were pools that seemed to reflect the multicolored effect of his nager. As she watched, and zlinned, the effect faded. The intense pure gold inner core engulfed her. "Die, Laneff? No. Not again. No."

"Shanlun, nobody can prevent it." *Least of all Jarmi*.

He drew her face close with a trembling intensity more profound than the restrained yearning in his nager. Then he kissed her thoroughly, his whole body responding. The totality of sensation cascaded through her until it was as if he were kissing every part of her.

At last, she drew away panting. "Do you know what you're doing to me?"

"When did you have transfer?"

"About five hours ago."

"Then I know what I'm doing to you. Or—is there someone else?"

Such panic she had never felt in a man before. But she *had* to admit it. "When I ran into you—I was looking for Yuan." The memory of that unfulfilled night gnawed at her, and as eager as she was for Shanlun, he, too, was suffering underdraw symptoms as well as the backlash of breaking his exclusive with Digen. Such stresses rendered the higher-order Tecton Donors both impotent and virtually sterile, until after their next good transfer.

"You love him?"

"No!" But that wasn't true. "Yes!" But that wasn't true, either. "I don't know! He's—he's so much like you!"

Shanlun denied that, and they talked for a while about Yuan's role in the whole affair until she related that Yuan had given her a finishing transfer after her kill.

Searching her face, as if trying to read her nager, Shanlun asked, "Could I win you away from him by doing the same sometime?" But there was no hint of nageric seduction in his nager.

"You're too Tecton straight!"

There was a tremor in his voice as he countered, "I'd do it, Laneff—if it would bring you back to me. If it was the only possibility, I'd do it. And more, a full transfer."

She was shocked. Of course, logically, the amount of selyn she might take would never be missed by any of his channel clients. *But the Tecton doesn't condone junctedness!* Yet Laneff found a greedy eagerness erupting within her which she could put down only by telling herself that Shanlun could be no more satisfying than Yuan.

Again, the puzzle that had tormented her rose again. "Shanlun ambrov Zeor, *who* are you, really? Who do you know these gypsies—their language, their customs, their channels? What kind of a name is Shanlun, anyway? And where did that Desha get off calling you Shan? You *look* like them, you know."

He looked down at his hands, folded quietly in his lap as he perched on a wicker lab stool. His nager stirred into a faint prismatic display, then washed out to pale gray.

"And where did you get that crazy nager?"

"I'm sorry, does it bother you?"

"No! And that's what's so intriguing about it!"

"The Tecton calls my type of Donor a Cardinal. And I'm at about ninety-three percent capacity right now. And that capacity is higher than most because I'm trained to serve the—" He broke off, glancing about suspiciously.

"This is private," said Laneff, having checked the place daily and found no spy devices.

"—to serve the endowed," he finished.

"Was any of that real?" asked Laneff. "It was another life, forever ago."

"It was all real. It's the training to handle that kind of emergency that gives my nager its peculiarities. The one time you accidentally zlinned me working, you discovered why I don't let it show most of the time."

Laneff remembered him bending over Digen, offering. "You never got that training in the Tecton," guessed Laneff.

He didn't answer her directly. "Laneff, I want to marry you—a permanent, sanctified union. I don't ever want to lose you again."

"Shanlun, you have to get it through your head. Jarmi was good—the best the Distect has for me, anyway. And she wasn't good enough. That means I'm going to die soon in disjunction crisis."

He searched her face frantically, then lowered his eyes to his hands again. They lay still in his lap, just as his nager lay still. But she thought he'd have charged about the room restlessly had he permitted himself the luxury.

"Let's lay that aside for the moment. I'm going to tell you something nobody in the Tecton except Mairis knows. I don't know if Yuan suspects, but it doesn't matter as long as he never *knows*. You already possess the greatest secret; the rest has to go under the same seal."

"You'd respect the word of a junct?"

"Digen was junct. Don't profane his memory. Azevedo is junct—by Tecton standards. Can you find it in your heart not to respect him?"

"Azevedo is junct? I don't believe it!"

"He is a channel—and more. Swear."

"I can't swear Unto Sat'htine anymore," she said, her hand going to the signet nestled between her breasts.

He caught her hand, and her tentacles naturally twined about his fingers. "Was your disjunction valid?"

"Yes!" Blood rushed to her face in shame at how she'd repudiated it all.

"Did you kill that terrorist out of craving for what you had forsworn?"

"No, but I—I was beginning to want a Gen, not a channel."

"And it was my nager that did that to you, wasn't it?"

"How did you know?" It was out of her mouth before she could stop the words.

"Laneff, you are not truly junct now, for your disjunction was valid, and it did not fail you. If you do not kill again—Laneff, swear by the validity of your disjunction, marry me, and together we'll fight for your life."

He dropped her hand, his nager closing around him so as not to engage her field at all. "But you must choose freely. Yuan, too, is offering hope. Do not bind yourself to me for the sake of something that may not come to pass."

Yuan, too, had only offered, and then made her choose. *They are so alike!* Suddenly, it occurred to her to ask, "Shanlun, what do you hate?"

"Hate?" he asked, bewildered. "Why would you ask such a question? Have you ever seen me hate?"

"No. But you must hate something."

"Why?"

His confusion was genuine. Laneff had zlinned closely to detect the truth, and his nager seemed open to her in his confusion. "Well, then, what is your enemy?"

"I pray that I make no enemy in life. I've never found anyone who required me for an enemy."

"That's the oddest answer I could imagine. What do you fight against in the world?"

"A wise man does not fight *against*. If necessary to fight, the wise man fights for his goal, choosing to preserve life wherever possible."

"Well, how do you feel about the Diet, for example?"

"The Diet?" He considered her. "I'm sorry, I can't hate them. They are terrified, and they live in a fantasy world. Their violence is a form of insanity born of terror, like a Sime in attrition. And there's only one way to approach that kind of blind terror: with love, not hate."

"You could *love* the Diet? After all they've done?"

With a throat-wringing near-sob, he nodded mutely and turned from her, rising to go toward the door. He moved with the jerky stiffness of an old man, such a sharp contrast to his normally fluid motions. This man, who had professed willingness to give her direct transfer in violation of his stiff-necked Tecton loyalty, who had proposed marriage in defiance of his Householding's custom, was willingly relinquishing hope of having her because he thought she hated the Diet for what they'd done to her and required him to hate as well.

But it's Yuan who's hagridden by hatred. Her whole life had been dedicated to eliminating a basic cause of hatred in the world, the killer Sime. The Diet required Yuan for their enemy. She wanted no enemies in the last days of her life.

She darted around in front of the slow-moving Gen, stopping him with hands on his shoulders, standing on tiptoe to reach. "Shanlun, would you have risked your life to save me, the way Yuan did, if you'd been close enough? Would you have fought for me—against the Diet?"

"May God give me the chance to demonstrate it, yes."

The bone-deep vibration of those words, carried on that powerful nager, made her shiver with the sudden fear that his prayer would be answered.

"Then I choose you, not Yuan. Because he hates. And that's—that's like being junct. He gets so—so vicious on the subject of the Diet—"

His eyes spilled over as he kissed her, grabbing her by the waist and holding her, feet dangling in midair. Then he set her down, breathless, and said, "There is no viciousness in you. Your first disjunction was genuine. It has held under the harshest of tests. Your second disjunction will be a rebirth that will set you free."

He spoke with an easy certainty that evoked an irrational surge of recognition in Laneff. *This Gen truly understands disjunction!*

Before she could recover enough to even think that there was no such thing as a second disjunction short of the grave, he went on, fishing his little silver starred cross out of his shirt and placing it in her hands. "Swear to me, by the validity of that inner choice you once made, by the inner harmony it gave you, that you will hold my confidence to the grave and beyond, and I will explain what you must know."

"By the choice I once made and the harmony it gave me, I swear to keep your confidence."

"To the grave and beyond," he prompted.

"To the grave," she repeated, and added, though it sounded silly, "and beyond."

He relaxed, circling her in his arms and his core nager. His face smoothed into that of a young boy, and his nager turned inward, drawing her into a realm of misty stillness, a point at the hub of reality, and then soaring with her on an updraft of ecstasy. Everything in all existence seemed *right*, embraced by love.

She came up out of it feeling refreshed, her eyes locked to his as he drew her gently down to duoconsciousness.

"How do you *do* that? What did you do?" she demanded.

"I'm sorry, I should have asked if you wanted to pray with me. But I have so much to give thanks for now that didn't exist a day ago! Forgive me?"

Pray? It hadn't felt like any praying she'd ever witnessed, but she said, "Of course. I didn't know gypsies prayed."

"As with everyone, many don't pray."

"But you are one of them, aren't you? You speak their language."

"I spent my formative years training under Azevedo, not in the Tecton schools. Then I was chosen to go to Digen because the Tecton had no Donor who could handle his Endowment."

"Azevedo taught you to serve the endowed? Then he is endowed? Are all gypsy channels endowed?"

"No! Azevedo is—exceptional in all ways. Azevedo isn't his name. It's a title. It means, well, maybe Wisdom translates it. I've loved him all my life, Laneff. But I can't go back—and I don't want to. I've chosen the Tecton, and Mairis—and Zeor."

"But you were scheduled to give Azevedo transfer."

"It wouldn't have put me out of phase with Mairis. Much. And I'd have been better able to serve Mairis for it, too. That's why Azevedo was waiting for me. But now," he said collapsing onto a lab stool, "he's got to go easy on Yuan." He looked into her eyes levelly. *"That's* what I was objecting to, in Yuan's office. Desha can't really handle Azevedo yet, and Yuan is totally inadequate. I'd been feeling very happy that I could finally repay some of what Azevedo had done for me. I was going to demonstrate to him all that I'd become through Digen and Zeor, hoping he'd then understand why I didn't go to him at Digen's funeral."

She frowned. "Azevedo volunteered to take Yuan in transfer. But the Tecton has left the gypsies alone because they never traffic in selyn except within their own tribes."

"Azevedo—and I—are not *really* gypsies, in the full historical sense. We go among the tribes, but we're not *of* the tribes. Yet we adhere to the codes, so you can think of us as a gypsy tribe, except we don't always observe taboo."

"Does your tribe have a name?"

"Yes, though I don't use it because I'm not of them anymore. But by the laws of the universe as I learned them from Azevedo, now that you've chosen me and I you, now that you've sworn an oath of secrecy, a way will open for us to live our lives out together, though the price may be higher than either of us guesses right now."

"Forgive me for thinking your faith naïve. I can't take a husband now or plan for the future. My life is cut off by a black wall maybe five months from now when I'm too strung out with disjunction crisis to work. A year from now I'll be dead. If any of the rest of my life is to have meaning, I can't afford to waste a moment of the time left me on developing intimate relationships simply for pleasure."

"We have all the time in the universe for that. Death will not part us, if we choose each other, forever."

He's crazy. Gentle, but raving.

As he did so often Laneff hardly noticed anymore, Shanlun answered her thought. "No, I'm not crazy. I'm just using a different model of reality than you use. With time, I'll teach it to you."

"A gypsy reality?" she asked. "Which includes mind reading?"

"No."

"Shan—Desha calls you Shan. Is that a gypsy name?"

He laughed. "Yes, it is. Desha has called me Shan since she was in diapers!"

"May I call you Shan?"

"Or anything else you like and I'll take it for my name."

His seriousness was mixed with such ardor that she had trouble keeping her mind on her question. "You haven't told me anything that ought to demand such a mighty oath."

He sighed. "Mairis is the only one in the Tecton who knows I'm from this tribe, trained by them, eternally oathbound to them. If others knew that there could be occasions when I'd cheerfully break any Tecton law, I wouldn't be trusted in the position I hold. If the Tecton took me away from Mairis and the endowed, demoted me to a mere four-plus Donor, I couldn't survive the under-draw for long. I've left Azevedo with no going back. There'd be no place for me."

She understood now how he'd given her great power over him. "But you won't even tell me the name of this tribe you won't go back to but are eternally bound to."

"I must discuss it with Azevedo first. But your oath means you're not an outsider anymore. Your oath protects not just me but all of us, just as if you were adopted."

She grinned. "An adopted gypsy! Like a children's story!" *Only this one can't end happily. I'm going to die.*

He scooped her onto one of his knees, as if she were a child and he was about to tell a story. Grinning back at her, he said, "These gypsies even have a little magic of their own. So it's possible, Laneff—oh, it's a very slim chance, but it *is* possible you may survive this. I'm going to fight for it."

He'd lost the fight for Digen's life, but then Digen had been very old. She remembered a small brown vial of medication against a white sheet, spirited away and never mentioned on Digen's charts. "I've been wanting to ask you: what was it you gave Digen?"

Startled, he set her on her feet again, holding her by the shoulders. "Now who's reading minds?" At her puzzled expression, he rushed on. "What makes you ask?"

She told him what she'd observed. "Obviously, it was something Digen was accustomed to taking for 'tertiary entran' so it couldn't have caused his death directly. But I can't blame K/A alone without knowing what that stuff was."

He sighed, and then thought about it. "Laneff, you now have the right to know all I know about it, which isn't much. But I have to consult Azevedo first. Frankly, I don't see how the information can help you. Your goal now ought to be to teach someone else to run your K/A synthesis. Mairis has had *teams* on it ever since you were kidnapped. Even in your own lab, nobody has yet duplicated your results."

She leaned against the bench, idly pushing flasks around. "I was afraid of that. Jarmi hasn't been able to do it yet. And I've got *nothing* until it can be duplicated." *This is supposed to be science, not magic. The operator doesn't count.*

She was still ragingly posttransfer, and the emotions of depression and hopelessness had taken over in the absence of sex. She plucked a bottle of the pure K/A crystals from a padded rack and turned it, watching the clean cascade. "It's so simple."

He took the bottle, turning it expertly, and said, "I wonder if—No. But . . . would you mind if I take this to show Azevedo?"

"What could he possibly do with it? We have to class it as poison until we know if it caused Digen's death." But she gave it to him, and he pocketed it.

"Would you try to teach Azevedo the synthesis?"

She scoffed, "He belongs behind a horse cart, not in a lab!"

Shanlun laughed uproariously. "Azevedo's a gypsy, so he must be ignorant and primitive?"

"I'm sorry," she muttered, crushed. Toying glumly with a half-empty beaker of trin tea, she sighed, "Things were so much simpler before you came!"

He slid off the stool and turned her away from the bench, his nager melting her tension until she leaned into his chest, listening to him breathe. His voice came as a rumble. "It's unhealthy to let post syndrome deteriorate into depression. And now that I'm here, there's no reason to."

Duoconscious, she was enjoying the texture of his nager counterpointing the dark velvet voice, hesitant to let herself enjoy it. "In a moment, you'll go all colored-confetti again, and spoil this."

"Colored confetti! You zlin in color?"

"Doesn't everybody?" she asked languorously.

He shrugged. "Perceptions vary. Do you like this better?"

He was all golden now, seductive as he'd been with Digen. "I wouldn't if I were in need. Or rather, I *would*—but—"

"But you're not in need. Zlin me."

He stood back an arm's length, his formidably trained Donor's attention wholly on her. It wasn't what Yuan had done. But Shanlun held out his hands to her, and she took them, stepping into the fierce core of his nager as if into a different world. Something of the same effect she'd felt on greeting him hours ago burst through her body, only this time she could identify it, for it lacked the painful intensity. *It's as if I were Gen!*

The tide of life itself that surges within the Gen, erupting into manifestation at the core of each cell in the form of selyn, surged now in Laneff, rhythmically washing away the detritus of death left by need. Each wave felt better than the last, drawing her to anticipate a further thrill with the next.

Her tentacles twined themselves about his cool, Gen

arms, complementing their deep, exploratory kiss. Without her volition, her laterals found contact, too, and his
welcome of that sensation she gave him brought exultation.
But even then, a tiny voice within had to reassure her: *it's
safe. You could never hurt him.* In that moment, though,
she couldn't imagine ever needing killbliss.

Hypoconscious, losing all touch with selyn fields, she
was aware only of the tactile presence of male skin, fine
tough male hairs, clean rough male pores, hard Gen muscle encompassing her as if she were a delicate treasure to
be protected. The sharp perfume of him stung her nose.

Yes, she thought, *this is much better than hysterics or
depression.* Never, though, had she experienced such abrupt
intensity before, not even in post syndrome. *Could this be
part of being junct?* She chased the thought and drowned
herself enthusiastically in pure sensation.

His response was a tender melting accompanied by a
surprising groan that was almost a sob of joy. As if he'd
been rigidly holding himself back, maleness throbbed against
her in long, even pulses. Breathless, he broke the kiss and
whispered in her ear. "I saw a couch in Jarmi's office. It
would hold two."

She hesitated. *What if he can't?* Considering that he
hadn't had the demanding transfer with Azevedo that he'd
been ready for, it was absurd to expect this to work. But if
she stopped now, she'd plunge back into the depths of
despair, or be seized by a three-hour crying fit. *What's the
difference, crying now or later?* And it might—just might—
work.

For answer, she locked her hands behind his neck and
climbed up his body. He carried her that way, to the
couch.

He took a very long time, leaving not a particle of her
skin unstimulated. Afraid he couldn't end it, Laneff barriered
herself from the sensations at first, but he was irresistible.
He played with her consciousness, coaxing her hyperconscious as if she were in need, and feeding his sensuality

into her nerves, pulling back to prolong the suspense and teasing her down to duoconsciousness where he tantalized her with symphonies of mixed sensations, and then plunging her into hypoconsciousness so that she lived in a skin flushed with expectation.

She forgot her fear of not finishing, forgot about the kill and her project, and rode with him up and down the levels of consciousness, unwilling to judge which level was better. The pace increased as he finally entered her; with every stroke he had her rippling through the levels of consciousness and finding the power of life in each.

She was astonished when he brought them both into intense climax, a crackling vortex of discharged tension, as well timed as any Sime could manage. Returning to her own world, Laneff thought, *When he's post, he's not so slow and thorough.*

He kissed away her tears of joy, catching his breath. "I've never been so happy, Laneff. It was as if I'd never had a woman before."

"You've never treated me like *that* before!"

He gazed down at her with a mischievous smile. "A Sime who's living on channel's transfer is a kind of virgin to be treated circumspectly."

8

MUTUAL ANNIHILATION

Laneff woke beside Shanlun, drifting in the rose-gold haze of dream. Reliving a familiar dream that unrolled itself inexorably before her mind's eye while she was caught in the supreme lethargy between waking and sleeping, she became once again a child enjoying the last days of childhood.

The golden warmth of spring wrapped around the two-story house surrounded by the bright emerald lawn and carefully planted saplings. The houses in the out-Territory neighborhood seemed cramped close together with only narrow strips of lawn and symbolic fences between them. Up the street, a machine was laying surface on a driveway. Across the way, a family was moving in.

Laneff got out of the car in front of the large house labeled with the number ten. After politely thanking the driver who'd brought her here, she exerted all her strength to slam the car door. It didn't latch. The Sime driver reached across and pulled it shut.

At ten years of age, Laneff was as tall as some adults, but her spindly arms lacked strength. *When I'm Gen,* she thought, *my muscles will grow.*

Holding that thought to her like a warm blanket, she faced the strange house alone, uncertain and shy. The car drove away. She couldn't make her feet move up the walk. She'd never been out-Territory before.

The cold, black, lonely moment broke when the screen door burst open and Fay ran down the path toward Laneff, her beribboned pigtails flying, her bright black shoes making clicks on the pavement. Joyfully, Laneff dropped her overnight case and ran to meet her friend who was squealing happily, "You came! You came!"

They danced around each other on the lawn, and then Fay dragged Laneff inside. The house held odd, heavy cooking odors, and the furnishings exuded a background of smells that added up to *different*. In a whirlwind tour, Fay displayed the family possessions with pride and explained things with adult-sounding confidentiality. "Now, this is where you'll get to sleep—right in my room. I made up the spare bed myself."

Closing the door, she began hauling out special treasures, chattering madly. Laneff remembered how she'd behaved the same way when Fay had come to visit her. They had met at a summer camp in-Territory, and become fast friends when they discovered they were both set on becoming Donors. Laneff had pleaded and begged until she was allowed to have Fay come stay with her at the Sat'htine children's dwelling where she lived. But she'd won only because she'd insisted on it for the Union Day holiday. Quite unexpectedly, then, Fay's parents had insisted that Laneff come to their house for Faith Day. The Sat'htine foster parents in charge of the residence had consulted Laneff's parents, and after much deliberation—during which Laneff piped up with urgent suggestions, begging and pleading and even crying until she was sent from the room, insisting she'd run away if they didn't let her go—the adults had permitted her to come, but only for two nights and one day in between.

That afternoon, Fay and Laneff played Sime Center with Fay's collection of Sime and Gen dolls; she even had a channel doll that lit up to show both the primary and secondary systems in the channel. When she was in transfer mode, the doll's channeling system was brighter. Otherwise, the regular system was brighter.

It had been the happiest afternoon Laneff could remember, but it was followed by the most difficult dinner ever. She was very careful to say "Mr. Ravitch" and "Mrs. Ravitch," but her command of English beyond that evaporated. The food was strange, and though they only gave her vegetables, she knew the gray stuff they were eating was meat. It stank. Her stomach revolted, and she just picked at her food.

But that night made up for the ordeal. She and Fay lay awake until nearly dawn just talking. In the small hours, the topic naturally came to changeover. "Since I'm a Farris," said Laneff, "and known *not* to be a channel, it's practically certain that I'll be a Gen, and a whopping good Donor, too."

"I'm gonna have to work to get that good," responded Fay wistfully. "But I have a cousin who's a four-plus Donor, and he says I have the personality for it."

Laneff woke to Fay's mother calling them to breakfast. She ached from overexcitement and lack of sleep and was wholly uninterested in food, but it was Faith Day today. Mr. Ravitch was already outside cutting the grass, and she and Fay were alone at breakfast, so Laneff got away with eating only a banana and some milk. "I'm saving my appetite for the party."

Soon, all Fay's aunts, uncles, cousins and their assorted in-laws began arriving. A swarm of children, tots to teens, thronged the backyard, playing tag games Laneff didn't know. But she ran with them anyway and pretended to belong. After a while, one of them took her aside and explained the rules, and she began to play in earnest. She even won a few times, and by the time Mr. Ravitch had a smoky fire going in the stone pit near the patio, she felt a warm friendliness among Fay's relatives.

The spring sun was hot, the air still, and the sky almost

Zeor blue. Some trees were in bloom, yellow daffodils around their bases. Women were spreading the table, ferrying pitchers of cold drinks and cookies to the children. Laneff drank and ate a couple of the big cookies, but they seemed to settle into a lump in her stomach.

Not wanting to run anymore, she sat down on the lawn. Soon, the girls joined her while the boys ran off to the front yard. From the open windows of the house, the echoes of utensils clattering against porcelain drifted around them. In some other yard, a radio played. The girls concocted a sedate game of "trin tea and truth" in which they lied and giggled.

Tardily, Laneff remembered the Faith Day gift she'd brought and sprinted upstairs to get it from her overnight case. She ran back with the flat, polished wood case and presented it to Mrs. Ravitch. Other mothers gathered around exclaiming, "How nice—a Faith Day gift from in-Territory!"

Mrs. Ravitch opened the case discovering the array of cheeses, each wrapped in a different-colored paper. She put the whole case on the table, making Laneff translate the labels on the cheeses.

The smoke from the fire hung over the patio tables during the entire festival meal, and the vile odor ruined Laneff's appetite. She ate a few bites of something she thought had meat in it, thinking, *Since I'm going to be Gen, I ought to be able to eat what Gens eat.*

Inside, after the meal, the television was turned on, showing the traditional Faith Day Pageant at Westfield's Border Stadium. It was the one familiar observance so far, and it made Laneff homesick. One of the men turned from the television, wiping his hands on the white towel around his waist as he returned to the sink where he'd been washing dishes.

"They've got heavy storm warnings up for tonight."

A chill foreboding shot through Laneff, and after that families began saying early goodbyes. Soon the house was empty again, bags of litter stacked by the back door, piles of clean dishes on the table. All the toys were out of the toy closet in Fay's room. "Those boys!" she stormed, about to go yell to her mother, but Laneff promised to help her put them away, and she quieted.

Outside, the wind picked up, battering trash against the house. Laneff huddled cozily under the blankets. Fay slept. Laneff, though, couldn't fall asleep. She didn't feel well. Her head ached and she had weakening waves of nausea. *I knew I shouldn't have eaten that stuff!* She held off as long as she could, then crept to the bathroom down the hall, closed the door, and by the night-light alone, she curled up on the floor by the toilet.

Gusts of wind drove torrential rains against the window, and whistling breezes filtered through the cracks, chilling Laneff. At last, though, she retched productively, and it was an immense relief.

Before it was over, both Fay and Mrs. Ravitch were with her. Laneff had wanted to come here so badly, had begged and stormed as never before in her life, and now she was shamed beyond measure. But Mrs. Ravitch seemed oblivious to that. She provided a mouthwash and a fever thermometer. Laneff had seen such devices on television, but had never had one thrust into her mouth before. A channel merely made lateral contact and zlinned for the problem. When Mrs. Ravitch took the thing out, Laneff said, "It's probably just another food allergy."

"But you do have a slight fever . . . "

Fay asked, "*Could* it be changeover?"

"Oh, shen!" swore Laneff. She'd never given that a thought despite all the years of training she'd had. Fay, whose only real experience had been the in-Territory summer camp, had gone to the heart of the matter. Laneff's own fingers found the tender spots along her arms where nerves and glands were developing to serve the tentacles that would be there in a few hours. "I should have known hours ago!"

Mrs. Ravitch cast a dark glance at the window and then ran a cool hand over the back of Laneff's neck, probing for the gland at the base of her skull that would swell during changeover. "We've got time. Fay, help Laneff get dressed. I'm calling the Center."

It was remarkably easy to follow Mrs. Ravitch's calm orders. When Fay and Laneff arrived downstairs once more, Mr. Ravitch was dressing while trying the phone with one hand. He slammed the handset down as they appeared. "Phone's out. I'll have to get the car out and see if I can get through to the Center chopper on the transceiver. Fay—why are you dressed?"

Mrs. Ravitch came in buttoning a slicker. "If we leave, we can't leave Fay alone. She'll have to come."

"Maybe not," answered Mr. Ravitch. "Fay, go over to the Milins' and see if you can wake them. You can stay there."

Laneff said, "I don't see how the Center patrols could be up in this wind." She was beginning to be scared.

Mrs. Ravitch let Fay out the front door, fighting to close it again. "Maybe, but don't worry. It's only about an hour's drive by car."

Laneff had overheard enough of the arguments against her coming here to know that it was actually about an hour and a half from here, and the Center was a small, minimally staffed out-Territory installation for collecting selyn and dealing with ordinary changeover. This was the first moment of her life when she was glad she wasn't a channel. Such an out-Territory Center would never have anyone on staff who could serve the voracious First Need of a Farris channel.

Mr. Ravitch tried the car radio to no avail, and Fay came back drenched pleading that she couldn't wake the neighbors. Then they were in the car, moving slowly through sheets of rain. The two girls had the back seat. Mrs. Ravitch sat beside her husband talking patiently into the car's radio. Fay coached Laneff through the rough transitions of changeover, holding her reassuringly, reciting the learned speeches with real conviction. It helped.

But in one place, a tree blocked the road. Another street they tried was flooded out. Laneff's arms hurt now, her new tentacle sheaths stretching with the fluids, the thinning membranes over the wrist orifices stinging.

Then the car radio crackled to life, and before long a bright light swept into the car, hurting Laneff's eyes. Mr. Ravitch opened his window to talk to a slickered man.

"Road's closed," said the man. "Fire."

"We've got a kid in changeover. Got to get to the Center."

"What stage?"

Fay answered, "Five, I think, but she's going real fast. She's a Farris, but not a channel."

Laneff could see the wrinkled face of the Gen by the light of his lantern. He chewed his lower lip, then turned away and called to some men. He stuck his head in the window again, and said softly, "Officer Swatek is a Third Order Donor, so don't worry now. He's going to lead you to the Center. If it takes too long, blink your lights at him, and he'll come back and give her transfer. Don't drive too fast. It's dangerous out there tonight."

As the moment drew closer, Laneff's world narrowed to Fay's warm body holding her. She held on, breath after breath. Her insides became a black emptiness, devoid of life, warmth. Despite all her training, the cold void within terrified her.

In desperate imagining, she thought she could sense the glowing halo of selyn around the adults in the front seat. *Am I zlinning?*

As the thought formed in her mind, the spinning world outside the car settled. They were in the courtyard of a large old stone building. Choppers were tied down under wind-whipped canvas. Windows were bright.

The officer who'd guided them dismounted from his two-wheeler and came to stick his head in the window.

At that moment, something ticked over inside Laneff and her hands convulsed shut into balled fists. Every muscle strained to press the fluids in her sealed sheaths against the wrist orifice membranes, to break them and free her tentacles. The spasm let up for a moment, and she was being pulled out of the car. Then it happened again, the world disappearing into sparkling blackness— localized balls of warmth that attracted her.

On the third contraction, her tentacles shot free into the cold wind, spurting fluid everywhere. The shock brought her duoconscious for a moment. She was kneeling in the rain, soaked but laughing wildly over the new freedom. Then the cold numb terror was back, and the world disappeared into shifting points of energy.

Bright ones far away made the nearby one seem the answer to everything. She reached for that ball of brightness. It withdrew slightly, and that shattered the dreamy state. Suddenly, she knew what she wanted, and she went for it.

Her tentacles lashed themselves about the bright Gen flesh, the four handling tentacles on each of her arms securing the grip so the laterals would not be dislodged.

Once she had the grip, the Gen yielded willingly. Selyn blasted into her consciousness for the very first time, and she surrendered to the reflexive draw, slaking the dark need that macerated her insides.

As she forced selyn to come faster, there was a sharp flash of searing white overload. The selyn changed, became harder and hotter, like a scream of delicious fright, as the Gen resisted. It cut through to her and lit up her innermost being with the exultation of Self over Other: sheer egobliss. But before it was enough, the selyn flow cut off abruptly. Ice-cold needles of pain showered through every cell of her body. She came to bare consciousness, dimly aware of the limp weight sliding from her wet, pain-weakened tentacles.

One framed moment etched into her consciousness: the Gen officer's head lolling to one side, mouth agape, eyes staring.

Then tentacles sought hers, her need still shrieking through her nerves, worse for being thwarted of satisfaction by the Gen who died too quickly. She yielded to the source of selyn that folded her in a bubble of blurred fields—a feeling of utmost privacy and bottomless selyn.

She began to draw again, seeking to re-create that moment of peak overload. A moment of struggle for control, and the instant of egobliss was on her again—but oh, so briefly.

She came to awareness again, the stinging rain, the cold bright lights, the surging hiss of rain blurring speech, the scratch of her clothing against her arms, all claimed her full attention. The glowing fields around people had disappeared.

The corpses of the people she'd killed slumped on the pavement frozen in grotesque positions.

She was renSime, never to be Gen, never to participate in the channel's service. She might have lived with that, but now she was also junct. The Gen who'd offered her transfer had known her to be only a renSime, and had been unafraid until her draw had built relentless pain, nerve burn and death. The Second Order channel had understood only that a Farris renSime had killed and still needed. He had not anticipated that her draw speed could kill him. Had he been prepared, he could have aborted on her—but, out-Territory, he had not even considered such a possibility.

That trip out-Territory had been the last time Laneff had prayed to get something she wanted, the last time she had dared to want something so urgently that she cast aside all thought of consequences. The price of getting what she wanted had been just too high.

Wakening, she nestled against the massive Gen nager, letting it fill her core with brightness so she could feel as if she were herself Gen, could sense her own selyn building outward in pulse after pulse of clean, sharp energy in eternal abundance.

Clinging to that illusion, she could admit to herself that her First Kill was still her standard of excellence, her standard of satisfaction by which she measured all other experiences. Small wonder Jarmi fell short, as did every channel who'd ever served her. Even the kill of the terrorist had not been the same. She had not gone at him with that same freedom from considering his feelings and the consequences.

Shanlun was right. What I achieved in disjunction has held. She knew that in two weeks, she would again go through turnover into need and become a threat to any Gen who couldn't handle her. She had nothing but her naked will to keep her from the kill, and for a renSime that just wasn't enough. The craving for killbliss would drive her at any Gen who experienced pain or fear, or who dared to offer her selyn, as that Gen officer had. In need, she would not dream of channels anymore, she'd dream of Gens—in deathscream. *And if that's not junct, then what is? I must be careful.*

Shanlun's arm circled her, heavy with sleep, possessive. Fully awake now, she heard a distant roaring, and zlinning she discerned a nageric turmoil to match the roar.

She sat up, shaking the Gen. "Shan! Something's wrong!"

He mumbled, then wakened smoothly. "What? What is it?"

She scrambled to dress. "Can't zlin much through these walls, but our corridor is full of people in battle dress!"

He struggled into his clothes. "Could be the Diet attack. What time is it?"

"Four twenty-three," she said, heading for her own office to grab up the copies of her notes she'd prepared for just this emergency.

The two of them were halfway to the lab entrance when the door banged open and shut behind Azevedo and the four gypsies. At the same moment, the speakers came on with a squawk and electronic howl. Then a coded horn call played twice through before it was cut off in midnote.

In the silence, Azevedo said, "That means the Diet has broken into the warren. Yuan has ordered all his people up onto the surface. He's prepared to blow this place up."

"Then what are you doing here?" asked Laneff. "This is a dead end." But that was irrelevant. "Never mind, we can get out through the hangar. There may just be time enough!"

She led them back into the corridor where the mob scene had abated. There were sounds of fighting in the distance, and the occasional blunted thud of an explosion. "If they get into the selyn batteries, we'll be in the dark!" said Laneff.

Behind her, the Gens linked up with the Simes, prepared to keep moving even in sudden darkness. She stopped beside Azevedo at the intersection with the main corridor. People were running, dressing as they moved. The fighters on watch were no doubt engaging the Diet raiders. These were the noncombatants and the Simes too close to need to be thrown into a melee against Gens.

Laneff pulled Shanlun up beside Azevedo, giving them directions to the hangar exit. "Stay with him, Shan. I've got to go make sure Jarmi woke up. She sleeps like a stone." And there was now a tang of smoke in the recirculated air.

She took off, weaving among the Gen figures, augmenting slightly. She'd gotten new shoes since her disastrous slip on the tile floors. And these floors were composition, not as slippery or noisy. But still she moved with utmost caution. Before long, she became aware of Shanlun behind her—and Azevedo with his gypsies strung out in a line behind them all. She shrugged. There was no time to argue.

Jarmi was dressing when Laneff arrived, and the Gen took time to ask the irrelevant questions Laneff had avoided. Exasperated, Laneff grabbed Jarmi's wrist and towed her out the door. "Didn't you hear the evacuation horn? *Move!*"

With the Gens to consider, Laneff couldn't augment.

She had to move at their speed. The air was choked with smoke now. The fans were off, producing an ominous silence.

Laneff guided them to the branch that let them out near the hangar and its wide exit. But here the ceiling had fallen in, dust thickening the air. Coughing, they retreated.

"I don't know all the emergency exits," confessed Laneff. They hadn't trusted her completely yet.

Jarmi had her bearings now, and still gasping from the long run, said, "I know a way. Here!" She opened a side door into a storeroom and led them into darkness. The lights refused to come on, and Laneff took Jarmi's arm, saying, "Which way should be out?"

"Straight across, there's a door into another storeroom that opens off Corridor Q-12, Sipples-Bay."

"I don't zlin any other door," said Laneff, scanning.

Azevedo moved to their right. "I do. This way."

With the Simes leading, they wound their way through the crates and bales of supplies. The door was locked but gave under the impact of three Simes. The other storeroom was also pitch-dark, and so was the corridor when they found it. Gunfire and explosions told of the battle in progress.

They had no weapons. Without instructions, the four Simes moved to the front, the four Gens bunched at the rear. They came to a bend, the last leg of the corridor to the hangar. Bright flashes strobed through the dark, loud cracks echoed when guns went off. Zlinning, Azevedo reported, "Five Gens with their backs to us. A barricade of large potato sacks. And beyond the Gens, two of Yuan's Simes holding the five off with rifles."

"They're probably shooting drug darts," supplied Jarmi. "But they might have live bullets."

There was a roar as a helicopter revved engines inside the hangar. The feel of the air changed as the big doors opened.

The two gypsy Simes, blond hair and pale skin making

them all but invisible in the smoky darkness, touched Azevedo. They seemed ready to pounce on the Gens. Azevedo gathered Laneff into a huddle.

"The Simes won't shoot at us. We can approach the Gens silently and knock them out. But we must not harm them."

His firm order was directed more to the gypsy Sime who seemed near turnover, but it was clear that, as was traditional with gypsies, Azevedo would not permit them to injure any Sime or Gen seriously.

Renewed billows of smoke belched from the air circulators and a distant whump marked another explosion. Jarmi smothered a cough. Laneff returned to explain their plan and ended, "Hug the wall and dash through as soon as the fighting stops."

Then, with all the craft of the wild, the three gypsy Simes led the way around the bend, advancing stealthily on the Gens who were shooting randomly into the smoke. Laneff's throat felt raw from the smoke, but she went hypoconscious anyhow, ignoring the coughing prickle, intent on not feeling Gen shock and pain.

The defending Simes zlinned them coming and held fire. The Gens hardly noticed that before the four Simes fell on them. Laneff's target went down as she got a hold on his throat, cutting off circulation to his brain. He went out quietly. The two defending Simes joined the fight, taking out one of the Gens. Before Laneff could turn around, all the Gens were unconscious.

Azevedo dropped his target Gen and whirled across the barricade of potatoes to where one of the defending Simes had dragged a Gen. The poor Sime's need had driven him to hunting mode, and he was now intent on a kill. But Azevedo swept the Sime's grip away from Gen arms before it was properly seated. Just as any Tecton channel might, Azevedo lured the Sime into accepting channel's transfer.

For one instant, the two of them were surrounded by a

blurred bubble of privacy. Laneff was transfixed, duoconscious, remembering how, at Digen's funeral, she had
been willing to fight for a transfer from this channel. Now
what she zlinned reminded her achingly of Yuan's selyn
flow. And the expression on the Sime's face, together with
the singing in the man's nager, made her wish she hadn't
taken that transfer from Jarmi.

As Azevedo dismantled his grip, the Sime looked down
in astonishment at the channel's tentacles, as if he hadn't
known he hadn't killed.

Then they were both coughing at a new, blacker smoke.
Azevedo, showing no signs of being in recovery after
giving that transfer, pulled the defending Sime with him
as he called, "We've all got to get out of here!" Their Gens
had joined them, Shanlun's field brightening the scene for
all the Simes. "How long will Yuan keep the hangar doors
open?"

"They're broken. Never close again," answered a defender.

Meanwhile, the two gypsy Simes had each hefted a Gen
body. Azevedo chose another, saying, "Come on."

Laneff picked one of the smallest, a woman, and slid the
limp body onto her shoulder. Still, the hands dragged as
she made for the open doors. Shanlun came up behind her
and picked up the woman's hands.

There were no more machines left on the hangar floor.
Overhead, the doors which had been camouflaged as a
hedgerow sagged inward, spilling dirt and thorned plants
onto the floor. They found a side exit stair that led up and
began to climb. Laneff struggled, aware that the others
behind her could not get out if she fell and blocked the
narrow stair.

And then they were out in the moist winds, chill with
oncoming storm. Clouds darkened the night, but Gen
nager hazed the whole farmstead like city lights.

And that haze was lurid with battle lust. Shanlun helped
Laneff set her burden down and placed himself next to the

gypsy Sime who was too near turnover. "Laneff, can you zlin any sign of Yuan?"

She scanned. The farmhouse was in flames. Craters pocked the once neat rows of crops. A stand of trees near a brook masked another emergency exit, and many Simes and Gens were gathering there. A wrecked chopper lay burning with no one alive inside. Other aircraft circled, some with Sime pilots—and some Gens. Laneff couldn't tell Diet from Distect and said so.

Azevedo observed, "He could be anywhere by now. Even dead. But he said he might have to blow the whole warren up. So I think we'd best get off the tunnels."

Jarmi said, "The nearest safe ground is that grove there."

Agreed, they moved in that direction. Before they'd covered half the distance, a fast plane swooped in from above the clouds and dropped something into the stand of trees they were headed for. In the split instant between the delivery of the object and the explosion, Laneff had time to yell, "Selyn bomb!" and to slide her burden to the ground, throwing her own body on top of Shanlun.

She nearly cracked heads with Azevedo, who'd also thought to protect Shanlun. And then the world exploded. To the Gens, it was a loud bright wall of power that swept over them. But to the Simes, it was also a flash of selyn movement so powerful it lit up their nerves even if they were staunchly hypoconscious. The blast turned everything transparent and died off so quickly it stunned like transfer abort backlash.

"Shenshay!" spat one Sime, naming it not swearing.

Bits of tree and rock, wet sand, splintered fence, and bloody shreds of flesh rained down. As it stopped, one of the gypsy Simes said, "This Gen is dead. A rock hit him."

"This one, too," said one of the defenders. "He'd taken three or four darts, and it only now got to him."

Three of the Gens survived. Hurting with shock, Laneff gathered her feet, holding to Shanlun. "We've got to move," she said. "When Yuan says he'll do something, he does."

"Yuan may be dead," said Azevedo.

"Where can we go?" asked someone.

"Into the bomb crater," said Laneff. "They won't hit *there* again!"

They staggered over the shock ripples in the ground around the explosion, then climbed and slipped in a mixture of soil, blood, and water, and scraped themselves on stones and splintered wood, until they scrambled down into the center of the bomb crater.

Mercifully, much of the gory mess was buried. And at the center, there was enough clear space to sit down. The war around them was undiminished, though, and Laneff followed Azevedo back up to the rim of the crater.

"Laneff, do you know the other emergency exits?"

"No." She turned and called, "Jarmi! Come here!"

The Gen scrambled up the loose slope, swearing at the splintered branches that caught at her. "What?"

"Point out to me the locations of the other emergency exits," commanded Azevedo.

Orienting herself, she pointed out six more locations. And with each one, Azevedo shook his head. "Bombed also. No one living."

"They've shut us up down there!" said Jarmi, horrified.

"Next will be the hangar bay. I don't know why they—"

At that, another sere explosion lit the night, from the direction of the hangar, but muffled underground. When rubble ceased falling, Azevedo said, "Defective bomb? *Where* has the Diet gotten these monsters?"

"The Tecton makes them," said Jarmi bitterly. "And only the Tecton. Ostensibly to excavate unpopulated rain forest, and to control concentrations of killer tribes in the South Continent mountains. Actually, they were developed for use against us."

"Let's not argue politics," said Laneff, and stopped, suddenly aware of a wisp of nageric static. Jarmi was between Azevedo and Laneff, with nothing but night blackness to Laneff's right. She turned now toward that blackness, scrambling along the branch-matted, blood-and-flesh-strewn ridge, zlinning intently. Azevedo followed, and Laneff said, "It's Yuan!"

"I don't—Yes! You *do* have remarkable sensitivity!" He turned to Jarmi. "Go tell everyone to stay there!"

He led the way toward the Gen, who was obviously unconscious and injured. On the level, they fought through rows of old grapevines. The darkness was nearly absolute, but the two Simes went unerringly to the lone Gen.

Azevedo turned the body over gently. "If I hadn't just taken transfer from him, his nager would have been strong enough for us to find him sooner!"

"If you hadn't taken that transfer," countered Laneff, "you'd be in no shape to help us now."

Azevedo ignored that. "He's going to live, Laneff. It's only some internal bleeding." A heavy section of fencing had fallen across Yuan's midsection as he lay supine, and a shower of large stones had followed. As they lifted off the last section of fence, they found a small box clutched in Yuan's hands. His grip tightened as he began to moan.

"Take his ankles, Laneff," ordered Azevedo. "We'll get him back to the others, and Desha will work with me to heal him."

As they reached the upslope into the crater, willing Sime hands helped them. Before long, they had Yuan stretched out on the bit of level ground at the bottom of the crater. False dawn had begun to pale the horizon. The sounds of fighting were dying away, and fewer aircraft roared overhead. The three Gen prisoners were conscious now, guarded by two Simes.

Enough burning wreckage had fallen that Laneff wondered if any of the Distect fliers had escaped loaded with refugees.

Azevedo and Desha had barely begun to work over the

Gen when Yuan fought to consciousness, mumbling, and then asking clearly, "Is everyone out yet?"

But it was obvious he didn't know what he was saying. A moment later, he glanced about, "What's this? What happened?"

Azevedo was concentrating, wrapped around in some channel's working mode that warped the selyn fields. Desha was kneeling behind the channel, her hands on his shoulders, her eyes closed, assisting him with all she had. Shanlun moved to kneel beside Yuan. In terse sentences, he explained how they'd come here.

"Then," concluded Yuan, "they've closed every exit. Most of their own forces are trapped down there, too—but then *they* signed on for suicide. My people didn't." His fingers began to fumble at the box, raising the lid. "What time is it?" Laneff told him, and he said, "That's twice the time it takes to evacuate the whole installation. Still—"

A roar cut him off, and he demanded, "What's happening?"

One of the gypsy Simes called down from the ridge, "They're landing planes. One just—" A fulsome explosion wiped out the words, and then the Sime finished, "landed in a bomb crater. Two more made it down—three—four. I think that's all—but they're fielding squads of men now." He turned toward them. "It can't be much longer until the Tecton shows up in force. We're not *that* far from a major city!"

"I've got to get up there!" said Yuan, struggling to move. But Shanlun held him down. "Azevedo is working on you. You'll bleed to death; besides, you're too weak."

Yuan subsided, but he called, "Tell me when the last of those men is offloaded. Are any headed this way?"

"Not yet," answered the lookout.

Jarmi, Laneff noticed, was clinging to Laneff's side. She put an arm around the Gen woman, knowing that the box Yuan carried must be the trigger for the hidden destruct charges. And some of the trapped must be Jarmi's friends.

Hidden as Yuan was in the cocoon of Azevedo's field,

Laneff couldn't zlin him. But in the growing light, his face showed just what she imagined he must feel.

The lookout called softly, "That's it. They're fanning out—searching I guess for survivors."

With the planes down and the explosions stopped, there was a huge ringing silence. Then the crack of a rifle. The other gypsy Sime joined the lookout, calling incredulously, "They're murdering the survivors!"

"Yes," said Yuan, "their own as well as ours! The filthy lorshes!" There were tears dripping unheeded from the corners of his eyes. A horrible grimace distorted his features, much like that of a Sime in killmode, and with a lurid curse, he rammed his finger home on the button set into the open box he held.

Azevedo flinched, his hands nearly coming up to protect his face before he recovered himself. Shanlun scrambled to his side, displacing Desha roughly, shrouding Azevedo in a brilliant shell of bright fluorescent confetti.

A distant rumbling waxed to a ground-rippling shudder. All eyes flicked about the crater looking for safety and finding none. The roar gathered and the ground heaved, then settled with a long, grinding noise.

Gen deathflash was lacing the nager like lightning, and every Sime sought the nearest Gen. Laneff clutched her throat to throttle her own scream and held on to Jarmi, hardly able to zlin the Gen's field even at contact for the blasting overload all about them.

Jarmi whimpered, unable to breathe in Laneff's grip. In the abrupt silence, nerves battered to insensibility, Laneff heard Jarmi's plea, and her heart melted. "I'm sorry! Oh, please, Jarmi, forgive me!" At that moment, this Gen was the most precious thing in the universe.

Catching her breath, Jarmi replied, "It's nothing. I just hope you'll learn your own strength someday!"

Meanwhile, Desha and the other gypsy Gen had joined the two Simes on the ridge. As her senses cleared, Laneff climbed the slope, Jarmi right after her.

The dawn light showed churned and puckered fields where neat, knee-high rows of crops had been. The vineyard was flattened. There was no sign of the farmhouse. Tangles of wreckage smoldered. In the distance, an irrigation pipe had broken and was spewing water into the air, spread by the light breeze into a mist. Nagerically, the entire field of pulverized and cratered mud was dead. But as they watched, the first rays of the sun struck through a slit in the clouds, and a rainbow arced over the grisly destruction.

Tears blurring her vision, Laneff turned to those below, but they required no report. Azevedo gripped Shanlun's shoulders once, hard, and then raised his face to the sky. The two rose and faced the rising sun.

As if by some unspoken signal, the four gypsies around Laneff and Jarmi also rose, facing east. The silence of the dead fields seemed to be dispelled by an even larger silence—the silence of living Sime and Gen nager, pulsing with life in clear concert.

It was only an instant, but the gypsies held them all breathless. Afterward, Laneff felt normality return, but now the horror was dispelled. Laneff went back down to Shanlun and Azevedo. Yuan had lapsed into unconsciousness. The others gathered around.

To Shanlun, Laneff whispered, "You call that prayer?"

"No," he answered. "Just a salutation."

Azevedo said, "We must move swiftly now. We'll require a litter for Yuan."

One of the Distect Simes said, "We can't afford to drag these three along, too."

Azevedo walked over to the prisoners, zlinning, then took one of the dart rifles and without preamble shot each of the Gens in the thigh. They each recoiled in anticipation of horror, but that faded as the drug put them to sleep.

Desha said something, objecting in the gypsy dialect. Shanlun answered, and one of the other gypsy Simes argued. While they spoke, Laneff heard the Distect Simes remark on how the gypsies will argue until doom strikes. They made shift to construct a litter out of the splintered wood about them and jackets they took from the three Gens.

The slit in the clouds had closed, darkening the day ominously. A damp, cold wind skirled about them. Laneff cut into the gypsy discussion. "It isn't so important where we go as that we get out of here—now."

Shanlun looked at her, surprised, and she decided they had indeed been discussing destination. Azevedo replied, "We're in Gen Territory here. It's imperative that we cross over before nightfall—sooner if possible."

Desha again objected in the gypsy language, though Laneff had once heard her speak perfectly intelligible Simelan. Azevedo answered, "We can if we must. We'll discuss it later." He went to talk to the Distect Simes who were securing Yuan to the litter.

"We'll head north," announced Azevedo.

"We don't accept a channel's leadership just because he's a channel," answered one of the Simes.

"There are six of us and four of you," said Azevedo, counting Jarmi as Distect. "We know this country. You're welcome to join us if you like."

There was a bristling moment, and Jarmi said, "I think Yuan would go north with Azevedo. Shall we wake him and ask?"

The Simes zlinned their burden. "No," one said. "Let's move."

They helped one another up the path they'd cut into the rubble on one side of the crater, and when they got to the churned ground, they circled to stay on the matting of branches until they reached a stream that was now cutting a new bed. They tromped along the watercourse until they came to the spot where it joined the old bed and continued on the rocky wet pathway.

It was hard going. The air was chill enough to bother

the Gens, so the Simes shivered, too. Before they'd reached the cover of a tract of woods, Laneff called out a warning. Moments later, Tecton reconnaissance planes zoomed out of the rising sun and circled the battlefield.

"Run!" called one of the Distect Simes.

But Azevedo overrode that. "Circle!" he commanded.

Immediately, the four other gypsies formed a circle with the channel, leaving the two Simes carrying Yuan balanced on their toes, ready to dash for the woods.

Azevedo motioned the Distect Simes to put Yuan in the center of the circle. "To move now is to attract attention. We must disappear into the landscape like a frightened rabbit."

The planes would carry Third Order channels as spotters. The sparse woods would not hide them then, nor would simple stillness. Jarmi complained, "This makes no sense."

"It will in a moment," replied Azevedo, arranging the gypsies in some special order and placing Shanlun and Laneff on the circle while herding Jarmi inside with the other Distect followers. Then he stepped into the ring with them. "Lie down. I'm going to put you to sleep." As they complied, his nager expanded to include the two Simes, Yuan and Jarmi inside a distorted shifting blur. He spoke to them softly.

At the same time, Desha and Shanlun got into another tart discussion in the gypsy dialect. Dividing her attention, Laneff missed watching the odd hypnotic sleep overcome Jarmi.

Azevedo turned back to his two Gens. "Now our secrets are safe from outsiders."

Desha challenged that, and Azevedo answered, "Shanlun vouches for her. She is sworn." Then, comparing Shanlun and Desha with one eye on the Tecton planes, he said, "Shanlun will work this with me."

A flush of pleasure suffused Shanlun's nager, but he protested, "I haven't since—"

Azevedo snapped, "They have a Second Order channel up there. Desha couldn't handle this. Come!"

As the gypsies settled cross-legged about the circle, Laneff was drawn in between Shanlun and Desha while Azevedo placed himself opposite Shanlun. The brilliant confetti nager faded into a dark-purple shadow. In the space of a deep breath, the entire circle turned to purple mist.

Azevedo seemed to reach out to embrace Shanlun's intensity within his own blurred nager, and the two flowed into that same oneness she'd zlinned in Yuan's office.

The bubble of nageric shadow misted and smeared by channel's shimmer grew to encompass them all, drawing them outside of time. She gave herself to that nonexistence, reveling in the freedom of existing in the now. She was no longer stretched on a torture rack between past and future. Enraptured, she contemplated the now and found it exquisite.

Reluctantly, she was drawn out of that contemplation to find that nearly an hour had passed. Three times, planes had looped low over the nearby stand of trees, but without spotting them. Azevedo bent over the Distect group, waking them one by one. The others were rising, moving stiff limbs, brushing ants and leaves off. Shanlun remained, eyes nearly closed, nager still as a tidal pool, shrouded in dark purple. His face was as wiped clean of character as if he were a babe. Yet she knew he was aware.

She rose, feeling as if she'd just wakened from the most refreshing posttransfer sleep of her life. Zlinning, she reckoned that the Gens had all produced more selyn in that single hour than they normally would in a day, though the Simes seemed to have used less than a fifth the selyn for an hour.

She bent over Shanlun, worried, but Azevedo intervened. "Not yet. Leave him."

He drew her toward the center. "Yuan wants to see you."

The Sosectu was propped up against one of the Simes. He smiled. "Laneff! It wasn't a dream. You made it!"

"I wasn't even hurt! But you—"

"I'm fine now," he said, but it wasn't true. He was hungry, cold, but only a bit weak from his injury which was healed totally. He pulled his feet under him, struggling to stand. "I'm going to get a drink of water. Join me?"

"In a moment," replied Laneff, glancing back at Shanlun. Yuan followed her gaze. "His people will care for him. Come." Unsteadily, he made for a nearby brook.

She knew, and Yuan knew, there was more to this moment of choice than a drink of water. Laneff compared the two Gens and wondered how she could ever have thought them similar.

Yuan shuffled toward the brook, not looking back to see if Laneff followed. But she could feel a thread of his attention on her. What they'd felt together was real. What he'd promised—and delivered—was real, and she was grateful. But what she knew Shanlun to *be* drew her to his side. That clear motion told Yuan all he wanted to know.

Azevedo, having checked each of the gypsies, now turned to Shanlun, motioning Laneff back. He hunkered down before the Gen, smiling, his nager reaching into the dark-purple shadow. Gradually, Shanlun grew aware, character returning to his face as he opened his eyes. He smiled up at Laneff, and it was as if she were engulfed by a rainbow.

Laneff asked, "Was that a demonstration of Endowment?"

Azevedo laughed. "No! Just part of the training that leads to the ability to control an Endowment."

The other Distect people and now some of the gypsies followed Yuan to the brook to drink.

Shanlun accused the channel, "No, that was no training exercise. You used yourself unmercifully."

"Nonsense. I'm more comfortable now. Not so post."

"You haven't been post since I left!"

They were arguing now in English, and Laneff caught a whiff of the same tensions they'd argued with before.

"The Tecton has taught you to be too domineering."

"And perceptive."

"If I can grant you the right to cope with your own problems, can you not grant me the similar right?"

"As long as you acknowledge the problem."

Azevedo wilted. "Yes, I know it's a problem. You've made your point, Shan. And we will take both of you to Thiritees. But I don't know about the others."

Yuan and the rest were returning from the stream. Leaning on one of the Simes, Yuan came toward Azevedo, and the old man went to meet him halfway. They discussed what to do next while Shanlun slipped his arm inside Laneff's so their forearms lay alongside each other, him gripping her wrist.

"You know why he's willing to take you with us?" asked Shanlun rhetorically. "Because he feels responsible for what happened to you at the funeral oration. His intuition—an Endowment of a sort—told him to come right over to me at the rotunda when you were talking to Mairis, and to insist I give him transfer, Tecton and Zeor notwithstanding. Then you'd have been on the platform with Mairis, out of reach of those terrorists."

She couldn't quite picture even Azevedo breaking through a security cordon and wreaking havoc with a Tecton Controller's transfer schedules. "Why didn't he do it then?"

"Because I refused him. So, you see, it's back in my lap again. If I hadn't been unable to control my nager, or if I cared for you less so it would have been easier to keep my attention off you, then you and Mairis wouldn't have had to decide to put you in that box."

There were other considerations, Laneff remembered. But he started her thinking, and as they formed up to move north together, she mulled it over and decided that many people had made responsible decisions contributing to the disasters they'd suffered. When she put it to Shanlun, he replied, "Yes, we've all had a hand in making this mess, and we've all got to pitch in and clean it up."

"Let's get out of here before the Tecton is back with ground patrols!" said someone, and without further argument they marched, Yuan's group accompanying them to the Sime/Gen border. The long, hard walk wearing House sandals made Laneff's feet hurt. And they were all hungry and tired when they reached the border, here marked only by a thick hedgerow set in a barren corridor between vineyards. It was raining, soaking and chilling everyone. But at least it kept the bees and flies down.

One by one, they wriggled through a small rabbit run through the hedgerow, snagging hair, clothing, and skin on the brambles. In the center it was dry, and Laneff was almost tempted to curl up and sleep. But she crawled out the other side and came out headfirst in Sime Territory.

Yuan and Azevedo were standing in the middle of the muddy road circling the fields. They'd walked together most of the day, conversing quietly. Now Laneff heard them at last in agreement. "Then," said Azevedo, "I'll be sending our messenger to you on the regular schedule."

"Not that there'll be anything to report. My organization can't be a voice in world politics again for a long time to come."

"Yuan, you're not *certain* the Diet also destroyed your other centers. You won't be until you get back in touch. Now, are you sure you can make it to Bayerne?"

Yuan glanced from his two Simes to where Jarmi stood beside Laneff. "We can make it," he assured Azevedo. "Laneff, I didn't deliver on all my promises. I can't hold you to yours. It could be a year before I could again provide you lab space." He eyed Jarmi. "Though we could still provide your transfers—and you might live long enough to use that lab."

He wanted her to come with him. And there was a part of her that responded. Her hand sought Jarmi's fingers. The Gen tightened her grip reassuringly. Jarmi didn't want to betray Yuan, but her nager told Laneff that Jarmi's first loyalty was now to her. On the march, Shanlun had explained that Thiritees held labs as well equipped as Yuan's, if older, and Azevedo had the authority to emplace her there. Shanlun was sure he and Azevedo could provide her the pure killbliss transfer she craved, and he'd pledged to stay with her, letting Mairis and the Tecton presume him dead. Labs now, and probably good transfers against labs later and only Jarmi; Yuan had lost his best channel, and *she* had been virtually useless to Laneff. Suddenly, Laneff was unable to stomach such a cold-blooded calculated decision. She asked, "Yuan, are you going to pull out of the alliance with Mairis?"

"Now it won't be necessary. We're going to disappear and let the world think we're *all* dead. At least for a while. That should help Mairis's political position. And, frankly, we couldn't help him much right now, anyway."

"You're going to rebuild—and so will the Diet."

"But it'll be years before they can do any damage. If Mairis's elected, by the time the Diet's organized again, there won't be a Gen in the world who doesn't have a Sime friend or business partner. The Diet's line doesn't work where people know each other."

"Do you still hate them?"

"Right now I'm too tired and hungry to hate anything but this rain."

Zlinning, she realized that his essential nature remained unchanged, though his spirits flagged now. Shanlun was glued to Azevedo's side, awaiting her decision tensely. He wouldn't go with Yuan. And she couldn't see herself chancing that, either. *With only Jarmi—no.* She turned to the Gen, squeezing her hand, "I'm sorry." Then to Yuan, she said, "I've got to go with Azevedo and Shanlun."

Yuan's shoulders slumped further, but he only nodded.

Jarmi looked to Azevedo. "Do you think you could take me along?"

Laneff found a smile blooming on her face, a grinding tension in her midsection letting go.

The channel answered, "It'd be awkward for you, Jarmi.

Gypsy tribes don't mix with outsiders. You'd have no friends."

Jarmi shrugged. "If I have Laneff, it's enough. And, I do know my way around her lab work. I can be useful."

"She could," declared Laneff, surprised she hadn't thought of that. "It would take a lot of time to train a new assistant." But she also knew there was no way Jarmi could be trusted with the secret of the Endowment and all the rest. "But, Jarmi, once there, you'd probably have to stay for many years. They won't let you go back to Yuan—after I die."

"Maybe you won't die."

"You've got to adjust to that idea, Jarmi. Think. After I'm gone, will you be glad to have left your life behind?"

Jarmi stared down at the mud with a pained expression, and Laneff realized everything Jarmi cherished had been brutally destroyed just hours before. Yet with an air of real decision, Jarmi said, "Yes. I want to be part of what you're doing." She looked apologetically toward Yuan.

Azevedo had zlinned her deeply as she spoke, and now he said, "Then I'll permit you to come with us."

As the two groups parted, trudging in opposite directions, Jarmi clung to Laneff both for balance in the slick mud and for security.

Laneff said, "I know why I'm glad you're coming. But why are *you* so happy, Jarmi? This is going to be hard on you."

"Laneff, you came back for me. It would have been saner for you to go directly to the hangar from the lab, but you went all the way back into the residence wing for me. I've never known anyone who'd do such a thing for me. I *couldn't* turn my back and walk away from you—not even with Yuan."

They trudged through the unrelenting downpour, some of them resorting to bare feet when their shoes were soaked. At dark, the Simes each took the arm of a Gen, enduring the increased hunger, cold, and aching muscles. Shanlun walked with Azevedo, and Laneff had Jarmi, zlinning the path through trinrose fields, apiaries, and clumps of houses.

Twice, Tecton patrols flew overhead, and once they crossed a road where buses whizzed by at speed. Then they came to a slideroad bed and had to wait for a train to pass. Later, they followed a road, taking to the drainage ditch when cars approached.

After one such episode, Jarmi reamed muddy water out of her face and said, "I hate to complain, but does anybody have any idea how much longer until we find something to eat?"

Azevedo apologized. "We all know where we're going. With luck, we'll be warm and dry and fed before dawn."

At midnight, they broke for a rest. Jarmi and Laneff huddled under a deadfall while the gypsies and Shanlun made one of their salutes. Afterward, *they* seemed refreshed, but Jarmi's fatigue and hunger dragged at Laneff. They slogged across alfalfa fields, skirted a new vineyard, scrambled through another hedgerow old enough to have been there when the Ancients held the world, and eventually came out in a gully sloshing through a torrent of dirty water.

A large clay culvert pipe emerged from beneath a roadbed. Above, houses were packed as densely as ever one saw them in-Territory. One of the gypsies worked at the mesh screen that closed the culvert and it swung aside.

"Now only our feet will be wet," said someone.

"Yeah, but with *what*?" commented another.

Yet, gratefully, they trooped into the dark. The center of the pipe was a juncture of two sections, both tall enough for them to stand upright. Azevedo and one of the other Simes scrabbled at the seam, and then another door opened, a narrow slit leading into even deeper darkness.

With trepidation Laneff followed, towing Jarmi and reminding her, "They say gypsies go where they will, without regard of civilized rules. This must be one of those ways—and no doubt a tribe secret."

"I won't tell."

In a double column, Sime and Gen together, Sime zlinning the way by the Gen's nager, they worked their way along an Ancient sewer pipe. Where it had crumbled, modern masonry had repaired it. It still carried noxious moisture.

"At least now my appetite's gone," said Jarmi.

It was slow going. Several times, they climbed up into side pipes, then down into another pipe, a warren as complex as if this underlay a city.

And then, without fanfare, they emerged into light, warmth, dryness, and clean air.

It was an underground room, connected to some sort of power system. The walls were white tile, and the refugees dripped filthy water on clean white tile flooring. An open rack at one side held an assortment of clothing—both traditional gypsy buff and beige fringed garments and ordinary street wear. Couches and chairs were scattered about the room, with tables, magazines, and a trin tea service. Doors opened in every direction. Two of them were labeled toilets.

"Now," announced Azevedo, "we can clean up!" He opened the toilet doors for them. Shanlun and the other Gen man made directly for one while Desha helped Jarmi toward the other. Laneff could just make out a row of shower stalls within.

Laneff said, "What *is* this place? I think we must be under modern P'ris!"

"We're on the outskirts, near the river," answered Azevedo.

"This is Thiritees?" asked Laneff.

"Just the entryway." He was zlinning her now, curious. "Come here, Laneff. I haven't zlinned you without the Gens around obscuring things. Let me make a contact . . ."

"Something wrong?" she asked, worried. "I feel fine."

He took her tentacles and made a brief lip contact. Pulling back, he tilted his head to one side, zlinning. "Yes, indeed. Why didn't you tell me—"

"What?"

"You don't—Oh, Laneff. I do hope it's on purpose. A Farris woman—a pregnancy is nothing to play around with."

9

THIRITEES

Shanlun stormed into Azevedo's den without pausing to announce himself nagerically. Laneff followed, feeling as if she'd touched off a volcanic eruption.

"You knew this three days ago!" accused Shanlun with none of the deference he usually showed the old man. His nager was in its neutral particolored confetti state, not forcing his emotional turmoil on the Simes about him, but his indignation was in his voice. "Azevedo, don't you see how this changes everything?"

"Shanlun!" said Laneff before the channel could reply, "I begged him not to tell you right away. Chances are that nothing will come of it; besides, *I* wanted to tell you!"

Fuming, Shanlun looked from Azevedo to Laneff and back. Gradually, his ire subsided. "My apologies, Azevedo. Permission to enter?"

He was already standing in the middle of the intricately patterned matting. Azevedo motioned with two tentacles, a gracious invitation to be seated. He was sitting cross-legged on a cushion set on a wicker platform surrounded by hanging plants and lit by a skylight. Tastefully uphol-stered wicker chairs and stools dotted the room. A fire-place filled one wall, the mantel strewn with huge fat candles and wax sculptures. Woven tapestries adorned the walls with abstract designs. There was no desk, no books, no files, yet Laneff had been told that Azevedo ruled the tribe from this room, as a Sectuib once would rule a Householding.

Shanlun took two strides toward the old man and crossed his legs at the ankles, easing himself gracefully to the floor. Laneff closed the door and hovered, unsure of the protocol. She was wearing gypsy costume—a floor-length skirt and hip-length tunic, hemp sandals, and wide hair band, all in pale beige. For disguise, in case she were seen by outsiders, they had dyed her black hair and eyebrows to a rusty blond and had given her a cream to use on face and hands that would bleach her complexion. She hardly looked Farris anymore.

Studying Shanlun's downcast eyes, Azevedo motioned her to a chair beside him, and said, "Or you may sit beside Shanlun, if you like."

She took the patch of floor matting beside Shanlun, feeling the ache of shame in his nager and wanting with unbearable intensity to soothe it away.

Azevedo closed his eyes, seeming to ignore them. At first, Laneff thought this the rudest possible rebuke to Shanlun. But the ambient settled into a calm she was loath to disturb, and presently she noticed Shanlun's nager changing. The stark contrast in color and brightness between the randomized chips at his nageric surface seemed to fade. The flecks danced less energetically, finally stilling and merging into a hazy solidity behind which the bright gold of packed selyn pulsed. His intense shame turned to chagrin and faded to a self-forgiveness.

At last, Azevedo said in the distant voice of a working channel, "Your feelings are understandable, Shanlun ambrov Zeor. You're personally involved here, a deep involvement."

"Yes. But it seems years in the Tecton have addled my perspective."

"But not your acuity. You're correct that this does change the situation."

Eyes like burning coals, Shanlun looked up at Azevedo, his hand stealing aside to grip two of Laneff's tentacles. "Is there anyone among the Company who has handled a Farris renSime's pregnancy?"

"I have, of course, put out the call for experienced midwives."

"I'm sorry," said Shanlun. "I should have realized you'd already be working on it." He added, "But even at best, she's going to have to be told everything. She can't survive this without hope."

Laneff quelled a leap of curiosity and listened.

Azevedo gathered Laneff's attention. "I do believe you can survive to be delivered. But we dare not fail to consider abortion."

Laneff had not thought of that. Objections burst into her mind, but before she could speak, Shanlun said, "No!" And then, worried, "It's a channel, isn't it?"

Azevedo nodded. "A female, unless I'm mistaken. But a channel will demand so much selyn of Laneff's system that she'll need transfers very frequently, and will likely go into disjunction crisis much sooner."

Scientific terminology in their outlandish accent, their gypsy costumes, seemed totally bizarre. Laneff laughed and then had to explain what was funny about disjunction.

"And that's the other thing," said Shanlun. "Azevedo, you've got to try to learn her synthesis—*now*, before she can't work anymore."

"Before that, I may have to go to see Mairis. If we don't have a midwife for her, we must beg one of the Tecton. No, Laneff, don't panic. We won't send you to their Last Year House. Zeor has a long history of cooperation with—gypsies. As Sectuib, Mairis can provide someone to care for you." He shifted his gaze to Shanlun. "Someone we can tolerate."

Shanlun put his arm about her, and she felt his inner conflict as he summoned bravery. "I'll go to Mairis. You must stay and work with Laneff while she can work."

Laneff choked on half-formed protests, dizzied by the speed with which events whirled around these two. "Shan, if the Tecton ever lays hold of you, you could be sent anywhere in the world and never get back here!"

"No. I'll go in gypsy garb, and no one but Mairis will know who I am. I'll tell him you're with Azevedo, and—" Bright hope and shyness warred with his apprehension. "Laneff, can I ask him to invite you to pledge Zeor?"

She'd thought about it often enough. Zeor doesn't marry out of Zeor. But Sat'htine was so much a part of her. "Shan, I'm a healer—"

"But as a healer, as in all parts of your life, you do strive for excellence. Even facing your own death, you have not ceased to *strive* for the best you can envision. You have always been as much Zeor as Sat'htine. Let Mairis judge it."

"I can't guarantee my answer."

Azevedo cut in, "There's no reason to be anxious about it, Laneff. You've plenty of time to make that decision. Meanwhile, you're safe here."

That's what I thought with the Distect! thought Laneff, aware that considering another life change, such as pledging a new House, did fill her with intolerable anxiety.

Azevedo turned to the Gen. "Shanlun, you're willing to risk your life—*everything*—for this child?"

"Yes," he answered without hesitation.

"Do you know why?" challenged Azevedo.

"Yes." He turned to Laneff, as if in explanation. "The impossible doesn't happen randomly. I haven't been tested, but I'm sure I'm at the absolute nadir of my own fertility. Yet this happened despite your precautions, too. This child is yours—and mine—and wants very much to be born now. I'm willing to take as much risk as you do to see that happen."

Laneff had spent three days growing into the idea, realizing that this baby was as important to her as her work, something to survive her. Yet Shanlun had arrived at acceptance within minutes of hearing the news. Her whole love went out to him, and she hugged him close, burying her nose in his chest and muttering, "Yes, I'm scared, too, Shan."

He kissed her. The nageric warmth was incredible.

Azevedo cleared his throat. "Then this is the plan. We'll begin immediately to determine why only Laneff can do this synthesis. Jarmi will continue the structure studies on the purified chemical you salvaged. If the Company can find no midwife, we'll send Shanlun to Mairis with a letter I'll write."

The previous day, Laneff had been assigned a musty old lab, much like the one she'd had in school. Now, she and Jarmi continued to gather equipment and set up their experiments again. Meanwhile, Laneff was welcomed into the community of not-really-quite gypsies from which Shanlun had come.

"Thiritees" was their word for library/school, and the entire top floor of the building housed a collection of ancient volumes that must have dated back to the Ancients. "This is all that's left of the great library of the School of Rathor, disbanded almost a century ago. Many of these books are copies of ones published by the Ancients—before mankind mutated into Sime and Gen."

Whole sections of that library, open to her only under Azevedo's guidance, described the science behind the Endowment. She didn't pretend to understand any of it, but she was interested. Her own child, they explained, would likely be endowed.

The School of Rathor, some of whose members called themselves the Company and traveled out disguised as gypsies, had been founded to preserve the mystical and esoteric lore of the Ancients and to add to that lore by experiment. Their central symbol was the starred cross—an ordinary five-pointed star superimposed on an equal-armed cross. It was the Company who had founded and maintained the safe ways out of Sime Territory for the children of Simes who established as Gens.

If she believed their claim, that certainly solved one of the oldest mysteries of civilization. To know that the safe ways were the work of the people around her made her happier. And Azevedo even began teaching her their language.

Shortly after that, Laneff was asked to attend three brief meetings, from which Jarmi was excluded, designed to familiarize residents of the building on new local laws.

Thiritees was established in a four-story brick building on a sheltered courtyard off a busy avenue in P'ris, a regional and district capital straddling a Sime/Gen border. The city was divided by a wide, oily river into Sime and Gen Territory, and the new experimental Embankment Zone where Thiritees was located. In the Embankment Zone, a mixture of Sime and Gen law prevailed.

The establishment of the zone was not merely the result of Mairis Farris's campaign, they were assured. The City Planners had been considering it for years. But the advent of the Digen coin suddenly made it feasible.

Laneff reported all this to Jarmi, saying, "This may make it easier to order from Sime or Gen Territory suppliers. Deliveries won't be so conspicuous."

They had a much tighter budget here, and less actual space. But Laneff had salvaged all the data from the expensive analytical machines, though her notes were a little mud-stained. With Shanlun's help, she was able to locate or borrow balances, desiccators, and distillation and filtration apparatus. And Shanlun found a renSime woman who was an expert glassblower.

"We'll have to recalibrate *everything!*" complained Laneff.

"I can do that," replied Jarmi, and set to work.

In a matter of days, they were ready to pick up where they'd left off. Jarmi began running the syntheses they'd planned to do as part of the K/A structural analysis.

Simultaneously, Laneff began to teach Azevedo the K/A

synthesis. They worked late at night, when Jarmi was asleep and they had the lab to themselves. Often they'd still be there in the morning, when Jarmi came in munching a sweet roll from the breakfast buffet.

Azevedo quickly demonstrated his mastery of the equipment, and within three sessions, Laneff had identified a familiar air to his manner. "You're a teacher—a professor!"

He pivoted on the wicker stool as he sat at the balance and smiled at her. "I've taught it, yes. But that was years ago."

Now she recognized the elegant battering all her equipment showed. "*This* is a school—not a lab!"

"A graduate school, yes."

Laneff recalled the groups she'd gone to those legal briefings with. Pregnant women, children, young men, but only a few of middle years. A typical college cross section.

But it was all housed in the one building that extended three damp stories underground, and rambled into a nightmare of wings and additions aboveground.

She'd often walked by the entrance to the living wing. The smells and noises and wild music were just like any gypsy encampment where you might shop for wickerwork. She hadn't seen anything that looked like a schoolroom, and she said as much to Azevedo.

"Our methods aren't suited to mass production of identical experts. And we don't differentiate between students and teachers. We don't have courses or curricula. But we do develop skills. Right now, I'd like to acquire one of yours."

"Well, I guess you're as ready as you'll ever be." He'd read up on her work as it was published, and now he'd read her previous month's notes.

So that night, she demonstrated her technique for him. Shanlun watched, commenting on the number of times he'd watched her do it for Mairis's experts. She had it down to a precise series of motions, pointing out to Azevedo each of the crucial conditions—where glassware had to be ultraclean, where weights had to be exact, where reagents had to be spectrometric grade and totally dry. And she could detail exactly what happened when any condition wasn't met.

He listened with rapt enthusiasm. The next night, when he began to duplicate her procedure with his own hands, she drew on a convenient chalkboard the diagrams of the various molecules formed during reaction. "If I had a three-sixty plotter, I could run up a display to show you in three dimensions."

"Don't worry. I've a fair imagination." He asked cogent questions about the activated states of the molecules and the bonding mechanisms. She sketched them, elaborating with hand and tentacle gestures, and sometimes full-body postures, creating for him something of the beautiful dance she saw in her mind as the reactions proceeded.

At one point, Shanlun remarked, "You seem to think of these molecules as personalities—friends, even."

Surprised at that notion, she could only nod. "And I sometimes feel you have to coax them to behave, like trained animals!" She laughed, a little embarrassed.

Azevedo smiled at Shanlun. "Isn't that what I've always taught you, Shanlun? Make friends with the universe!"

They worked until well past dawn, Shanlun leaving after their routine midnight break, when Laneff went to the public kitchen for a snack. At that time, everyone else in the building congregated in the large briefing room where they'd had the legal meetings. For those few moments, an intense silence fell over the building that penetrated the ambient nager, as it did at dawn, noon, and sundown.

When she asked about this, Shanlun told her, "We mark the passage of time with a salute—you might say because time is a sacred part of the material universe. It's too easy to be caught up in personal affairs and forget one's relationship to the eternal."

Weird. Laneff reminded herself not to ask such questions, and that afternoon she got down to running the analysis on Azevedo's product, allowing for excess moisture since it hadn't dried for a full twenty-four hours. Her last sample was filtering down the chromatographic column when Shanlun came in beaming.

"What's the good news?" asked Laneff. She was a bit tart with him, more tired than she should be after such a light day's work. *Don't think about it*, she told herself silently. *Miscarriages are very common among Farrises*.

"We've got an apartment! You and me, and Jarmi. And room for the baby, too. You'll have your own kitchen!"

She zlinned him. For the first time, she believed he really *would* come back—and stay with her, always, or until she died. *If he can*.

"What's the matter? You complained about the spices in the food from the main kitchen, so I thought—"

"It's not that." She told him how she felt.

"Laneff, you've chosen me, and I you. By Zeor custom or here, we'll be married." He took her in his arms. "This is for real. This is forever."

Jarmi came around the workbench. "This apartment is on the family floor, right?"

"Yes," admitted Shanlun, letting Laneff go.

"Do you think it'd be all right if I keep the room I've got?" She turned to Laneff. "I'll come stay with you when you're in need, but—I just wouldn't feel welcome up there."

She'd been warned, and she wasn't complaining, but Laneff's heart went out to her. "I don't mind, but—"

Shanlun said, "It's all right for a while, but there'll be a group of transients coming through in a few weeks, and there'll be as little privacy where you are as on the family floor."

"But can we keep it that way—for a while?"

"Sure, Jarmi. But you'll have a home with us, when you're ready." Then he inquired about what Laneff was doing, adding, "Azevedo will be along in a few minutes."

The channel arrived nearly an hour later, announcing, "Well, that's *it*. I just heard from the last group. Nowhere in the Company, nowhere in all of Rathor, is there a midwife with experience of Farris renSimes."

Laneff turned on her stool to change the collector under the dripping column, mentally timing it. Her hand was shaking. To Shanlun, she said, "When are you leaving?"

She was trying to be brave, but she thought it would be easier if *she* were going to sneak in and talk to Mairis while Shanlun stayed behind and worried. *If Mairis goes all Tecton, and decides I have to go to a Last Year House before he'll help me . . .*

His arms came around her, and he turned her on the stool, his nager enfolding her until his overwhelming optimism suffused her whole system. Then he kissed her with real passion. Even though she was far past being post, she enjoyed every second, but she had to break away to change the collector again. "Don't distract me right now. The fractions come out at close intervals. Jarmi, take number one over and dry it."

Laneff worked mechanically, her mind whirling as she assimilated the news. If she'd gone with Yuan, pregnant with Shanlun's child, she'd have been hysterical to get back to him. She had the best possible chance here, but the sinking feeling at the idea that Shanlun had to leave her now, if only for a few days, verged on panic. Only by total concentration on the work under her hands was she able to still the shaking in her fingers. Her work was the one haven of peace in her life.

Shanlun and Azevedo watched her quietly for a while and then left for their sundown salutation. When they returned, Jarmi had gone to dinner, and Laneff was just calculating the results of the analysis, holding her breath as the numbers flashed on the screen before her.

The door had no sooner closed behind Azevedo than she blurted out, "It's perfect! You did it! I can't *believe* it!"

"We must send word to Yuan," said Shanlun. "And Mairis has a right to know."

"Don't tell anyone until we double-check these results. And Azevedo has to do it at least twice more with the same or better results. We can't report out on—"

"Absolutely correct," agreed Azevedo, as if giving her a lab grade. He bent over the results on her screen, then ran the graph strips from her new gas chromatograph through his fingers. She'd packed the column herself but still didn't rate it as reliable.

Azevedo said, "I wish we had some of your original data to compare this with. There's a lot of water in it, too."

"I have a second group running right now," said Laneff. "And Jarmi's doing a third—which should be perfectly dry—right on the heels of this one. But this is definitely the very best anyone but me has ever gotten. You can do it! Now, can you do it again?"

The channel grabbed a light beige smock from beside the door. "Let's find out!"

Laneff started to follow him out of the office into the lab, but he waved her away. "Shanlun will have to be leaving in the morning. You two deserve a night off together. Besides, I have to see if I can do this without your nager interfering."

Joyfully, Shanlun scooped her out the door of the lab, not giving her a chance to ask what in the world her nager had to do with a simple chemical reaction.

She found that he'd spent some of the time while she was doing the analysis in setting dinner in their apartment. There was a soup she'd made, an artichoke, avocado, and mushroom dish from the main kitchen, sans the awful spices, and some nut bread with a tofu-and-tahina spread that he must have bought in some regular supermarket.

As soon as he had made sure she'd eaten enough, he said, "We must do something to celebrate your victory."

"It's not a victory yet, just a breakthrough. Let's clean this up and go back to the lab to see how Azevedo's doing."

"No. He asked us to leave. He's probably sent Jarmi off, too. If this is going to work, he's got to be alone."

She got up and started to clear the table. "That's nonsense. He's been watching me—"

"When do you get your best yields?" he asked point-blank.

She stared at him. She'd never correlated it, but— "Laneff, I watched you, lived through all that in the Hospital/Center with you when you were trying to get Mairis's experts to duplicate your results. They still haven't done it. And they *won't*. I *knew* Azevedo could do it. Doesn't that tell you something?"

She nibbled sauce off the end of one handling tentacle. "Why did you think Azevedo could do it?"

"Because I guessed what you were doing differently from all the others who tried, and I recognized it as a technique Azevedo had taught me, although I've never been very good at it. And when I found out you zlin in color, I realized you visualize a lot. You dream in color, too, don't you?" At her nod, he went on, "You can't work a synthesis *without* visualizing the molecules! And that's the essential technique necessary to get good, clean yields of kerduvon."

"Ker—what?"

"Kerduvon. The mythical extract of the mahogany trinrose. We call it moondrop. It's what I was giving Digen because it helps control tertiary entran, among other things—"

"Wait a minute!" The other half of her puzzle, the exact cause of Digen's death, had been put aside under the press of events. "Why are you telling me this now?"

"Because Azevedo has given me the discretion to do so." He took her hands, pressing them together between his huge, cool Gen palms. "Laneff, I had it in my mind, when I found you alive, that if I could get Azevedo to accept you, we could use kerduvon to disjunct you."

"A *drug* that disjuncts? Nobody could possibly have

kept such a secret! I don't believe it! Disjunction is—is—is a private and personal *hell!*" She had once thought this Gen of all Gens understood that. "No drug could—"

"No, kerduvon doesn't *disjunct*. It's *very* dangerous, Laneff. It acts on the central nervous system to wipe away certain types of neurophysiological programming. That's all it does—*blanks* the Sime's programming. What new programming takes its place is a matter of your choice—and that of the Gen working with you. One slipup and both Sime and Gen could end up permanently insane—or dead."

Assimilating that, Laneff said, "It'd be worth the risk."

"Kerduvon tends to cause abortion or miscarriage."

It was too much. Laneff's hands flew to her face, muffling a gasp. She understood now the firmness of Shanlun's nager, the tension in him.

"Laneff, you can survive until the child is born. I'm going to bring an expert, and we have Azevedo and Jarmi. Staving off disjunction crisis for ten or eleven transfers is not an absurd goal. And after that, we can risk kerduvon. There *is* a way for all of us, Laneff, if we have the courage to take it. I can't offer certainty—only hope. And that's better than no hope, isn't it?"

Strangling a cry of anguish, she nodded. Her body relaxed. "Oh, I've been so exhausted lately," she said, her shoulders slumping. "I know that's no excuse when so much depends on this, and there's so little time now. I keep telling myself I must do things today because I'll only feel worse tomorrow, but—" He held her snugly. "Shanlun, what am I going to do without you here?"

"Try to teach Jarmi the synthesis. I don't know if she has the well-developed ability to visualize, but she knows the theory best. If you can teach it to her, you have something to publish. And I'll be back in time to give Azevedo transfer."

"What if Mairis taps you for his transfer? Or the Tecton—"

"I'll find a way. Azevedo needs me now. And so do you."

He began kissing her seriously, but she leaned away to ask, "Shan, you've got to get me a sample of this kerduvon."

"Azevedo will get it for you whenever you ask, though I don't know what good it will do—"

"Neither do I, but it's the only hole left to plug. I've got to know what's in that stuff, and how it interacts with K/A in order to exonerate K/A of causing Digen's death."

"Our best chemists have tried to analyze moondrop for generations. It's a very complex mixture, and we've never—"

"Can you get me any publications on it?"

"Certainly, but not in any language you know."

"Get me a translator then. Surely there's a graduate student around here who'd like to get their name on my project."

"We don't work that way."

Suddenly frustrated beyond endurance, she cried, "How *do* you work then! Nothing around here makes any sense! Shidoni-crazed motives and ass-backward customs, inedible food, and imagination controlling chemical reactions—"

She scrubbed at a tear, and he handed her a tissue.

"I'm not going to cry! I'm not post anymore."

"I remember how I felt, those first few years in the Tecton. For a time, I was sick with it—like being constantly shenned. Nothing works the way you expect it to, not the plumbing or the people. And it isn't the big things but the little things that finally get to you. For you it's worse because you're weakened by the pregnancy, and you've been snatched into a second, totally foreign, culture. Oh, Laneff, I *wish* I didn't have to go."

"Then send somebody," she said, knowing it was silly.

"I can't." He broke away from her and paced, then looked back at her as if measuring her strength. It made her stand taller. He said, "There's more news. Our messenger to Yuan returned. The bolthole where he said he'd be—it was a bombed-out ruin. Unidentifiable bodies everywhere. The Tecton picked up those Diet Gens we left in the crater. News blackout on what they've gotten out of them, if anything. Mairis is making a round-the-world tour, campaigning. The Digen coin is a big success most places. Mairis's experts still haven't duplicated your synthesis. And even so there have been six attempts on Mairis's life."

"He—"

"No, he's not hurt. Some of the Distect supporters are still with him; one died protecting him. That attack on Yuan's labs was just the opening shot in an all-out war between Diet and Distect. In every major city there's been violence, bloodshed and pain enough to provoke Simes into the kill. But not one Sime has killed because of it. The vast majority of the world is coming to *see* where the Diet is wrong about Simes in general. Support for the Diet is cooling off.

"But with all this, security around Mairis is very tight. Paranoia is a survival trait for him now. If I were him, I wouldn't *believe* a note delivered by just any gypsy—not if it asked me to send one of my best out into the mists. Remember, he thinks I'm dead—and you, too. He's not going to send anyone else into that kind of danger. So I've got to go and choose one person to come take care of you. And I want to be back before you hit turnover—or, failing that, at least before hard need. You and Azevedo are in phase . . ."

"That doesn't give us much time," said Laneff. Her cycle was already perceptibly shortening, as always with a channel fetus.

"I'm going to leave no later than noon tomorrow," he said, coming to enfold her in his arms. "And you're right, that doesn't give us much time."

It was the first time she could recall him failing to read her thoughts, and she suspected it was deliberate. He bent and kissed her with a single-minded dedication that she couldn't resist. They had their own bedroom now, and they used it.

Sometime past midnight, he lay back exhausted and fell

into a typically heavy Gen sleep. She reveled in it for a while, and then got up, took a snack plate from the refrigerator, and went to the lab

As she'd suspected, Jarmi was there, having slept the late afternoon away and found herself too wakeful to laze in bed all night. "Hungry?" asked Laneff.

"You know me by now, don't you?" asked Jarmi investigating the plate. "Oh, yum, *real* food!" she said, tasting the nut bread. "Here, I've got some hot trin tea. Let's eat!"

They took the tea and nut bread to Jarmi's desk, set across the end of one workbench, and Laneff said, "Tomorrow, I'm finally going to get a sample of that other drug Shanlun had Digen on when I gave him K/A! They call it kerduvon around here. We're going to have to figure out how to analyze the stuff, but if we can, maybe we can figure out what caused Digen's death. Did the cadaver tentacles arrive?"

"Yes, they're in the refrigerator. I'm afraid there isn't much I can help with on those selyn conductivity tests!"

"Don't worry. I'll be back to start them as soon as Shanlun leaves in the morning. Meanwhile, you're going to have to do an analysis on this kerduvon sample, at least find out what kind of trouble it'll give in the chromatograph."

"It'll muck up the column for sure."

"I'll figure on repacking the column and make some extras."

Licking honey off her fingers and tentacles, Laneff got to work analyzing Azevedo's yield of the afternoon. Jarmi puttered around awhile and finally fell asleep on a cot they'd had brought into the lab. Just before dawn, Laneff had some preliminary results: Azevedo's yield had been immeasurably close to the theoretical yield for the equations. And it was nearly pure.

When she told Shanlun as he was dressing, she let her dismay show clearly. He threw back his head and laughed. "I know what you mean. It's enough to make anyone wish to be an endowed channel!" Then he sobered. "Well, at least now we know the secret. And all that's left is to teach it to Jarmi!"

10

NEED

The noon sun beat down on the courtyard. Laundry hung on sagging lines in sunny corners. Bedding lolled out of windows like heat-struck tongues. The cacophony of colors dazzled the eye, and the riotous play of swarms of children numbed the ear. A buff-clad man leaned out a window, beating a dusty rug, sending clouds of dog hair into the light breeze. A woman who was fixing a bicycle in one shady spot yelled as a group of children waded through her tools playing Sime/Gen wars and laughing in high shrieks.

Laneff stood in the cool of the main doorway with Shanlun. They were waiting for his car to be driven up from wherever it was stored. The gypsies in the surrounding buildings, Laneff had discovered, were "real." And they accepted the Rathorites with a respect bordering on awe. No outsider ever penetrated this deep into the courtyard. Looking at the spectacle, smelling the heavy odor of their cooking, Laneff could understand why nobody would want to.

"You said Mairis is on this side of the ocean now. How will you find him?"

"Read the newspapers. I can read languages I can't even speak, and *we* have friends all over. All I have to do is find a certain tribe, and they'll get me in to see Mairis."

"I *don't* understand! You're going to wander around the countryside until you find this gypsy tribe you've never met before and just tell them to sneak you past the tightest security cordon this continent has seen since the time of Kishrin the Eighth?"

"Before I went to Digen, I was trained by the Company. Gypsies do not wander around at random. And they leave clear sign for their own to follow. Finding them will be easy. Getting to Mairis may be harder. I don't want to announce myself to the whole Tecton, so only Mairis is to know I'm alive."

Privately, she doubted Mairis would go along with that. "The other thing that worries me is that message from Yuan that Azevedo got this morning." The development had delayed Shanlun's departure by a few hours. Yuan's first refuge had been destroyed before he got there, so he'd gone on to his second choice, sending a message by a stray gypsy. Now, Shanlun was to be the first of Azevedo's regular messengers to call on Yuan.

"Look, Yuan's place is right on my way, and I can carry a message from Yuan to Mairis. Azevedo insists Yuan has a right to know of the baby—and your success."

Laneff didn't quarrel with that. And Azevedo was right that Yuan really could use the encouragement. "The Distect hideouts are all targets right now. It's dangerous to stay overnight with Yuan!"

"True. But Mairis is also a target."

Laneff had no idea why the Rathorites were so supportive of Yuan and Mairis both. When she asked Jarmi, the Gen had answered that Azevedo had been around ever since she'd met Yuan. It'd never occurred to her to question it. To Laneff, the Rathorites were gypsies that were nuttier than most gypsies, and there was no way to fathom their motives. Yet it was obvious that something deep in their way of life was congruent with Digen's dream of Unity—and Yuan's: Sime and Gen living together without fear or distrust. And to that end, they unquestioningly took all sorts of risks.

With a shudder, she turned into Shanlun's arms. "There are so many dangers!" But she held back the plea *Don't go!*

At that moment, the car nosed through the archway from the street and crept down the narrow alley between gypsy-occupied buildings into the courtyard, scattering children and weaving politely through laundry lines. It drew up before the door, a pale-beige jalopy lacking one fender and with a rack of empty chicken cages on the top. The front cargo compartment was tied down with hemp rope that dragged under the car. One shattered side window was taped, but the tires were new.

The Sime woman driving it got out. Laneff knew her as a Rathor instructor. "Shan!" said Laneff shocked. "You're not going to drive *that* halfway across this continent, are you? You'll *never* make it!"

He laughed, as did the driver. Shanlun said a few placating words to the driver in their dialect and told Laneff, "Selitta wouldn't give me a run-down car, Laneff!"

Laneff closed her mouth over her outrage and just looked at him. He laughed again and tugged her toward the rear of the car. "Start it up, Selitta!"

She got in while Laneff was treated to a view of the engine compartment. The engine housing was clean, and much smaller than the fittings had originally been designed for. Obviously new. The selyn battery was likewise of the latest design, and a spare battery also shimmered brightly with packed selyn. As Selitta started the car, Laneff zlinned the smooth clean running of the engine.

"Good!" called Shanlun. "Now run the jiggler."

Another, smaller selyn-powered motor coughed to life, producing noise and vibration such as the car had displayed on entering the court. Now the selyn fields wavered like those of a truly decrepit car.

"See? It's a disguise. The brakes and bearings are all new, but disguised. It's Selitta's specialty."

As the woman stopped the motor and got out, Laneff apologized. "It's a great disguise!"

Shanlun picked up a patched and stained canvas bag filled with his things and tossed it into the dirty-looking back seat of the car. His costume, like the bag, was worn and tattered-looking, fringes missing here and there. Nothing was left of the crisply formal First Companion in Zeor who had stood beside Mairis throughout the funeral ordeal. With his white-blond hair combed down over his forehead and the oddly gypsy mannerisms he could adopt in a moment, not one reporter would recognize him even if he were standing beside Mairis.

He turned to Laneff, letting his nager pale to a chalky white flecked with only an occasional blip of color and his stance degenerate into pure gypsy. "I'm just another wandering gypsy. I've even got legal border-crossing tags that say so! I won't be recognized, so stop worrying!" He kissed her quickly, then got in and started the motor, adding the vibrator to it.

As he moved the car out of the court, expertly maneuvering around children, dogs, chickens, and laundry, he waved goodbye.

To blot out the thought *What if he doesn't come back?* Laneff plunged back into the lab work, setting all their projects in motion at once, and then starting Jarmi on learning the visualization trick for synthesizing K/A. This required giving Jarmi an entire refresher course in organic reaction mechanisms.

Going through it all a step at a time brought back to Laneff how she'd played with the other isomer that could result—the one that ruined the synthesis when it occurred. *Must research that thoroughly sometime*, thought Laneff. It was possible that this technique could make the other isomer pure just as it could this one. *Maybe there's some use for it?*

But she could only make note of it and dismiss it now. When Jarmi was sleeping, Azevedo joined her, showing her how to synthesize kerduvon from the raw extract of mahogany trinroses. The rich red-brown flowers were now grown in botanical gardens all over the world, but Azevedo said, "Up in the mountains, we have ancient fields of them. Conditions are perfect there—and we get much richer yields of moondrop from those harvests."

"Does it make any better trin tea?" she asked, recalling the fact that the professionally grown ones didn't.

"No; tastes horrible." He showed her how to concentrate the extract from the dried flowers, steam-distill off the fraction of active kerduvon, cook it, then vacuum-distill it. Instead of a molecular mechanism, though, he had her concentrate on a decorative old starred cross he wore around his neck. It was jeweled, flashing a dozen colors like Shanlun's nager.

"Visualize the symbols picked out by the jewels," he commanded. "And the colors are extremely important."

"Is this your molecular symbolism?"

"Goodness no! Wellll—actually, there is a relationship. But just try it; visualize it while you work."

She learned it under his supervision, then spent another whole night running ten simultaneous procedures, filling two whole benches with apparatus and doing everything the same except what she thought about while working on it.

The one she did without any of the visualizing came out black—almost devoid of the product according to the qualitative test Azevedo had provided her. They graded through dark brown, brown, light brown, all the way to nearly transparent yellow, the one where she'd given her all to the visualization. Azevedo's own product was a pale yellow, the color of Shanlun's nager.

She was staring at the row of vials when Jarmi came in, looking drawn and weary. "Jarmi, I don't believe this. I just don't believe it. It can't be happening—not by any theory of science I've ever heard!"

While looking over Laneff's results, Jarmi said, "But isn't this what you've been trying to get me to do?"

"Yeah. I think I've been expecting you to fail—only then, what will become of K/A?" She sat down on a wicker stool, picking idly at a stray wisp of the tough fiber. "But if you succeed, how can we possibly report this in a respectable journal?"

"I don't think we'd be anywhere near that point, even if I succeed today! First you're going to have to teach it to several really respectable experts. When it's become something 'everybody knows,' *then* you can write it up."

Laneff slumped on her stool. "I probably won't live that long."

"You know what's wrong with you? Tomorrow is your turnover day—I'll just bet!"

"Three days early?"

"You *are* pregnant. You haven't been getting enough rest."

"It can't be affecting me this soon," pleaded Laneff, but she was thinking of the solicitous way Azevedo hovered over her when he visited the lab—which was often.

"Well, we'll talk about it tomorrow. Meanwhile, let's get this mess cleaned up. I was supposed to try the K/A synthesis on my own while you do the conductivity studies."

They worked industriously all day long, and when it came time for Jarmi to quit, she said, "Let's just set up the analysis for tomorrow." Laneff had noticed how the Gen was putting in a couple of extra hours each night.

They worked until Jarmi was weaving with fatigue and Azevedo came in and shooed her to bed. "And when was the last time you slept, young mother?" he asked Laneff.

She admitted, "Just before Shanlun left."

"Then off to bed with Jarmi—or you're going to have a very rough turnover!"

"But—" There was no arguing with such a channel.

Laneff said, "We won't know whether we've succeeded until these analyses are run. I was going to start them tonight—"

"No. That's an order."

On the way up the stairs, Laneff had to admit that her knees and feet were glad for the respite. She caught up to Jarmi on the third floor and confessed that she'd been run out of her own lab by a ferocious channel.

Jarmi commiserated. "Look, maybe we can get into one of the kitchens and fix us something decent to eat."

"I've got a kitchen all to myself, remember?" And she rattled off the list of ordinary ingredients she had in stock. "Think you could make a meal off of that?"

"Sure! Let's go."

Cooking together turned out to be even more fun than lab work. They discovered they had a lot of food prejudices in common, and apart from those of the gypsies around them. Laneff actually enjoyed the taste of the food Jarmi made while thinking that if Azevedo was right about turnover, it was probably the last meal that would taste good for a long while. Laneff even dutifully remembered to take her new vitamin tablets.

Over the empty dishes, Jarmi looked around at the apartment: an open living room with breakfast nook, a tiny kitchen, a hall leading to three bedrooms and two bathrooms. Jarmi had never seen it before, and Laneff was suddenly ashamed that she hadn't decorated the bare walls. Everything was done in the style she'd come to think of as "Old Gypsy Standard."

But Jarmi let out a wobbly sigh. "It's almost like home." Her voice broke on the last word, and after a moment's struggle, she broke into tears. "I'm sorry!" she gasped.

Laneff moved her chair over beside Jarmi, supplying tissues and then crying with her because the nageric power of the Gen was overwhelming. Afterward, they both felt wrung out, and Laneff took Jarmi into the sitting room, where they shoved books aside and sat on the cushion-strewn wicker couch.

"That's why you've been working so hard lately, isn't it?" asked Laneff, feeling like an idiot for not knowing.

"No," she answered. "Well—that room got to be so empty with you gone. It was like home, only there was no Michen to come visiting, no Gilbert, no Tanya, no Sissa . . ."

She'd have gone on listing her dead friends, but Laneff put a tentacle over her lips. "I wish I'd met them."

"They were a little afraid of you—oh, not *that* way. Afraid of what you meant to all of us. Afraid of the gossip about anyone who so much as spoke to you. And now they're all"—she strangled on the word—"dead."

She held the Gen through another siege of tears, worried that perhaps Jarmi had chosen to come here to avoid the ghosts she'd have to face with Yuan's group. Jarmi eventually quieted, then drifted slowly into sleep, clutching Laneff's tentacles as if they were life itself.

Laneff slept half propped against the Gen and woke just after dawn, confused by the presence of Azevedo's nager. And then she realized he was at the door.

Disentangling her hand from Jarmi, she went to let the channel in. She didn't feel rested, and moving away from Jarmi, she felt the familiar sinking sensation of turnover.

"Laneff? Here, let me." Azevedo did something with the selyn fields as she opened the door, and she felt better. Jarmi sat up, grinding sleep and the crusts of tears out of her eyes. "Who? Are we late—did something happen?" She lurched to her feet, her beige pants wrinkled, her buff blouse twisted.

"I just came to invite you to breakfast," said Azevedo.

He came to zlin my turnover!

Seeing the disarray in the kitchen, he said, "I'll assign someone to give this place a daily straightening for you. Now, come along. The trin tea will be getting cold!"

He gave them only moments to wash up, and then they

were climbing stairs to the roof where tables were set among huge potted plants. All the way, Laneff argued that she wasn't hungry, and Azevedo insisted that the growing fetus had to be properly nourished. As good as his word, he had a whole new regimen of vitamin and mineral supplements laid out for her along with a ration of yeast tablets.

Laneff found the nut bread went down all right, and she could manage the fruits, but no way could she get near the gypsy idea of porridge. It reeked. By the end of that meal, Azevedo had guaranteed to search all of P'ris if necessary to find Laneff foods she was more accustomed to.

The rest of that week, she and Jarmi spent running the analyses of the various products they'd accumulated. Laneff set up three new gas chromatographs, experimenting until she found a column packing that didn't die after one run of kerduvon. Jarmi analyzed her own K/A product, doing two more runs and analyzing those before she reported to Laneff, "I think I can almost do it now. At least these are fifty percent higher yields than I got before."

She was referring to the runs she'd done at the Distect labs, but avoided calling it home.

"That's—interesting," said Laneff, looking over Jarmi's shoulder at the notebook page displayed on the computer screen. "I don't want to believe this. I'm not going to even try until I've looked at it *after* transfer. Print it out. I want to take it upstairs and study it later."

Jarmi punched up the printout and the photocopy machine lit up, flashing out the pages of notes. "Have you calculated the kerduvon results yet?"

"I've been afraid to. Need makes me cowardly."

"Hardly!" laughed the Gen suggestively. "But it probably blunts your curiosity about anything not Gen." Her fingers danced over the keys of the pad. "Mind if I run the calculations for you?" she asked as Laneff's notes appeared on the screen. "Shidoni!"

Anybody who'd been working this analysis regularly

hardly had to calculate to see the similarity between the kerduvon components and those of the K/A Jarmi made before learning the visualization technique. Jarmi looked at Laneff.

"Yeah, I saw it. It scares me still. Go ahead and run the calculations."

Jarmi had re-created the calculation program she'd worked out in Yuan's labs. With a few key strokes, she had the results flashing before them. Jarmi's nager jumped with excitement, while Laneff felt morose. At that moment, Azevedo walked in. He'd taken to seeing them at breakfast and dinner, Desha joining them now that the channel, too, was in need. It was close to dinnertime, and he entered projecting appetite at Laneff, but as he read the ambient, he shifted to more neutral fields until he could see what they had on the screen.

As he studied the figures, his fields crystallized around him into an opaque egg—an effect Laneff had never zlinned before. He reached over Jarmi and punched up her notebook, scanning to her recent analyses, split the screen, and compared the two analytical runs. He studied Laneff's struggle to find a column packing that would work. He looked over her calibrating runs of his pure K/A, and compared that to the kerduvon samples she'd just finished running.

"I don't believe this," he said at last.

Jarmi burst out laughing. Laneff couldn't supply more than a smile and an explanation to Azevedo.

"Laneff, do you realize that the best minds of Rathor have been trying to do *this*"—he pointed to the results of her gas chromatography—"for centuries!"

"The gas chromatograph hasn't been around that long," said Jarmi.

"Well," he amended, so facilely that Laneff was instantly certain that Rathor had the instrument long before the rest of the modern world, "I mean trying to analyze moondrop."

"There's a lot of stuff in this mixture that I don't know anything about," answered Laneff. "But I've been analyzing the vile mixtures my synthesis produces for years, and I've invented a few kinds of column packs to handle it!"

"You don't seem to realize what this implies," said Azevedo.

"If it's true," said Laneff, depressed, "it means that I murdered Digen Farris. With an overdose of kerduvon!" She was wishing more frantically than ever that Shanlun was back. He and Mairis were the only ones who could say for sure if that was the case.

Azevedo brought his fields back into the channeling mode by some dissolving sort of effect. Softly, he said, "It also means that you've *synthesized* moondrop—something long thought impossible. In fact, it was once a religious premise!"

"It isn't really moondrop," argued Laneff, somewhat horrified. "I told you there's a lot of odd organics in the natural stuff. I've got one of the active ingredients!"

"Two," returned Azevedo. "There're two isomers."

"But nobody knows what the other does!" replied Laneff.

"Your K/A has two known properties," he said. "It stops selyn flow in placentas. And it mitigates the transfer abort reflex. Kerduvon has several other properties, some of which *may* be attributable to the *other* isomer."

"What properties?" asked Jarmi.

Azevedo merely said, "Why don't you synthesize some of the other isomer, and let's run a few quick tests on it. *Then* we'll compare it to the known properties of moondrop."

Shanlun had said she could disjunct using kerduvon, but not until after the baby was born. *Kerduvon is an abortifacient and a disjunctant.* Could it be that K/A is the abortifacient and K/B is the disjunctive agent?

Unbidden, a feeling she'd had while making love with Shanlun came back to her—the feeling that she *was* Gen. It had been a feeling of *wholeness* that went beyond Sime and Gen. Everything in the universe was a component of something larger.

With a blinding insight that shook her to the core she *knew* beyond all reason that K/B had to be natural to the *Gen* metabolism, as K/A was to the Sime. If K/A fit into receptors on the selyn-transport nerves, then perhaps K/B tied into the central nervous system of the Gen—perhaps the brain surface receptors. The state of junctedness might cause irreparable imbalance in that complex biochemistry, causing the producers of the substances to atrophy. *And that's why people die in disjunction as adults?*

"Laneff," said Jarmi, perhaps for the tenth time. "You can't stand there slack-jawed all night. Tell us what you're thinking."

Azevedo's hand came to her arm, cradling the tentacles gently. "First, let's get some dinner into her."

Laneff went without protest, lost in thought. Interrogated over the meal, she said, "I'm just feeling so *stupid*. This has been staring me in the face for years. I couldn't see it!"

"But you didn't know anything about moondrop. You didn't know that your compound actually occurs in nature!"

"Well, it—or something awfully like it—occurs in the Sime body! You know we produce within ourselves all the pharmacopoeia we really require. Kerduvon isn't so much a drug as it is a vitamin! Maybe there are even traces of it in trin tea!" She held up her glass to look at it.

"You're exaggerating," said Jarmi. "This is going to be decades in the researching stage." She shoved her chair closer to Laneff. "She's in need, can't you zlin? Laneff, you'll have the strength to deal with this in a few days, when we've had our transfer."

"A week, you mean," said Laneff, realizing that she'd never discussed the problem of transfer with Jarmi. *Time goes so fast!*

Azevedo leaned across the table. "Not quite a week. Laneff, you're deeper into need than mere passage of time would indicate. Your transfer should be moved up a few days. Don't let depression swallow you whole. It's just part of life. Take it in stride."

Laneff zlinned the old channel next to Desha, who was for him a not-quite-adequate-but-best-there-was Donor. Azevedo knew whereof he spoke. *But are Jarmi and I even that closely matched?*

Without being asked, Azevedo zlinned Laneff and Jarmi, comparing, and pronounced, "Jarmi's selyn production is increasing slightly. She'll be ready for you when you are for her. But"—he probed them seriously—"Jarmi, you do realize that this may in fact be the last transfer you'll have with Laneff until after the baby is born? Your capacity is just not going to match hers when that channel fetus starts to draw selyn in earnest."

"I understand," replied Jarmi gravely.

"Azevedo," said Laneff, hesitant. He brought his attention to her, and she had to just blurt it out. "Maybe it'd be better if you give me transfer this time, too?"

"Laneff!" cried Jarmi, and the bereft tone sliced through Laneff's heart.

Azevedo, studying her, zlinned Desha. "Are you still Tecton enough to accept a channel's judgment?"

"Yes."

"*I* think you'll do better on Gen transfer this time. And of all our Gens, Jarmi really is your best match here. Her willingness is also a big factor in that. Now, it *is* up to you, Laneff. I know Tecton renSimes aren't trained to make these decisions for themselves, so I will advise; but here, it is ultimately up to you. At least it is until Shanlun gets back with your physician."

She studied Azevedo and Desha, seeing channel and Companion, but not the eager harmony Shanlun's nager made with Azevedo's. And even she could see his need now, the graven lines carved deeper around his eyes, the weary shuffle to his stride, the pallor that occasionally underlay his leathery tan. *He just doesn't feel up to me,* she concluded.

Later, when they were alone, Jarmi said, "I thought you were completely post after our transfer; I thought you were satisfied."

The tremulous fear of rejection in the Gen made Laneff reach out to her. "Oh, Jarmi, you were marvelous. I was as post as ever I've been!"

"But?"

"But," admitted Laneff. "But. It wasn't—exactly—what I'm going to be craving in a transfer."

"You mean—I didn't get the right tone of killbliss?"

How can I discuss this with a Gen! "Well—yes."

"Don't worry! I told you it takes practice. I'll learn. But you've got to be honest with me. I thought I had it right; you didn't let me know—"

"I'm sorry. . . ."

Jarmi took Laneff's hands, letting her fingertips rest near the wrist orifices. *"This* time we'll get it right!"

With Shanlun gone and Azevedo declining, its was Laneff's best course. *At least I know this time that I won't kill her!*

For the next few days, they labored to clean up the lab and set up the new work. Laneff ran several large batches of K/B, having to purify it several times of the K/A that came with it. She couldn't seem to twist her mind around into the reversal of the formulas. But she was determined to have enough of it on hand after her transfer to launch right into the new work.

This could be the big breakthrough! In the back of her mind was the nascent idea that she might separate the selyn-flow inhibitor, which was probably responsible for the abortifacient effect, from the disjunctive agent. It was the abortifacient, she was sure, that was what she was using to detect Sime fetuses. The Rathor statistics showed that kerduvon caused abortion in just the right proportions for it to be aborting Sime fetuses, the ones dependent on selyn from the mother. Her test would take a tissue specimen from the placenta and check its selyn conductivity with and without K/A. In Sime fetuses, the conductivity would drop markedly under K/A—and thus, K/A introduced into the womb would have killed the fetus!

It has to be the K/A fraction of kerduvon that's causing the abortifacient effect!

There were two possible approaches: remove K/A from the purified kerduvon mixture and see if the remainder still acted as a disjunctive, or produce purified K/B and see if *it* acted as the disjunctive.

She set Jarmi to work trying to coax their chromatographic technique to extract K/A from kerduvon while she worked at nursing higher and higher yields of K/B out of her synthesis. Meanwhile, she ordered cadaver brains, both Sime and Gen, through Azevedo's supplier, knowing it would take weeks to get them.

The bench work was tedious and draining. Time after time, she stopped herself from snapping at Jarmi or Azevedo—or the crippled old Sime man who came daily to clean the apartment. She tried telling herself it was just loneliness for Shanlun, but then came the nightmares.

The first shattering episode came as she stretched out on the lab cot to wait for a solvent to clean out one of her columns. Her feet hurt, and her back hurt, which was hardly surprising since she'd been at it for nearly fourteen hours without a break. So she gave herself a half hour to relax, knowing she couldn't sleep because of the need gnawing at her.

But she drifted just under the barrier of sleep, where half-waking she watched dream images of all the Gens she'd ever known flitting across the screen in her mind. Each nager had an individuality she'd have recognized through a closed door. She dwelled on each Gen nager, savoring the memory, entertaining the tactile fantasy she'd never let herself indulge in when she'd known them: tentacles around cool Gen arms, moist Gen lips on hers, rich fabric of nager penetrating—penetrating . . .

No! She started awake, heart pounding, disgusted at herself for she realized every last shred of her disjunction conditioning to seek a channel when in need had gone. She was vulnerable to almost any Gen now. And most of them were vulnerable to her.

She still had twenty minutes to wait. Fixing her thoughts firmly on Jarmi, she lay back, staring at the gray ceiling. She had to let her eyes close.

She was a child again, playing with channel dolls, fantasizing what it would be like to be a channel.

She was a channel, experiencing each month the full force of need that the Tecton protected renSimes from— because, tempted, any renSime would kill helplessly. And she was in need now, stretched out on the contour lounge in the transfer suite of a big city Sime Center. Her Donor would arrive any moment now. She could afford to savor the essence of need, to probe her fear of it. She could rely totally on this Donor.

The door opened, and the room flooded with sparkling gold, like a cascade of powdered gold caught in sunlight, creating a brilliant rainbow of joyful color. The tall blond Gen who followed that nager into the room was a trim, handsomely muscled man, with clean smooth features, calm in the anticipation of real pleasure—the slil only the First Order four-plus channels and Donors could share.

He spoke, voice as cool as his ineffable skin. The calm penetrated, surety replacing her fear. Need became a pleasure too intense to bear. Anticipating her, Shanlun joined contact, letting his nager turn to a sunlike furnace that raised her intil beyond all flesh-and-blood limits until she was seizing his selyn, drawing it into her dark, aching void in pulse after pulse, giving Shanlun the same life-worshipping satisfaction she was taking . . .

No! She woke sweating, her ronaplin glands aching as ronaplin oozed from her lateral wrist orifices, the laterals themselves peeping from their sheaths as if searching for the reality behind her dream. She wiped herself, thinking,

Idiot. It could never be like that with Shanlun. I'm no channel.

She forced herself to get up and find something to do until Jarmi got there at dawn. The Gen was aware of Laneff's strain and went out of her way to be kind. Several times, she tried to start a conversation about the qualities of transfers, but Laneff shied from it. That night, Laneff was determined not to let the nightmares overtake her again, so she rested sitting up poring over her notes.

And she fell into a light doze, head cradled on her arms. She was in the disjunction class at Teeren, The Rialite Last Year House, going on their first excursion. The class was taken into the closed wing where the in-crisis cases dwelled.

They were obliged to watch a disjunction attempt. A Sime woman with long, stringy brown hair and a twisted scar on her calf was brought into the disjunction theater. The room was built on two levels—an open pit surrounded by balconies where students could watch undetected because of the thick selyn-field insulation woven into the glass.

Laneff had a front-row seat, peering down into the white circle of the floor. A trained Gen Donor stood to one side; a Tecton channel to the other. The brown-haired woman was in need, her long-fingered hands clutching themselves nervously. There were dark hollows around her eyes, and dreadful fatigue in every line of her body.

The woman stood, searching between the two offers of transfer, zlinning the fields and comparing them. Laneff knew that to disjunct was to choose the channel, to choose freely to eschew all transfer contact with Gens forever. She watched the woman in the scene below, begging her silently to choose the channel, to be free and live.

She took a step forward, wavered toward the channel, another step, arms reaching out embracing both channel and Donor, and then she plunged, swift as lightning, for the Gen!

The contact was joined before Laneff absorbed the fact, and as she gasped, the Gen below was thrown clear of the Sime as if by an electric shock. The Sime woman fell to the white floor, convulsing, thrashing and screaming. Instantly, the channel was on her, fighting her movements, capturing her arms to force a lateral contact.

One moment he had it, the next she ripped free. Again, and again they fought, the Gen now joining the battle. The Sime's struggles became ever more feeble. Laneff caught only glimpses of the twisted grimace on the woman's face, but it turned her stomach to see such agony, for she understood it now. A trained Donor couldn't be killed by a renSime, and only the kill could sustain that woman's life.

Gradually, the thrashing subsided. Laneff's fingers against the glass no longer registered the vibration of muted screams. At last, the feeble protests, the mewling cries of desperation, ceased, and the Sime woman slumped into a boneless heap—forever still, forever free of need—dead.

No!

She woke, mouth gaping, throat open in what might have been a soundless scream or a retching. Her tentacles were clutched around her fingers so hard she had to pry them loose and wait for the pain to stop before she could resheath them. *It shouldn't be this bad yet! I've so much more work to do!*

All the next day she could hardly think two thoughts connected. She was sitting despairingly over the disjointed scribbling that should have been a cogent experimental plan, when Azevedo came into the lab.

"Oh, at last!" said Jarmi. "Azevedo, *will* you talk that stubborn woman into quitting for the day?"

Azevedo came close, zlinning her. "You're hungry, Laneff, and tired. When was the last time you took a shower? When was the last time you even poked your nose out of the lab?"

She couldn't remember. "Not very long ago." *Three days?*

Jarmi came over. "I cooked her a marvelous dinner last night, but she wouldn't come up to eat it. And when I brought her a tray, she left it untouched. I still have a good four portions in the refrigerator upstairs. Azevedo, why don't you and Desha join us for some really exotically spiced food?"

The channel smiled, coaxing Laneff to her feet by tugging on one elbow. "Laneff, I have about as much appetite right now as you do, but Desha will be hungry. She's got her class out in the courtyard drilling them in coordination. Why don't we just pick her up on the way?"

Agreed, they shut down the lab. Laneff grabbed a journal to read during the break, aware of how behind she was in her reading. They climbed the front stairs to the courtyard door where she'd said goodbye to Shanlun, and she asked Azevedo for news. "Nobody has heard a word, nor has there been anything from Mairis. But Shanlun can take care of himself, don't worry."

She discovered to her dismay that it was a torrid summer day outside, with lowering clouds and no wind. The city drowsed about them, people outside the gypsy bands living indoors under air conditioning. The gypsies, however, preferred nature unalloyed and had their windows open. As always, gypsy children, dogs, cats, and family tumult abounded in the yard.

Amid all this, Desha had a class of young Simes jogging around and around the courtyard, leaping obstacles, tossing objects, and chanting. Meanwhile, their fields were doing the oddest gyrations, flickering through a wide inventory of emotions and degrees of intil. In the center, near the fountain, Desha trotted about in a smaller circle, tracking them and shouting instructions. Among the Simes, Gens wove some sort of braided pattern, further churning the already dizzying nager.

Laneff had never seen or heard of anything like it.

Gypsies watched from the open windows, as awed as Laneff, but amused by people who'd work so hard in such heat. Azevedo beat a straight path through to Desha, spoke a few words, gesturing toward the doorway where Laneff and Jarmi waited, and Desha called out something to the class. They stopped in their tracks, folding gracefully down to rest.

While Azevedo and Desha spoke, other children scattered about the court began to yell, running toward the alley that led to the main street. It was no game. The Simes of Desha's class rose, most augmenting slightly, and followed the children to the mouth of the alley, forming a cordon.

Azevedo walked along behind them, Desha at his side. The children's yelling became belligerent and rose to hysterical pitch as they swarmed into the alleyway. A second-story window opened over the alley, and a Sime man leaped to the ground just in front of the children, facing the distant street. Another window opened farther down on the other side, and a Sime woman leaped out.

Laneff looked at Jarmi. "Invasion?" They shrugged at each other, then began walking across the court. They'd always had the impression that this place was deliberately kept private, but they'd never seen an outsider attempt entry. They were barely halfway across the court, mixing with the Gens of Desha's class as they pulled into position behind the Simes. The ambient nager was thick but firm with a kind of menace in it.

Through it all, though, Laneff zlinned something familiar. *Gen.* She ran, augmenting, leaving Jarmi far behind.

She came even with Azevedo as he breasted the double row of Simes across the alley mouth. Cutting through the cordon, she zlinned the Gen nager. Not Shanlun. *Yuan!*

Azevedo, too, had made that identification. "Desha!" he called over his shoulder, running down the alley. The close, damp stone walls framed Yuan, cloaked from hair to boot tops in a forest-green and chocolate Householding

cape, woven with heavy insulating fabric. He was swaying
on his feet, facing the two Simes who'd jumped down to
challenge him.

Unable to muster the strength to speak, he crumpled to
the ground—unconscious. Laneff arrived at his side just as
Azevedo did, opening the cloak to find a bloody mess of a
shoulder wound, pluming selyn—and roaring *pain* through
Laneff's raw nerves. The thrill of that washed the
shock away, and she went hyperconscious, soaring into
high intil and lusting after killbliss as she never had before.

The next thing she knew, with a rending shock, she was
in Jarmi's arms, two channels shielding her from Yuan's
pain. She barely had time to catch her breath when two
more Simes arrived with a stretcher, and they bundled
Yuan off into Thiritees, leaving only two Simes behind to
explain to the gypsies.

Several anxious hours later, Laneff and Jarmi were called
to the Thiritees infirmary. Laneff thought she had her
reactions under control, more worried now about Yuan—
and Shanlun—than about her own peaking need.

The infirmary was located on the top floor of a two-story
addition to the building that stuck out at an odd angle to
the bathhouse wing. It was painted inside in dozens of
colors, with filtered lighting adding more color—*like living
inside Shanlun's nager*. Speakers provided soft music and
potted plants hung everywhere, flowering in many colors.

Azevedo came out of one of the rooms. He seemed tired
but triumphant. "It wasn't as bad as it looked. The bullet
went cleanly through his shoulder, nicked a tendon. But it
should all heal very nicely now. He's lost a lot of blood.
This must have happened three, four days ago. Laneff—
you should take transfer before you try to talk to him."

She shook her head. "The longer I can delay, the better
chance my baby has of being viable—when I die. It's not
bad, now." She nodded to the two channels who'd worked
to stabilize her. "They're good. Thank them for me."

Azevedo said something in the Rathor dialect, and the

two channels responded politely. But he was zlinning Laneff the whole time. "All right," he agreed, "but they have to come in, too. I can't do it all." He seemed like a weary old man. *Need is eating him up, too. He's waiting for Shanlun.*

As they entered the sickroom, Azevedo muttered instructions to the two channels escorting Laneff. A sort of misty cocoon formed around her in the ambient nager. Jarmi was like the sun, hidden in a fog just tattered enough to show a glowing disk. Yuan was another diffuse center, like the moon.

Two channels flanked by their Donors attended Yuan, one on each side of the high wicker-frame bed. A wicker nightstand held a lamp, lit because the drapes were pulled shut. There was a pitcher of a dark fluid by the bed. The whole room was done in shades of orange and cream. Yuan was propped up against a huge pile of pillows. "Laneff!" His eyes slowly refocused. "Jarmi!"

"Yuan!" they said in unison, then Laneff asked, "What happened?"

Azevedo added, "We all want to know everything, but now isn't the time for details. Is there anything we must know *now?*"

Yuan swallowed, thinking. "I don't know how to say this. I think—I'm not sure, understand—but I think Shanlun is dead."

The silence in the room broke as someone translated for those who hadn't understood Yuan's Simelan dialect. And then the shock echoed even through the damping nageric fog.

Gradually, the story came out, amid many halts. Shanlun had found Yuan in the small depot which he'd chosen to go to if the first had been hit by the Diet. He'd gathered his lieutenants for a conference, taking stock of the losses which were still going on. His Distect forces, however, had given as severely as they'd gotten.

Even handicapped by their Sime contingent's being unable to operate out-Territory, the Distect organization had been able to cripple the nerve center of the Diet. Nevertheless, the Distect was in ruins. Top executives had been assassinated, funds were choked off, communications broken down.

"I told Shanlun to tell Mairis that the Distect was gone. I told him to tell Mairis that if they wanted me to, I'd come out in the open and repudiate our alliance with him in person. But I also told him I didn't think this would be a good idea. Given time, I can rebuild."

"There's been remarkably little of this in the news," said Azevedo. "The assassinations were attributed to organized-crime syndicates."

Yuan nodded, obviously hurting, but Laneff felt none of the pain. "And the rest of the violence has been reported as mysterious fires, explosions due to sewer gas, and they're calling my headquarters labs a sinkhole!" He frowned. "I've assumed Mairis has been requesting the media to downplay it. He *is* winning in the polls now."

"That depends on which poll you read," said Azevedo.

Laneff hadn't read any papers, and the building had no radio or television. "Yuan, *what* about Shanlun?"

"The Diet—I believe it was the Diet—hit us just before dawn, when he was about to leave. Everything went up in fire and smoke—one of my Simes killed, and I was too slow to stop one of our newest recruits from shooting him down. I pulled a burning timber off Shanlun, and we dragged each other away from the building. I'm not sure when I got shot. Somewhere, I passed out. When I woke up, I was alone. Some branches had been piled over me, and I was half buried in earth—though I expect my nager was plain enough to zlin. I *hurt!* All but three of my Simes were dead, and the others burned or suffocated in the basement of the farmhouse we were using. We were out-Territory, you understand; I shouldn't have had Simes there, but we really had no place else to go. Most of my

Gens were dead, too. We took a *lot* of those shendi-fleckin' Diet lorshes with us, but we're effectively dead now. That was all the rest of my leadership! I should have died with them!"

Denial rung in Azevedo's nager, but he said nothing until Yuan looked up at him. "Shanlun wasn't among your dead?"

"Not that I could identify. He's the crazy hero type. He *might* have gone back into that building. Burned like *that*, there's no way we could have identified his body. He wasn't even wearing his Householding jewelry!"

"I don't believe he's dead," said Azevedo thoughtfully.

"We have to face facts," said Laneff, gritting her teeth. "He's probably dead—or, worse, prisoner of the Diet!"

"I didn't think Shanlun would have just left me like that. So when I couldn't find him, I hiked on down the road, across the border. Found some picnickers and stole the cloak—House of Gabriel, I think. Got to return it . . ." He trailed off into sleep.

One of the Gens took the glass from his hand, and silently they all left the room. "I imagine," said Azevedo out in the hallway, "Shanlun told Yuan how to find us here without realizing how badly Yuan was wounded, and then went on with his mission."

He's in need and wants Shanlun. It's wishful thinking. But everything in her cried out for it to be true. She couldn't bear to lose Shanlun after everything else. Yet another side of her, a self that seemed a stranger, said, *It's better this way. Now, when you die, he won't suffer this.* And the baby would live on after both of them.

Later, while Jarmi was boiling some noodles in the kitchen of their apartment and Laneff was snapping some raw green beans into the salad, Laneff confessed her split feelings.

"I've felt a little like that myself," replied Jarmi. "Too many shocks in too short a time—and now this. I mean, even Azevedo has lost touch with reality! He thinks Shanlun survived! We've seen how the Diet works."

At Laneff's stricken expression, Jarmi left off stirring the boiling noodles and came across to lean on the counter beside Laneff. "I know you loved him. I know you felt something for Yuan, too. These things tear a woman apart!"

The Gen, too, had lost dear ones brutally, and her sympathy came from a deep personal knowledge. She'd lost weight, lately, from poor appetite as well as overwork, and maybe silent grieving as well. Laneff had expended selyn recklessly in augmentation that afternoon when Yuan arrived. The shrieking intil was gone, but the need ached to the bone, and she was ready to take Jarmi in transfer right then and there—but the noodles boiled over. The Gen jumped to rescue the pot.

Laneff held her breath, half wishing the Gen would burn herself and send that indescribable thrill through the air to trigger her off into a thoughtless hunting-mode attack. *What am I thinking?* She forced herself to breathe, to take her fist down from her mouth. "Jarmi, don't be surprised if I just suddenly—"

The Gen turned from the steam as she drained the noodles. "What? I thought you were all right?"

Laneff nodded. "But I was just hoping you'd burn yourself!" Disgusted, Laneff buried her face in her hands.

Jarmi came and pried her fingers loose, her steam-reddened hands soothing Laneff's tremors away. "It's all right. I understand now. Oh, Laneff, I didn't realize! When those terrorists set you up, that man had been deliberately *hurt*. No wonder! Of course, now I understand it all, Laneff!"

Laneff noticed a nageric shift in the room. Azevedo and Desha were at the door. Pulling herself together, she went to let them in, and the four of them shared a dinner from across the ocean, completely free of all the pungent herbs and spices favored by the gypsies.

Laneff could barely stay duoconscious long enough to

smell the memory-laden fragrances, let alone taste anything. She nibbled a few bits, forcing herself to swallow. *If Shan is dead, this baby is all that's left of him. I must eat.* She choked down a few more bites and then swallowed her vitamins.

Azevedo likewise was unenthusiastic but doing his best. The two Gens ate ravenously, Jarmi delightfully detailing her sauce recipes for Desha. Afterward, they were clearing off the table, and the two Gens were in the kitchen washing dishes, when Azevedo leaned over and commented to Laneff, "It's obvious what condition we're in, isn't it?"

She shrugged. "I think it'll pass. It's just intil."

But he zlinned her at intervals for a while, finally saying, "In this channel's opinion, I think you two ought to transfer tonight—before you precipitate it unexpectedly."

"Is that an order?" asked Laneff.

"I don't order that sort of thing. I zlin that you've got yourself set on Jarmi—and that's good. But with intil such as you're displaying, you might go for some other Gen."

"You still think Jarmi's the best choice for me right now?"

"Gen transfer should help stave off disjunction crisis." Then he added, "But if for some personal reason Jarmi is unacceptable to you—I *am* here, Laneff. Always."

The assurance in his nager helped Laneff relax. The two Gens came to the bar that divided off the kitchenette, and Desha called, "I suspect you're talking about us!"

Azevedo straightened. "Now what else would two Simes in need be talking of?"

Jarmi laughed. "Two overstuffed Gens, of course." But there was strain in the humor all around. Shanlun's absence at this time—when he'd been so sure he'd be back—then Yuan's report—all left a black hole in the nager.

Desha took Azevedo off almost immediately after that, and Jarmi confronted Laneff. "He's right, you know. We ought to do it tonight."

Laneff realized that somewhere in back of her irrational

mind she'd treasured the hope that Shanlun would return to give her transfer—as he'd once promised he might, to win her from Yuan. She thrust all that aside and told Jarmi, "Yes. I do want you. You're comfortable—and good for me."

"And I want you. Nobody has ever been like you!"

Jarmi's nager engulfed her, full Gen attention penetrating. It wasn't anything like a trained Donor's attention—but it was Jarmi. It seemed to Laneff that this Gen was the only stable, dependable thing in life. Familiar. Comfortable.

At last she dared to relax, to give in to the lure of sweet Genness. *This is the safest way. Azevedo's right, I'm dangerous like this, and Jarmi's my best choice. Besides, tomorrow I'll be able to work for a change!*

The sitting room was an alcove off the bedroom, adjacent to the dressing room and shower. It had a huge picture window, facing west—and the blank side of another building. The westering summer sun had turned the overcast to rose and gold, and the light from the window blushed the white-painted wicker furniture to pink. Laneff went to the window, expecting Jarmi to sit on the odd little transfer bench that was upholstered over a wicker frame.

But the Gen turned to the shower room. "I've *got* to shower first. All I'll want afterward is to sleep!"

Thoughtfully, Jarmi left the shower room door open so Laneff didn't lose touch with her nager and panic. Laneff pulled a stool in front of the door to bask in the Gen nager. "I'll want to shower, too. I spilled—Well, you don't want to know what I spilled on myself today!"

Jarmi leaned out the door to toss her dirty lab coat into the laundry chute. "I'll tell you what I broke if you'll tell me what you spilled." The humor was forced but Laneff appreciated the attempt.

As Jarmi stepped into the shower, Laneff raised her voice and said, "One of the bottles of kerduvon. But it doesn't matter, I'll make more tomorrow. What did you break?"

"Our only, it-costs-seventeen-hours-to-make steam-distillation column! What else!"

"What?" Laneff came up off her stool. "Oh, no! Now I can't make more kerduvon tomorrow!"

"You forget," called Jarmi, "what you really have to have loads of is the K/B fraction. You know, we should make a rule to take a holiday the day before a transfer. Neither of us is in such great shape."

From inside the shower, Jarmi was working on the nager. As she waited, Laneff couldn't help but think of Shanlun. His face—his silly nose, and sunburned forehead, and tactile voice that sent shivers up her spine, and that incredible sparkling colored nager—and his touch on her tentacles. *Oh, dear God, don't let him be dead!*

Everywhere she looked some personal item of Shanlun's loomed into consciousness, as if his nager lingered in the air.

She got to her feet and stripped off her filthy clothes. As Jarmi was finishing, Laneff edged around her into the shower saying, "Don't bother to turn it off!"

Before Jarmi had her wrap tied, Laneff was out of the shower, toweling off and slipping into a wrap. "Why are Gens always so *slow!*" she complained, only half joking.

"All right," said Jarmi. "I'm coming. I'll just let my hair dry in the air."

Laneff was waiting on the lounge when Jarmi finally came out of the bathroom, wearing a terry robe over her gown, and with her hair wrapped in a towel. "How do I look?"

"Who cares. It's how you zlin that interests me."

"Just what I wanted to hear!" Now she did take a seat on the transfer bench. They had once discussed the piece of furniture and noted how it was used in various paintings hung about in the halls. "Like this—right?"

Laneff sat, facing the opposite direction, half turning to take Jarmi in transfer position. "Not bad, actually."

Laneff moved to close the contact, but Jarmi fended her off. "Not so fast. You've lost your edge. *This* should help!"

The Gen raked her long, hard fingernails along her own forearms, leaving instant red welts that sent stinging shivers through the nager and *hurt*. It wasn't the same as the pain from Yuan's bullet wound, nor the terrorist's broken ankle and torn hand, but the pure, allover sensation weakened Laneff's nerves to renewed intil.

She went hyperconscious and didn't even hear her own growl of savage frustration as she seized the Gen's sensitized arms. Selyn erupted into her system at first lip contact. Laneff soared on it, drawing with all the pent-up yearning.

Quickly, Laneff was drawing at her peak speed, easily matched by Jarmi. Euphoria held her transfixed on the brink of satisfaction. Pain still burning along her arms, Jarmi deliberately resisted the draw, taunting the half-crazed Laneff to further effort. Helplessly, she drew selyn against the Gen's resistance, and the pain increased, and her satisfaction came nearer, and she increased her draw speed, and the pain increased until it was the exquisite torture of real satisfaction run full to completion.

She came out of it weeping for the unexpected joy of it, knowing that with transfers like this she could avoid disjunction crisis and bring Shanlun's baby to life. Everything was solved.

The Gen opposite her slumped into a boneless mass of terry-cloth. "Jarmi?"

The nager had gone flat. The screaming alarm in Laneff was not echoed by the pain of transfer burn. She wasn't breathing. She wasn't producing selyn. "Jarmi! Wake up!"

"No! No!" Laneff screamed, a long inarticulate wail of anguish. "No!" Then the choking sobs came.

By the time she could go to call Azevedo, Jarmi's hair had dried.

11

CHANCE

The longest night of Laneff's life passed in a blurred kaleidoscope of impressions: shock/horror/sorrow veiled behind nageric cushions //spinning images of walls, paintings, doors//faces looming/stretcnermoving/candles/mirrors/ flowers/bells/silences/bursts of tears/low-voiced conferences over her head/trin tea and medicine forced on her/ sleep at last.

She woke floating in Yuan's nager, convinced she'd had a particularly ghastly nightmare—until she saw his face, worn, sunken, tattered by weight loss and pain, while in herself there was no trace of need. Sunlight leaked around drapes. A dimmed lamp showed his reddish-blond hair, freckles and his gingery eyebrows over sunken eyes. And he'd shaved his mustache. His nager, darkly mottled with trauma and exhaustion, held a tender luster void of all recrimination.

With a cry, she wrenched free of that hypnotic nager and twisted away, facing the opposite side of the bed. She determined to stay that way until he left her alone.

With his good hand, he stroked her shoulder, freeing her hair. "All right. Take your time. We have all day." He eased himself gingerly down on the pillow she'd vacated, his own illness weighing heavily.

She wondered how—and why—he'd dragged himself here to be with her, and marveled at his stamina. But it was only a fleeting awareness. The warmth of the man brought the memory of Shanlun sleeping soundly in just that spot, in just that position. On a tide of anxiety, she thrust herself free of the blanket and plunged across the room toward the dressing alcove—and the refuge of the shower.

The wicker transfer bench was gone. The empty floor space stopped her—almost worse than if the thing were still there, gleaming whitely. In a flash, she relived the entire experience. Her knees buckled. Without the strength to fight it, she let herself slide to the floor mat, her night dress caught awkwardly under her knees.

But the tears wouldn't come. Not again. Only wave after wave of self-loathing answered her seeking for tears. Grief was a refuge denied.

Yuan worked his way to his feet awkwardly, then swayed slowly to her side, favoring the arm bound in a sling. She felt every twinge in him, distantly, without need, without intil. She shied into hypoconsciousness, unwilling to think about it. His shadow over her was like a tangible thing. His voice laved salve over her scream-torn ears. But his words echoed those in her mind. "You killed Jarmi."

It was no rebuke, no accusation. She couldn't divine how those words could carry such intense compassion, especially coming from him—Jarmi's Sosectu.

"She loved you so," whispered Laneff, throat raw from screaming.

"Say it, Laneff. Say, 'I killed Jarmi.' "

She vaguely remembered screaming. Then, for a long long time, she'd been unable to move, or do or say anything for the endless repetition of those words. Catatonic, they'd called her. She wanted now to respond.

Her throat opened, then clenched shut over the words. Mutely, she shook her head, her guts cramping. Every nerve in her was on fire with Jarmi's selyn.

"Say, 'I killed Jarmi,'" he insisted with remorseless compassion. "You have to say it, Laneff, out loud. Say it and accept it."

She felt as if her very mind tissues were about to tear open, spilling mental bile that would burn her brain.

He went to one knee, gasping as he clutched his shoulder. Then he put one hand on the small of her back, his Gen coolness taking the fire out of her. He let his hand smooth upward along the curve of her spine as he urged her, "Tell me about it, Laneff—tell me how good it was—and terrible. Tell me what Jarmi felt."

She hadn't been able to tell them how it had happened. When she'd found Azevedo beside Yuan's bed, she'd only been able to strangle a wail and point in the direction of the apartment. But the channel had known from her nageric state. Running under full augmentation, gathering attendants with shouts, he'd pounded into the apartment and to Jarmi's side, halting only when the hopeless silence of her nager was clear.

How good it had been. Tell a Gen how good it was to kill? His hand stroked her back, pausing just where the selyn-transport nerves joined the spinal axis, sending a seductive relaxation through and through her.

She straightened away from that touch, unwilling to yield the tension that held down the realities.

His hand hovered. "Tell me how good it was, Laneff."

She turned, unable to believe his nager, searching for the condemnation she knew had to be in him somewhere, searching his face for a hint of it. But it wasn't there. He knew very well—how good it was.

A sudden inward rending, and she threw her arms around his neck, burying her face in his good shoulder, blurting in total catharsis, "I killed Jarmi! I killed her and I didn't even know I was doing it! I thought I could live forever on such—such—such transfers! But it was killbliss. And she *hurt*, and died! I—ha-ha-ha-hate myself!" Dry sobs wrenched at her chest, burbling upward, unstoppable.

Hours later, when it abated, he helped her shower and dress and then to eat a little. There was a private funeral. Yuan officiated in Distect style, reciting formal words and then calling Jarmi his most dedicated follower. They took her body away in a rattletrap truck to the gypsy burial ground, far out in the wilds.

After that, they left Laneff pretty much to herself. Yuan stayed in the apartment, sleeping on a narrow cot in the sitting room. He cooked for her, made her get out of bed and dress, but let her sit for endless hours just staring at nothing. Azevedo came, often with Desha. She knew when they'd had transfer, and watched as Azevedo suffered from the inadequacy. But he came to make her feel better—to sit quietly or talk randomly of the life of Thiritees, the children, dogs, students, weddings, and graduations. Every once in a while he mentioned that her lab was standing empty.

Yuan, too, spent hours talking to her. Gradually, time became structured into morning, noon, night. The rhythm of passing days became the tension of approaching turnover. The baby was developing. Morning sickness seized her, and she had to urinate more often.

The brisk quickening of need prodded her thoughts into motion again. Azevedo was sitting with her—had been the entire day, lurking in wait for the renewed hysteria at the first touch of cold need. Instead, she turned to him and shocked herself by saying, without preamble, "She raked her own arms with her fingernails."

Azevedo stopped in midsentence, bewildered.

Yuan, who'd been preparing dinner, charged out of the kitchen. "She—what? That fool!" Setting aside the bowl he was carrying, he knelt before her, taking her hands in his cool, damp ones. "Then it wasn't your fault, not at *all*. That was a stupid thing to do with you!"

Azevedo asked, "This is some sort of Distect practice?"

"We've worked out a few such evocations to prod listless need. Jarmi hadn't learned any of them, but people talk."

"Then Jarmi, too, was responsible for what happened. She used a technique she didn't fully understand."

"But why?" asked Yuan. "Laneff, did she also resist your draw?"

She nodded mutely.

"And she felt pain?" prompted Yuan. Again Laneff nodded, and he added, "That's part of the technique, but it got away from her. Why would she be so desperate?"

Azevedo pulled back. "*I* told her this would be her last transfer with Laneff until after the baby was born!" And then he frowned. "She was so depressed. Working like that, not eating, having no one to share her grieving for all the lost ones. To have come here only for Laneff, and then to fail with her—I should have realized! I should have monitored them!"

Sitting on his heels in front of Laneff, Yuan put his face in his hands, driving his fingers into his reddish-blond hair. "They obviously weren't as well matched as I thought—"

Laneff saw the responsibilities like reflections. At Jarmi's funeral, she had seen a device Azevedo had told her symbolized Thiritees: a cube made of half-silvered mirrors. Inside the cube, a candle burned, its flame reflected in all six reflecting surfaces, infinitely in all directions, and visible from outside the box through the half-transparent walls.

She hadn't been able to get that object out of her mind. Now she saw one thing it meant. If one person did something, another responded, and another responded to that, out to infinity, each acting in free will, each responsible for the results. *But it's all one!*

For an instant, the heady insight she'd had when they discovered K/A and K/B in kerduvon came back to her, the vision of Shanlun and Mairis blending and becoming a Unity, of Shanlun and Azevedo in eager harmony, all crowded into her awareness. The whole universe was made of one piece, infinitely reflected. Just find the axis of symmetry, and it would all make sense!

They stayed with her all that night, and she slept as well as possible at turnover. Refreshed, at dawn she asked Azevedo if she could go to the dawn salute with him, and he was delighted, though Yuan wasn't allowed to go.

She ignored the nageric gymnastics and contemplated that cube of half-silvered mirrors. The candle wasn't lit, but she could imagine it as she had once seen it.

Afterward, she told Azevedo, "I've got to get back to work. I was so *close;* I can't give up now."

"Your lab is as you left it," he assured.

But the first thing Laneff saw when she flipped on the lab lights was that a cat had had kittens in the nest of a fallen lab coat. She hissed at Laneff, hardly bothering to move from nursing the little ones. They seemed to be about two weeks old.

Prowling among the benches, Laneff swiped a tentacle through the patina of dust, broke a cobweb, automatically checked the thermostats on the thermal baths, and found where a ventilation grate had fallen out, admitting the mother cat.

As she toured, she saw Jarmi's desk littered with things just as she'd left them. Jarmi's analyses in progress. The neat bottles of Jarmi's own products. The screaming, haunting presence was overwhelming.

She made herself bring the mother cat a bowl of milk and egg, and then left the lab. The next day, and the next, she fed the cat, but could do little more than dust and make a few tentative attempts to clear away Jarmi's things.

One morning, Azevedo found her there. "Somebody," she said, "should have been carrying on while I was—ill."

"Laneff, I could perhaps assist you, but I don't understand this well enough to design and execute the bench work. What you've done here is beyond what Rathor has been able to accomplish in centuries! You may make it safe for the last of our secrets to be released!"

"Secrets?"

"Kerduvon. Laneff, think. How would the out-Territory Gens of your grandfather's day have used kerduvon? To abort every Sime fetus—even at risk of the mother's life or sanity! How would it have been used in-Territory? On every junct who wanted it, regardless of how ill prepared. 'Rejuncting is not a terrible thing; you can always disjunct again.' Only it doesn't work that way; it's no miracle solution. But its constituents, used by properly qualified channels, may do great wonders to transform this world. And *you* will be the one to solve the problem!"

Together they cleaned the place up, and Laneff sat down at her desk. She found the disjointed mess she had left and decided it was born of the craziness of need, so she chucked it.

Hours whizzed by. Later, Azevedo came back, got hissed at by the cat, sidestepped, and came to her desk. The entire day had passed. For those few hours, Laneff had thought only of cadaver brains and K/B receptors and how to prove their existence and function. Not for weeks had a day passed so quickly.

She set Azevedo to work the next day, trying to find a way to remove all the K/A from a kerduvon mixture. She set to work on the cadaver brains that had finally arrived. Despite the tightening of need, she was able to work, and that made the need easier to bear.

Over dinner, they talked of the experimental design, and she explained her hypothesis of the composition of kerduvon. "Nature put the two active isomers back to back, in the mahogany trinrose. The trin plants are a mutation that appeared about the same time as the Sime/Gen mutation, and I *saw* this in your candlebox. Optical isomers are reflections; Sime and Gen are reflections of each other; I've now proved K/A is present in detectable abundance in Sime nerve tissue; K/B *has* to be present somewhere in the Gen nervous system, and I'm betting on the brain. K/A is the transfer-abort fraction;

K/B has to be the disjunctive. It *has* to be that way or nature isn't symmetric; but nature *is* symmetric."

She explained how K/B would have to be present in Simes in extremely minute quantities, and K/A would likewise be present in Gens in minute portions. "An adult can't disjunct because the ability to create K/B has totally atrophied. Somehow, kerduvon restores that ability."

Azevedo liked the hypothesis and helped her brainstorm a series of experiments that might prove it. Laneff began to feel she understood what it was she had synthesized and how it worked. She even began toying with the idea for a test that could be administered in childhood to determine Sime from Gen before changeover/establishment. But first she had to determine how K/B behaved on brain surfaces. The task was simply enormous and required a team of laboratories. She had to get enough proof in hand to publish something that would get people started on this line of research.

With the crude equipment of the school and Azevedo's help, she designed a small exploratory experiment and began the work. In spare moments, she pored over the notes she and Jarmi had collected, assembling data and creating tables to show that her synthesis was indeed repeatable. And she pondered how to broach the subject of the importance of the operator's visualization. She had no scientific reputation to lose and wouldn't have to live with the rejection that would no doubt follow publication because she'd be long dead of disjunction crisis. *If not here, then in a Last Year House. There'll never be another Jarmi.*

But as she worked on the paper, she had to admit it required more data. She ceased to struggle to oust Yuan from her apartment on the grounds that she could care for herself now and convinced him to come work in the lab and learn her synthesis. Seeing Yuan daily in Shanlun's chair, at Shanlun's place in the kitchen, and using Shanlun's shelf in the bathroom, watching him daily doing

Jarmi's work, sitting at Jarmi's desk, only increased the tension between them. And it was worse because Yuan turned out to have the worst technique of any lab assistant she could imagine. *How did he ever pass basic pharmacology?*

Azevedo had infinite patience, but Laneff often yelled at Yuan and then had to apologize. At one point, she accused him of playing mud pies in her lab, and he came back belligerently, "Perhaps I *don't* really grasp the importance of what you're doing, but I think you grasp it too tightly, Laneff!"

"What in creation do you mean by that?"

"You're hiding from need by burying yourself in this work—like Jarmi did!"

"She wasn't *hiding*," Laneff retorted. "She was dedicated to banishing the kill! She knew what it means to be renSime, even if she was Gen. She not only worked in this lab until she dropped from exhaustion, she tried the craziest stunt in the Distect arsenal in hopes of keeping me on my feet long enough to finish this!"

Azevedo broke it up, then, before it could turn into a real fight, and sending Yuan off to eat, he fed Laneff trin tea and yeast tablets, saying, "I think you understood Jarmi's motives better than the rest of us, but don't discount her very real depression. She was fighting off coming to grips with her personal losses by her furious dedication to something vast and impersonal—your research, and, through it, you."

"No. She wasn't impersonal, she wasn't Tecton. I was something deeply, intimately personal to her." And she sketched for the channel what life in the Distect warren had been like for Jarmi, excluded from the one-to-one Sime/Gen relationships which were the foundation of Distect philosophy. "And then I came, and gave her the first real taste of the pleasure she'd always fantasized transfer to be." She related the course of their first transfer. "So, you see, there was nothing mercenary, nothing of the Tecton distancing in it for her. She wanted to give me what I'd given her; surely as a channel you can understand that! The great ironic pity is that she succeeded!"

He looked down at his hands, toying with his tentacles as if working out a difficult arithmetic problem. "And she took *pride* in being able to 'handle' you? It was a matter of personal pride for her to be able to satisfy you?"

"Pride? No—but well, you might say that . . ."

He looked up at her, head tilted to one side, duo-conscious. "Did you know that Gens can experience a kind of egobliss?"

"Egobliss is just another word for killbliss, so they can't—"

"No, no. They are two completely different things. Think, Laneff." He zlinned her deeply, then returned to duo-consciousness. "You no longer have the capacity for egobliss. You gave it up at your first disjunction. But remember what that first kill was like? You were lord of the universe, and that Gen was so much cold meat for your use. Your ego, your sense of being totally separate from all creation, was fed in that kill, and engorged, inflamed, and torn from its moorings in the lives of others. The disjunction year was spent making that sick ego fast and repent and see itself in others. Didn't they make you watch disjunctions?"

"Yes," whispered Laneff, hoarsely. "Oh, yes."

"And when it came your turn, you chose the channel because the channel had something within that bespoke kinship with your inner self, understanding of what life meant to you."

"How did you know?"

"It's often that way in a true first disjunction. The affinity for a fellow Sime becomes stronger than the attraction to a reflection, the Gen. The channel gives you access to the Gen without danger of egobliss."

"Danger?"

"But after a first disjunction, the craving for killbliss is still there. The Tecton treats that craving as pathological, denying its existence in every Sime, nonjunct, disjunct or junct. Killbliss, Laneff, is simply another word for the physical satisfaction of need, the repeating of the experience of First Kill, or First Transfer. It is only at second disjunction that a new "first experience" can be imprinted on your nervous system. What you will crave and what you will experience will feel like killbliss, but it should not be necessary to burn a Gen to get it."

"You're talking about the kind of junctedness of the endowed, aren't you?"

"No, not really. We share a third experience, textually different from killbliss, and indescribable. We call it slilbliss."

There was a sadness in his nager that told Laneff it was this experience Desha was unable to give him. *Oh, where is Shanlun?*

"Slilbliss," repeated Laneff. "Slil is the experience of the four-plus Donors who can read selyn fields and sense selyn motion directly during transfer. What could slilbliss be like?"

He shook his head and gave a gypsy shrug. "Maybe a mutual sort of egobliss/killbliss, a moment of perfected ecstasy shared." He brushed that aside. "My point, Laneff, is that *you* had long since given up egobliss—but Jarmi had not! She was not your perfect reflection, not the right transfer partner for you. When you satisfied her, you were left wanting. When she satisfied you, she was destroyed. Think of the candlebox, Laneff. The people we see surrounding us are reflections of ourselves. Each of us lives inside a candlebox, unable to see the real selves of those around us, able to see only reflections of ourselves. To even glimpse others, one must extinguish the egoself, if only for a moment's meditation."

"And I'm imputing motives to her that are really my own?"

"That might have indeed been within her, however buried. You can see them where we can't, but we can see what you can't."

It was like the infinite tangle of responsibilities she had seen before when contemplating Jarmi's death. Digen's death, too, had been the result of decisions and responsibilities made by Shanlun, Mairis, herself, and even Digen, reflecting infinitely in all directions, ultimately becoming a single Unity. In both cases, she had made decisions that had led to disaster by long, involved chain reactions. Things she started to do just didn't come out right.

"Can you see what's wrong with me?" whispered Laneff.

"No," he answered quietly. "You are inside your own candlebox, you alone determine the distortions in the reflections you see. Look out around you, and see yourself."

She looked.

She looked at every crucial decision in her whole life. She had begged and pleaded, and prayed to God to be allowed to go and visit Fay Ravitch. And that had led to her killing in First Need. From that day, she had regarded herself as handicapped because of being renSime and disjunct, vulnerable to the temptation to kill. She had compensated for that handicap by always playing it safe around Gens, always opting for the safest transfer.

She'd played it safe when she accepted Mairis's suggestion of going into the visitors' box, rather than onstage beside Shanlun. She'd played it safe when she'd let Yuan take her to his headquarters, promising her a Gen whom she couldn't kill, but who could satisfy her and keep her alive. She'd played it safe coming to Thiritees, where there was a channel good enough to handle her, and Shanlun whom she certainly couldn't kill and who claimed he could satisfy her—and Jarmi, too. She'd played it safe choosing Jarmi the first time, but that had led to her getting pregnant so that Shanlun had to go out into danger which had probably taken his life. And she'd played it safe choosing Jarmi over Azevedo, and that had led to her killing Jarmi.

By failing to risk herself, she was murdering those around her.

A plan was forming, a daring plan, a harebrained scheme that any real scientist would be ashamed of hatching. But it would cut ten years of throat-clearing out of the process of airing her results in the proper journals. If she was right, she and the baby would live, and never kill. If she was wrong, they'd both die, but nobody else would have to.

If she won this gamble, the whole world would see that the kill wasn't the essence of the renSime. It had been Digen's dream, and Shanlun's, and Jarmi's. It was Mairis's life's work, and he had a chance to succeed if she could show concrete results: one adult junct disjuncted. And with that success on record, her project to identify Simes before birth was as good as completed. Those were stakes big enough to be worth a couple of more lives. So many had died in senseless violence already.

"Yuan was right. I was hiding in my work. I hadn't given a single thought to my next transfer, because the whole idea scared me. I knew what I had to do—and I knew I wouldn't do it."

Azevedo waited, one hand spread over her lab notes, the other resting on his knee. When she didn't go on, he prompted, "And what do you have to do?"

She couldn't read a thing in his nager. So she took her courage in hand and said, "No matter what, you would be giving me my next transfer. But I've decided you're going to take moondrop with me, and be Gen to me. Not after the baby is born. Now. *This* transfer is going to be *it* for me. I'm not hiding anymore."

"You'd sacrifice your child—"

"No! *I* will take K/B! Azevedo, the preliminary tests show that it *is* absorbed onto Gen brain surface, molecules fixing themselves in a definite array. My work has shown that K/A fixes onto Sime fetus placenta, inhibiting or even cutting off selyn flow to the fetus. *That* means K/A is the abortifacient fraction of kerduvon. There might be other chemicals in it that contribute to that effect, so I'm opting for pure K/B, which my theory says must be the disjunctive agent."

"And what if the impurities contribute to or control the disjunctive effect?"

"You said yourself it works better, safer, when it's purest."

"That has been our experience," he conceded, but argued, "but there's no reason to do it now. We can save this as a last resort, continuing the research to improve our understanding. I've sent another messenger to Mairis—while you were so ill. The security cordon was so tight she couldn't get through at all. Rumor is that a big Diet attempt on Mairis's life is cooking. So I sent a messenger to your father. Sat'htine can surely find us a Farris expert who can handle your case. We've been lucky so far you haven't suffered complications. Why try to precipitate them? I'd have a hard time facing your father's expert if I'd participated in a drug experiment with you—and made matters worse."

They argued for hours, but Laneff was adamant, the fire of her new vision of herself driving her. She'd never felt so sure about anything before. But Azevedo, too, was intransigent. She'd never thought to meet up with such entrenched scientific orthodoxy in the midst of a gypsy camp.

At last, she stood, gesturing with hands and tentacles as she paced. "You're not the only channel in this outfit trained to handle that stuff, and there are Gens who know how, too! I'm not going to be stopped this time!" She started toward the lab door.

He called after her, "Whatever you do, *don't* try to involve Yuan in this. He has the nageric power, but a total lack of the control necessary. He'd leave you both insane."

If, she thought, *K/B itself is responsible for the hallucinations—which hasn't been established.*

Frustrated, disconsolate, she stalked out into the halls to walk off the spurt of fury that had built when Azevedo had denied her. *I feel betrayed. It's nonsense. He'll do my transfer—even if only his way. And he thinks he's not Tecton! Ha!*

She realized she knew not a soul she could go talk to. She regretted not paying more attention to the language lessons, trying to develop contacts among the other sudents. And her feet knew only one path through the sprawling building: the one to her apartment.

She found the newspaper outside the door. She usually had no time for it, but she took it inside and threw herself onto the floor cushions in the sitting room to read. All the news seemed strange, continuations of events she'd never heard of. But when she got to the back page of the world political news, she stared.

Mairis's face leaped out of the page, paired with the photo of a woman she'd never seen before. The caption identified her as Hajene Malry Remuns, a newly declared candidate for World Controller. She was calling people to come back to traditional basics in Sime government, not to take risks with the world balances achieved at such great cost to our ancestors.

She wasn't opposing Mairis directly. He never mentioned her in the interview published with the pictures. But they stood for opposite paths. With a shock, Laneff realized the election was barely a week away now. And the published polls suddenly indicated Mairis was trailing Remuns by nearly 20 percent.

In a sidebar, Laneff found itineraries for the two candidates. The day after tomorrow, Mairis would be touring the Embankment—the Sime/Gen mixed-law experiment. *Here! The day she ought to be having transfer.*

She punched up the newspaper service on her own screen and discovered that the parade route of Mairis's tour would pass right by their court. There was no mention of Shanlun.

I have to see Mairis. He has to know about Shanlun, and the baby—even if none of us survive.

Visions of herself being shot crashing his security lines

danced through her head, but she dismissed them. She grabbed up the paper and plunged out the door, heading down to the lab to find Azevedo. *This changes everything!*

Her path through the front lobby was blocked by a surging crowd of gypsies knotting themselves around the front door. Somewhere among them, she caught a whiff of Azevedo's nager, and as she squirmed toward it, her senses keen with need, she sorted through Azevedo's formidable nager and found—*Shanlun!*

She leaped ahead, breasting the crowd, leaping up and down to cut a path, yelling with the rest of them, "Shanlun!" She flung herself into his arms.

He staggered back under her weight, and she realized he'd lost a lot of weight. Her hands found something under his shirt, and zlinning, she discerned a huge scar running across the backs of his shoulders—a burn scar.

It barely registered in his nager, which was replete, sparkling pyrotechnically with relief, joy, anxiety, tension, and even—Laneff drew back surprised—overtones of guilt.

When everyone had said their welcomes to Shanlun, Azevedo had Yuan summoned, and they all met in the privacy of Azevedo's office.

Yuan came in as they arrived, embraced Shanlun, and said, "I've never been so glad to see someone! You've got to tell us all what happened to you!"

But Laneff sensed a reservation in Yuan that distressed her. The two men had never been friends, but—and then it dawned on her. Why had Yuan nursed her, when he was the one who required nursing? Hoping that her affection would turn from the presumably dead Shanlun—to himself? Of course, then he wouldn't rejoice too much if Shanlun turned up alive. *Could I have been so blind? Or did Yuan hide it so well?*

He wasn't one to put the pressure of his emotions off onto another. He'd been willing to wait patiently for her. Her heart went out to the man, and her whole being turned from hurting him. Yet the presence of Shanlun filled her with rising hope flooding upward against the downward tide of her own increasing need.

Shanlun would work the disjunction with me, no matter what Azevedo says. And afterward . . . She remembered how Shanlun made love into a celebration of life.

Azevedo served trin tea all around, his nager trembling as he neared Shanlun. He let his tentacles linger over the Gen's fingers as he gave him the glass of hot tea in its wicker holder. Shanlun let his eyes close raptly at that touch, then met the channel's eyes and nodded, "Soon."

Azevedo, she realized, had been severely shorted in his last transfer, repeatedly losing Shanlun after anticipating him. He'd be ready for Shanlun about the time she would have to seek transfer. She chided herself for regarding Azevedo as a rival; what had she to offer Shanlun? And Shanlun, with that nager, could serve them both without ever noticing!

The byplay did not escape Yuan. He strove to mask his disappointment, and Laneff understood that he'd been anticipating serving Azevedo. *He doesn't realize he was inadequate, just as Jarmi didn't!*

Azevedo took his tea and folded himself cross-legged onto the cushioned platform amid the arc of plants, under the skylight, as they took places all around at his feet. He said, "So *you're* the one arranged for Mairis to come here!"

Shanlun asked, "Have the marshals come here already?"

"No. You know they'd never get through the alley! The tribes would never let Tecton officials in here, regardless of local law. The marshals will have to content themselves with sealing us in here for that day."

Shanlun sipped tea. "Do you think you could talk the tribes into letting Mairis in here? I've told him everything about Laneff. He wants to zlin her condition and then leave someone here with her; he's not sure who yet. It depends on her."

"He could even give her transfer," mused Azevedo.

"No!" said Laneff. *He can't work kerduvon!*

Shanlun raised an eyebrow at her in silent query, but Azevedo answered. "There has been—an event—while you were gone."

Azevedo and Yuan looked to her, and Shanlun followed their gaze, frowning, head tilted, hands held in the gypsy position of inquiry. In his rough gypsy traveling clothes, he still looked gypsy, not Tecton.

The silence stretched until Laneff said, "I—killed—Jarmi."

"Oh, Laneff!" Shanlun cried in sympathy. He set aside his glass and came to her, enfolding her in his arms, his cheek next to hers. His nager was politely neutral, not engaging with her needing body at all, yet soothing, and carrying the honest throb of sorrow he felt. Then he sighed, pulling away, kissing her forehead. "I should have seen that coming. She was too eager and lacked the strength of discipline."

Azevedo said, "Yuan and I also felt our part of the responsibility for it. But Laneff has suffered the most."

Shanlun resumed his seat, asking the channel, "But the baby is all right?"

"Couldn't be better, though I'm glad you're here to coax her to eat! She argues too much with Yuan."

Shanlun flashed the other Gen a brilliant smile, and Azevedo told how Yuan had put aside his own injury to care for Laneff, and Yuan told his side of the tale from when he woke under branches near the burned-out farmhouse to when he arrived at Thiritees, ending, "So now it's *your* turn! What happened to you?"

"Oh, I was the one who covered you with those branches, and then I went back to see if I could save anyone from the fire. Only a few of the Diet got away. I got one woman out of the fire, but she was dead. I passed out from smoke, and the next thing I knew, I was in the back of a truck, a Diet prisoner. When they camped for the night, leaving me for unconscious, I escaped, flagged down a car, and rode to the nearest town. I was going to call—either one

of our locals, or even Mairis's private number. But I
passed out again on the street. Woke up in a hospital, and
they identified me by fingerprint and retina scan.

"Mairis sent a squad for me, and they squashed the
news coverage under his security blanket. I tried three
times to get word to you, but I didn't want to take any
foolish risks, and . . ." He shrugged a gypsy shrug.
"Azevedo, I've never seen anything like this. I had to
escape from Mairis's traveling team."

"He wouldn't let you go?" cried Laneff.

"He didn't have the authority to! The World Controller's
Security has taken over. There've been innumerable attempts on Mairis's life. It's quarantine to go near him!" He
smiled tightly. "He didn't think I could get away. Now
I've almost no way to get word to him until he shows up
on our doorstep. He plans to stop the cavalcade right in
the street out there, and spontaneously—at random—
investigate our dwellings here."

"You told him—about Thiritees?" asked Azevedo.

"Just what Digen knew, and that Laneff's here."

Azevedo ran fingers and tentacles through his thick
white hair. "I don't see any way to convince the tribes to
let him in; but I'll have to try."

When Shanlun and Laneff were alone with Yuan in the
apartment, Azevedo off in conference with the leaders of
the surrounding tribes, the inevitable moment came when
Laneff had to relate to Shanlun all the details of what had
happened with Jarmi. Yuan told of her illness, and she
hardly recognized the story from his point of view.

Hurting, as if he himself had killed, Shanlun wrapped
her in his nager and said to Yuan, "Thank you. I'm so glad
you managed to get here."

"Yeh, but what will Mairis think when he zlins my
presence? He's not likely to miss it, you know!"

"I've told him all about you. You may be in trouble with
Tecton law for kidnapping Laneff, but Mairis is on your
side because you kept her alive and well. With his backing,

the legal problems can be straightened out, though I don't know if the Tecton will want to put you back to work as a First!"

Yuan frowned. "Shanlun, I'm *not* Tecton. I don't want to go back. And I honestly don't care *that*"—he snapped his fingers in the gypsy manner—"for Tecton law!"

Shanlun eyed him levelly. "You're feeling defiant because you're overdue for transfer, and I just came along and took your best prospect away."

"Mairis himself couldn't make me feel Tecton!"

"I know," answered Shanlun kindly.

Fuming, Yuan said, "I'll go make dinner."

Then Laneff had to tell Shanlun of her progress with kerduvon, and her plan to use K/B on herself. "And that's what we're going to do. Azevedo said you know how to use it."

"That's an insane plan!"

"Anything else is insane, too. You've never been junct. What do you know!"

Shanlun squeezed her shoulders. "No hysterics. Listen, there's no reason to contemplate desperation yet. At least not until after Mairis can examine you—and after I've taken care of Azevedo. He's in no shape to do such a high-tolerance job right now."

"And what can Mairis's examination tell you that Azevedo doesn't already know? That I'm junct? That I'm healthy for now? Shanlun, I want this baby—and I want to live to raise her!"

"And that's what Mairis wants, too! You don't know what he went through to arrange this meeting! His advisers say he's losing the election, and this stop isn't going to gain him any votes. With so little time left—"

"Then he shouldn't come."

"Do you honestly think *he* wouldn't? His own security won't be able to stop him. You mean a lot to him, Laneff, and not just for your project. For *you*. I asked him; he told me he'd be delighted to accept your pledge to Zeor, if you can survive disjunction. I told him he'd better mean that because I was going to see that you survive! He meant it."

How will Dad feel if I pledge Zeor? He'd lost members before, but never one of his own family. *But Sat'htine isn't really my House anymore*, she realized, and her father was Sectuib enough to recognize that kind of personality change.

Shanlun kissed her lightly, aware that she couldn't respond sexually. She let her tentacles ease onto his arms, hyperconsciousness overtaking her. His nager responded gently, masking his core from her even at such close range. Carefully, without denying her the selyn she craved, he disengaged contact, and brought her down to duo-consciousness.

"Shan, I don't know if I *can* take transfer from a Gen. I'm scared of Gens now. They die too easily!"

"You can't hurt me, or Yuan, no matter what, so relax. This evening, you're safe. And tomorrow we'll face tomorrow."

"How gypsy!" remarked Yuan with mock scorn from the doorway.

"Yes, I suppose," replied Shanlun evenly. "But I don't know what I am anymore, or where I belong, except with Laneff. Anywhere with Laneff."

They ate the good food Yuan had prepared, and then Shanlun went off in search of Azevedo, admonishing Yuan to make sure Laneff got enough sleep. Laneff marveled that Shanlun couldn't conceptualize Yuan as a rival lover, and that Yuan had put all of that aside for Shanlun. *No matter what they say or think, they're both Tecton Donors to the core!*

But Shanlun hadn't been raised Tecton, and she wondered if his lack of jealousy was simply gypsy-Rathor. She didn't know, but she knew she loved him for it.

Shanlun turned up the next morning for breakfast, reporting that Azevedo had spent most of the night with the tribal leaders and was back there again this morning. She realized the gypsy tribal politics were as complex as any

Tecton hassle, and the Rathorites might be held in awe but they weren't bosses by any means.

Yuan was called to the infirmary where his Donor's training could help a Sime who'd been injured, and Laneff took Shanlun down to the lab.

Immediately when she opened the door, Shanlun fell in love with the kittens, who had become socialized through constant handling, though Laneff thought they preferred tentacles to fingers. Shanlun insisted on feeding the cat himself and then sat on the floor and fed the kittens with little drops of milk on the ends of his fingers. She watched, thinking of the way Yuan had virtually ignored the brood, and was reassured she had the right man.

Eventually, Shanlun peeled the last of the kittens from his shirt, put them all to nursing, and rose. "That's the most incredibly marvelous thing. Laneff, somehow, this whole mess is going to work out right!"

"Funny, that's just what Azevedo said when he saw the kittens, and I felt the same way. Illogical, but—"

"No, it's not illogical. Life has a certain symmetry, and when one can find the axis of reflection, lots of unrelated things form patterns that make sense. And that's an intoxi-cating beauty that's everywhere about us! Haven't you seen the candlebox yet? The symbol of Thiritees?"

And that led her into a discussion of her discoveries and her hypotheses. Just being within his nager cleared her head of the fog of need enough that she felt she was making some sense.

Azevedo found them there, having gathered Yuan from his work. "The tribes won't go for it. They don't pay much attention to World elections, and don't know who Mairis is other than Sectuib in Zeor, and they don't care." He shrugged. "I could have told you that last night."

"I was sure you could sway them," said Shanlun.

"I tried. It's going to look bad when they turn him away."

"But Mairis has never claimed gypsy support, and everyone knows we keep seclusion."

"Maybe you shouldn't have told the tribes," said Laneff. "Mairis could've slipped through before anyone knew."

Azevedo and Shanlun shook their heads. "That alley is guarded. No one gets in without being recognized!"

She looked at Yuan and remembered his arrival. He could have been tossed back out in the gutter. She wasn't sure she liked gypsies anymore.

Azevedo sighed. "We've got to get word to Mairis."

Yuan said, "Surely you could get through to him by phone, Shanlun. They know you're alive."

"His phone operators know me, true—but the call would be traced. I'm in trouble for leaving without a security pass, without waiting for a proper Tecton Assignment for transfer! Those paranoids will probably be thinking I've gone to spill state secrets or set up a trap for Mairis. Anything I might say would be interpreted in that light. Besides—our purpose was to get Mairis and Laneff together." He nibbled a fingernail. "Azevedo, what exactly *is* her condition now?"

"You're not thinking of exposing her to that crowd! The streets will be full of people—even nondonor Gens!"

"Suppose she has transfer before Mairis gets here?"

"No!" Laneff objected. "I'm going to disjunct this time!"

Ignoring that, Shanlun asked, "*Would* she abort off a Gen?"

The channel had zlinned Laneff deeply on many occasions. "Maybe," he admitted. Then to Laneff, he added, "Not as big a possibility as you think. The baby is draining you. You're a mother. You'll do what you must for your child to survive."

"I could do the transfer," said Yuan. He overrode objections to add, "I know I botched it the first time, but I'd do a lot better this time."

The similarity to Jarmi's attitude put Laneff off at once, even not considering that Yuan couldn't handle kerduvon.

"No. Please, no. Azevedo, can't a renSime get channel's transfer around here without begging for it?"

"I told you, if that's what you really want, it's available for the asking, and gladly given."

"So I'm asking, but I'm also insisting on kerduvon and K/B. I've made up my mind."

They didn't argue, but she felt their adamant refusal. And she was afraid Yuan would offer to try it. At the moment, she could decline. But would she be able to resist him later?

That evening, Azevedo went again to the tribe leaders, insisting the effort was doomed, but trying anyway.

Shanlun went with Azevedo for their transfer appointment. Laneff spent the time pacing and fretting. She'd had another go-round with the adamant channel and Shanlun. Where they'd been gently putting her off before, they were now insisting the entire thing was out of the question, and any self-respecting scientist should know that. As she plunged into real need, they weren't humoring her anymore. They were trying to control her firmly.

But I'm not a cripple who has to be taken care of! The thought surprised her. They weren't treating her a whole lot differently than she'd been treated all her adult life. And she'd always accepted it without question before. *And it always got me in trouble!*

Meanwhile, the marshals arrived to sift the contents of the court buildings for assassins, found they couldn't gain admittance even to the courtyard, swore lustily in several languages, and finally settled for the cordon that Azevedo had predicted, sealing them all into their dwellings until the cavalcade had passed.

This didn't sit well with the other gypsy tribes. Within hours, several harassing incidents had been directed at the marshals stationed at the mouth of the court: a bucket of dirty water—or worse—slopped onto them; the dogs got loose and bowled over two of them before gypsy children rounded them up, accidentally downing more of the mar-

shals in slippery dog leavings; and then windows opened
all around the court and gypsy music filled the air, several
different pieces played at the same time, as near as Laneff
could tell.

In the first three hours, the entire troop of eight marshals was changed three times, but they were sure their
cordon held. Meanwhile, gypsy commerce continued over
the rooftops and through the Ancient sewer accesses. The
marshals, native to the Embankment, veterans of dealing
with gypsies, knew their efforts were futile as well as
unnecessary. But orders were orders.

By the time the cavalcade approached in early afternoon,
the gypsy adolescents were in the spirit of things. The
courtyard, ordered cleared by the marshals, teemed with
disorderly youth, dancing to the music, creating confusion.

Yuan, Azevedo, and Shanlun were watching from an
upper window with Laneff. Shanlun's field was rock-bottom,
lower she thought than after a transfer with Digen. And
Azevedo seemed in a fine mood. He commented, "They're
trying to make the place as unappealing to Mairis as
possible, hoping he'll just skip the stop."

Shanlun said, "If we could get him away from Security
we could bring him in any number of other ways."

"That might be possible tomorrow, if he's still in town."

"He won't be," said Shanlun morosely. Then, straightening, he said, "I'm going down there and crash that line.
The worst they can do to me is fine me for deserting my
post, escaping arrest, maybe disturbing the peace!"

Laneff had prepared for this moment. She wanted to
see Mairis—to have her pregnancy checked out. She wanted
to tell Mairis all her discoveries, but not without proof.
Not while she stood junct.

Azevedo had had his transfer, and a splendid one if she
was any judge. *There's no reason now not to do it.*

From the capacious pockets of her beige smock, she
produced the two small vials of liquid she'd prepared, one
of the purest moondrop, Azevedo's own synthesis; the

other her own K/B, purified and dissolved. As Shanlun turned from the window, she uncorked the K/B and downed it in one gulp just before Azevedo struck the vial from her hand with one tentacle.

"Laneff!" he cried, horrified. "Not here! Not like this!"

The two Gens added to his cry. She tossed the remaining vial, neatly labeled, to Azevedo. "Let Mairis be turned away now. We can find him later, and see him officially!"

Azevedo frowned at Shanlun, saying cryptically, "There's no blackroom prepared!"

"The lab's windowless," said Shanlun. Then, "The kittens! Yuan, don't ask questions, just run and get those cats out of the lab. Make sure you leave the lights *off!*"

Laneff began to feel a little woozy and looked about for the hallucinations to begin, to confirm her theory. But there were none, and she was beginning to be scared.

Yuan's nager itched with puzzlement as he sidled past Laneff. She tried to scratch his itch with a tentacle. The poor Gen was in such a hurry, he hadn't time to scratch his own nager. *If this stuff doesn't work, I'll never get another chance to scratch him.*

Azevedo caught at her hand, his tentacles made of clear blue sparks. They hurt where they touched.

She flinched away, impatient for the confirming hallucinations. It had surely been nearly two hours since she'd swallowed the stuff. The sun was shining directly into the window; the brightness was unbearable, and it was increasing rapidly. *The sun is falling!*

There was panic in Yuan's nager now as he fled past her. *He knows, too. The sun is falling!*

Suddenly, it was unimportant to wait for the hallucinations to begin or for the chemical to make her sick. People had to be warned.

With a mighty tug that nearly unrooted one of the tentacles Azevedo was holding, she broke away and pounded after Yuan, augmenting with all her strength.

Giddy, she flew down the stairs, crashed through the

gawkers piled around the front door, and tore through the whirling dancers in the courtyard, shouting.

They took her for part of their game of deviling the marshals and collected around her as she ran at the cordon. Behind her, Azevedo, far outdistancing Shanlun, was gaining. Then she was in the alley. The cordon of marshals had their backs to her, the tumultuous noise of the gypsies masking Laneff's approach.

She breasted the cordon, the slightness of her body fitting cleanly between the shoulders of two burly Gens. The two Simes on either side of the Gens reacted fast enough to get a tentacle hold on Laneff, but Azevedo hit the line at that moment, and three of them went sprawling, dragging Azevedo down with them.

The swarm of children fell on the marshals, laughing gleefully, but she didn't pause to watch. She plowed into the standing crowd, shouting in every language she knew, "Hurry, hurry. The sun is falling! Tell everyone. The sun is falling!"

It was already so bright that she couldn't see. She was certain her optic nerve had been destroyed. But zlinning, she made her way along the street, leaving astonishment ringing behind her. She thought surely the weight of that rising astonishment would buoy the sun up long enough for everyone to find safety, as she would.

Running, shoving, she cut across the line of bedecked cars creeping along with their waving dignitaries. She spooked an honor guard's camel mount and made it out a side street. Here she had the sidewalk to herself.

Running under high augmentation, she barely felt need against the euphoria of hunting mode. People began to pour into the street behind her, spreading her message by their shouts, and the shouts themselves rose like doves carrying blue ribbons of peace to the warring heavens. And it seemed the sun was slowing in its fall!

She was glad she'd seen it in time; perhaps humanity

had a chance after all. She ran. She didn't know the city, but something about the place seemed familiar.

With the Simes on her heels, gaining on her again, she beat a jagged path toward that familiarity, wondering when the hallucinations were going to begin. But that hardly mattered if the world came to an end before she had a chance to disjunct.

She came out of the narrow streets fronted by a thick-walled stone building into a huge, flat, round area, grassy fields and a few scattered trees, benches, strolling couples.

In the center of the area was a dark stone monument, a huge replica of the starred cross. The sun was falling right onto it. Yelling her message, she leaped over the plastic chain fences and ran up to the monument.

Sandblasters had been working to clean the monument, their scaffold on the ground, cables pooling about it, and the men themselves were gone. An open padlock lay beside the equipment, security forgotten as the men went to lunch.

The monument itself stood on the two splayed points of the five-pointed star, the fifth point shooting straight upward. The equal-armed cross, carved out of the same solid piece of pink granite as the star, was suspended in the air just high enough for people to walk erect under its bottom flange.

Laneff's plunge carried her into the exact spot where she had once stood while her name had been inscribed on this very monument, the Monument to the Last Berserker.

The memory of that day rose crystal-clear, and the wrenching thrum of her oath to be the Last Berserker seared through the veil of insanity. She found herself standing, cold, in the midst of the plaza, unaware of how she'd come there save that *this* was the moment her life had been focused on, the moment of the Last Berserker.

The long run under augmentation had sharpened her need to the pitch it had held at First Need. There were Gens about, alarmed now by the sudden appearance of a haggard Sime gypsy. One or two of them were Donors, aware of her need and moving automatically to her aid.

No! No matter what, I won't kill! No matter how much I want it—I won't! But she was only a renSime. Her resolve meant nothing before the relentless onslaught of physiology. A woman cannot resolve not to give birth; a renSime cannot resolve not to kill.

The swarm of pursuers boiled from the outlet of the street she'd raced down a moment before. With an anguished cry, she seized up one of the scaffold cables, yanked its looped end free of a bossing, grabbed up the padlock and with desperate, clumsy movements passed the cable around the narrow end of one of the star points that touched the ground. She wrapped the cable around her own body, twisted it through its own loop, and fastened the two grommets together with the padlock, ramming it home with a thundering snap. With her waning strength, and in the disorganized insanity of attrition, there was no way she could get loose to attack a Gen.

Safe.

She surrendered.

12

RENSIME!

Laneff fell into the sun, blinded by brilliance until all seemed black.

And after a long time, far in the distance, a tiny light blossomed. Instantly, like fireworks, echoes of colored reflections exploded all about the glimmer. She took heart in her aloneness and wanted to glow like the little light. She ached and yearned—and was kindled.

She felt the surge of will brighten within her, a smile. And then dots of brilliance danced all about her, herself reflected back a billion times a billion times. Dazzled, she twisted away, only to find more and more dizzying reflections.

In self-defense, she fixed on just one of those dots. It loomed larger and larger, took on individual characteristics, face, hair, peculiar little nose, wistful smile in a round face.

Jarmi!

She twisted away. Another face: red-blond hair, mustache, beetling eyebrows, sunburned nose, fierce joy. *Yuan!*

She fled. *Azevedo!* Another direction. *Shanlun!* A twist away. *Digen!* And again. *Mairis!*

She was surrounded in every plane not by just one Jarmi and one Shanlun, but by thousands of them, spinning around and around, shouting a babel of languages at her. She clenched her fists over her ears, squeezing her eyes shut, and dove into the black silence within her.

But it was a cubical house that twisted through another dimension; a tesseract within the soul. She sped by the light of herself into a cubical room walled round with mirrors. And she was a zone of quantum mechanical incandescence, converting the essence of eternity from one form to another, emitting excess energy in every plane and dimension.

Her emissions dopplered back at her as they reached the ends of reality. She saw herself reflected back at herself in a globe that was bigger inside than out. All alone, she thought she'd go mad. She ran and ran off to the wall at the end of the universe.

But she couldn't get there. She smashed into an invisible plate of mirror which reflected herself back at herself and reflected all that was behind her, making it seem infinity was ahead of her.

She pivoted and ran to the nether end of the universe. And again smashed into a clear wall and confronted herself— guardian of eternity that would not let her pass.

What do you want of me! she wailed. *Let me out!*

Look at me, was the answer.

She resisted forever. And after that, she looked.

Jarmi!

She looked into a mirror, and someone else looked back. But it wasn't someone else. It was the Gen who lurked inside of herself, buried but not dead, buried and eternal. It was like using a dental mirror to look at the back of a tooth in another mirror. She knew it was the inside of her own self, a self she could never see directly.

If I'd been born Gen, I'd have been Jarmi. I'd have done the same. Jarmi had considered herself a crippled Donor, and had spent her whole life limping, favoring that crippled side of herself so that when she finally did lean on it, it buckled under her.

The truth of self-knowledge was so painful that Laneff wrenched free of the fascination and fled, only to fling herself against yet another barrier. She looked at herself in this mirror and saw Digen. Or was it Mairis? Ferociously dedicated to a Cause: however necessary the Cause might be, however laudable the capacity for total dedication, the ferocity betrayed the true motive: escape from self-knowledge. *There's only one way to be safe from self-knowledge, and that's never to look closely at the people around you.* Digen had looked only at people's virtues; Laneff looked only to eliminating their faults.

Eliminate the kill and cure what's wrong with humanity. But what about what's wrong with myself?

She had to flee from that, to run forever, until she crashed stunningly into another barricade across infinity that was infinity.

Yuan!

Yuan hated the Diet for hating Simes, for fearing the kill when it was really themselves who were committing suicide. There is no such thing as the kill; it's only that Gens commit suicide. That was the basic tenet of Distect philosophy. The ultimate crime in the Distect was to use a Sime to commit suicide. But a self-destructive Gen just naturally ended up doing that. So the ultimate crime that Yuan hated was self-destruction. And she had never met a more self-destructive person than Yuan Sirat Tiernan ambrov Rior. The hate itself had turned on him and compelled him, like a junct in need, to destroy everything he'd built.

True, he never blamed anyone else for his misfortunes. But he couldn't quite see for himself that he himself was actually to blame. So he came out to squash self-destruction with the same ferocious dedication she herself pitted against eradicating berserkers.

I hate berserkers the same way he hates the Diet; I hate because I am a berserker.

Surrounded by herself in many guises, she understood herself and became one with herself, seeing her own face

superimposed thinly over the faces of others and knowing
that they saw themselves in her and were at one with her.
Keeping herself company, she was not alone.

A tremendous feeling of belonging, of Unity, overcame
her, more powerful than pledging a Householding. *We are
the same yet individual.*

And all of us are junct. She toured the walls of her prison,
greeting the multitudes gathered at infinity, channels,
Donors, donor Gens, and nondonor Gens, and renSimes.
All junct, all dedicated ferociously to self-destruction.

Junctedness, then, is not a property of renSimeness.
Self-destruction is a human preoccupation, and the kill is
our way of cooperatively doing that.

She relived the four kills that she had made, and from
this new perspective of *being* the Gen while also being the
Sime, she saw herself ripping savagely at her very substance to satisfy an inner lack that really couldn't be reached
that way: *like a hungry wolf gnawing chunks out of its
own leg!*

She looked out of the mirror at herself, long canine jaws
dripping blood that plumed selyn in a mist about the
drops.

She fled, but the echo of that vision was everywhere
until she fetched up in her father's arms, in his Farris
channel's nager so infinitely Gen. She looked up and saw
two crippled renSimes leaning on each other, trying to
pretend to be Gen, needing to be Gen to someone.

The grotesque image repelled her. She stumbled away,
confronting everywhere the reflection of her face with the
wolf's snout sticking out, dripping blood, her own blood,
her own selyn misting off to infinity.

She stared at the image that stared back as if in a
contest of wills. *No, that's not the essence of renSime, nor
the essence of me. It has been, yes, but it doesn't have to be.*

The colored-ball models of her two compounds, K/A
and K/B, floated into her vision, mirror images perfectly
suited to this infinite but limited environment. The uni-

verse was constructed on pairs of opposites that were nevertheless identical: channel/Donor; Sime/Gen; Actor/Reactor. Who was responsible?

She had seen how everything that had happened to her was the result of a decision she made independently and with full personal responsibility. But she had also seen how each event was just as much the result of the decisions others had made, independent of herself yet a reflection. Each of them in the scenario was both Actor and Reactor, each reacting to something that happened before.

She stood outside of time and looked at the events since her changeover/kill, and looked backward in time from that moment, and looked and looked to infinity. The reflections dazzled to infinity and beyond until she could go no further than some abstract First Cause, a Prime Mover whose Word began creation. God.

She saw those energies weaving down a Jacob's ladder of twined pylons that supported manifest reality, a brilliant gold current, a flood of pure undifferentiated energy that poked through the mirror-screen that surrounded reality and emerged as the tiny zone of phase conversion at the core of every soul, Sime and Gen alike.

She saw how channels were able to dam up this energy, refusing to let the polar-opposite Sime and Gen come into direct contact, to let the essence of life flow forth and celebrate the full unifying force of the Will of Nature.

But renSimes were unable to do this. The renSime would always succumb to the will to live, no matter the cost. The renSime could be the Force of Nature.

The Gens could choose to oppose that force, and die, or acknowledge their oneness with it, and celebrate life.

Each could choose, each was Actor and Reactor, each personally responsible, but none totally responsible. To change, they must change as a group. Yet to change as a group, they must each change first separately. Reflections within reflections, where all opposites were identical.

The dripping beast jaw that protruded from her face began to dissolve. She pulled herself up to her full height and, back straight, head high, she turned without haste and calmly walked away toward her new destiny, free at last of the fear that had made her flee.

She came to where the invisible barriers had always stopped her. The sea of reflected faces dimmed, thinned, and evaporated, smiling calmly back at her as they died away.

The barrier they had formed turned to gossamer and parted before her until she came to a reflection that had no reflection of its own, as if it existed in the instant of its own creation, before reflections could be bounced back.

Shanlun and Azevedo. More than just faces. Whole and complete bodies. Whole, complete nager, joined into Shanlun's scintillating pyrotechnic display.

They were dressed in emerald-green ankle-length robes that enveloped their bodies. Azevedo wore a headdress of three tiers piled on top of each other making him very tall, with folds of white cloth shrouding his neck and hair, exposing only his face to her view. Their sleeves were elbow-length, cut full and loose, exposing forearms.

Each wore a jeweled starred-cross emblem on his breast, and the emblems glowed preternaturally.

I never found anyone who required me for an enemy, Shanlun had once said.

Oh, yes you have, Shanlun. And it was me. But I don't want that to be anymore.

Let us change together, offered Shanlun, as always answering her unspoken thoughts.

Choices precipitate consequences, thought Azevedo. *If you would return to the real world with us, you must return as someone. You cannot be everyone when you dwell on the other side of the mirror. You must become only one of the people within you. You must choose which one.*

How?

By choosing the source of your life, replied Shanlun. His

headdress was a simple glowing green cloth draped about his head and down around his shoulders, fastened under the chin. He shook it back now, as a woman shakes back her long hair. *I've come to be that source to you, if you choose me*. And with the same shaking gesture of his head, he disengaged his nager from Azevedo's and stood resplendent, though pale beside the channel.

Azevedo added, *And I am your other choice*. His nager sparkled with the scintillating effect she had come to associate only with Shanlun.

Though separate now, the two of them blurred together. *They had transfer*, she thought.

Do I want to return to the real world and live without what they've had? For that bliss was not only forbidden to every renSime, that peculiar perfection Azevedo and Shanlun shared was slilbliss, unattainable by any renSime.

But then her new perspective took hold. There was no way she could evoke any trace of any sort of bliss in Shanlun. But Azevedo was like her father, a channel needing to function as a Gen, wanting very much to give.

She moved toward Azevedo. She zlinned no blocking or damming up of the life force within him. He was open inside, all the way to infinity. And at infinity, within Azevedo, whirled the vitality of Shanlun.

Remembering her years taking transfer from Tecton channels, Laneff knew that they'd be horrified at Azevedo. The Tecton channel presented the renSime with the pleasure his Donor had experienced at his previous transfer, modulated by the channel's Sime sense of relief from need. But there was no way any renSime could discern via the channel which Gen had provided for the channel that month. Selyn was anonymous in the Tecton.

The disgust that rose in Laneff was identical to the disgust she had felt when confronted with her own junctedness. *That anonymity creates and perpetuates junctedness*.

But Azevedo was offering her Shanlun in his full glory, plus all the Sime's own satisfaction modulating that glory.

She went for it, a decision that came from the very center of her new being. Perception and action were one.

She entered a cloud of scintillating powdered gold that whirled and coalesced into a brilliant sunfire, a swirling, boiling locus where the primal life energy of creation surged through into reality.

She was a dark aching void, frozen with need and aware that the need had passed into attrition. It was only a distant, dull aching that had nothing to do with herself. But the warm sun suffused her, melting her, surrounding her in gold dust fraught with happy rainbows of life.

And need returned, a shrill knife of voracious pain.

"She's coming around!"

Azevedo had a long-handled, snub-nosed cutter with which he snapped through the cable binding her. Her body slumped but Shanlun's hands caught and steadied her.

The numb cold of attrition left weakness behind, but need drew strength back into her limbs. The Gen left her on her own two feet and backed away, his whole attention trained on her. The channel, likewise, backed away until the three of them occupied the corners of an equilateral triangle.

But her choice was made. It remained only to force her numb body to stagger toward Azevedo, two, three steps, four; reaching out with her hands, tentacles spread, she let the brilliant, dancing gold draw her forward, seizing contact with his offering laterals, dragging herself upward as he bent to offer lip contact.

Need became intense pleasure, transmuted to ecstasy as the warm pulses of selyn flowed into her system. Suddenly, she could sense her body using selyn in little pulses, in a very characteristic rhythm all her own, a thuttering like her own heartbeat. The incoming selyn harmonized perfectly to create a new, syncopated rhythm to dance the joy of life.

Each pulse was formed of billions of tiny flecks of colored nager, sizzling with a thousand rainbows like the heart of a diamond reflected to infinity. She tasted and savored each one, letting it fill her whole being with delight. Each tiny little pulse expanded within her void and filled and fully satisfied her, only to be followed by a new pulse that filled her faster and satisfied a renewed and sharper need.

Faster and faster the pulses came until it was one continuous stream of molten golden joy warming and renewing herself. The pulses rose simultaneously from within her own cells, as if she were Gen, and from outside herself, given freely and in love for the joy of causing joy. And the given was received for the joy of causing joy.

Delight built upon delight, thrill upon thrill, not wearing out her nerves but leaving them more sensitive to the next surge of even more intense shared giving/receiving in the dance of life. It built and built to exquisite repletion that went on and on until she was wide open to her very core.

She was Gen, full to overflowing with selyn, delighting in the filling of need. She was renSime, thrilled by Gen delight. And she was channel, living and reliving the most ineffable experience in creation—or out of it. Slilbliss.

She was all of her Selves at once, dancing her love of life in syncopated harmony.

She came up out of it laughing, gasping, reluctantly letting Azevedo dismantle the contacts.

He shouted out a tremendous roaring laugh and picked her up and swung her full around before setting her on her feet again and hugging her close. "Oh, Laneff," he groaned. "Oh, dear God, you've learned to be renSime! That was so beautiful. Thank you, Laneff, thank you."

He was crying, almost as if he were post.

And she was crying, too, genuinely post. *I've never given a channel transfer before!*

Shanlun's field and arms came around them both, and he was laughing, too. He kissed her. Then he kissed

Azevedo on both cheeks. Then he kissed her full on the mouth and didn't want to stop.

She didn't want him to. It helped her keep and store up the feeling Azevedo had given her, and she had given him. *I am ren*Sime*!*

"Naztehr." Mairis's voice, Mairis's nager.

Shanlun relinquished the kiss, slowly, promising more later, and turned, cradling her in one arm while his other hand rested on Azevedo's shoulder.

"My Sectuib. May I present my wife. And my mentor."

Mairis zlinned her critically. Then he held out his hands to her, tentacles spread. "Step out of there for a moment and let me zlin you, Laneff. I can hardly believe what I sense here, though I witnessed it myself."

She stepped out, offering her hands confidently, for Mairis didn't zlin like a Tecton channel now. He was like Azevedo. *Endowed. What Azevedo did to me was a trick of the endowed channels.*

As Mairis examined her, she realized a dense crowd had formed around the plaza, newscameras mounted on trucks or newsmen's shoulders, crowded the front rows, held back by dark-clad security forces. A bank of microphones was already being set up right under the starred cross, the classic setting for a major news conference.

But the ambient nager of the crowd was dark, disapproving, doubting, rejecting—yet openly curious, excited by portentous events. Her senses were ultrakeen, the world vivid in both sound and color as well as nagerically. She had no trouble spotting Yuan, inconspicuous while standing, gypsy-clad, just three arms' lengths from the security cordon of the Tecton guards. As she watched, Yuan faded back into the crowd and was gone.

Mairis grinned at Shanlun. "Your baby's fine, and your wife is disjunct—again!" Then he turned to Laneff, flashing a grin toward Azevedo, "Will you stand with us now before all the world and show them what we can do—united!"

"Yes," replied Laneff.

EPILOGUE

On the very first day of spring, Tansy Farris was born to Laneff Farris ambrov Zeor and Shanlun ambrov Zeor, First Companion in Zeor.

By Householding custom, the wedding was held on the day of Laneff's next transfer, just after she pledged to Zeor through Mairis. But in defiance of Householding custom, the officiating channel at the wedding, Azevedo, was not even a House member.

The celebration lasted until dawn, when the small contingent of gypsies attending retired for their morning salutation.

"Aren't you going with them, Shanlun?" asked Mairis, watching as the buff-and-beige-clad forms left the pavilion that had been set up on the lawn at the World Controller's residence.

"With your permission," replied Shanlun, "my place is at your side, my Sectuib."

In the months since her disjunction, Laneff had come to appreciate the difference between Mairis and Azevedo. The Rathor channel was just too much—too potent—for any mortal to accompany for long. But Mairis was real, a flesh-and-blood, mistake-making, advice-taking person. Shanlun worshiped Azevedo, but he could live with Mairis. And she felt the same way.

"My permission for your presence is always granted. But I'll never hold you away from him."

"I know," grinned Shanlun, one arm around Laneff.

The guests had all left now, and workmen were cleaning up the mess. Laneff looked around at the aftermath, the glow of another perfect slilbliss transfer still warming her, and making her eager for her husband's bed now that she'd recovered from the birth. "Tomorrow, then, I can get back to the lab. I've only been away three weeks in all, and I'll bet I won't recognize a single report on my desk!"

"Not so fast," said Mairis. "You've got a series of personal appearances to make first. If we're finding this hard to believe, imagine how those who've never zlinned you disjunct and healthy are taking it?"

"But—" protested Laneff, having forgotten she'd agreed to travel. "Not *yet*—not *now!* There's so much to do—"

"Laneff," replied Mairis, "do you remember how hostile that crowd was around the starred cross? Until you and I stood up there and *showed* them your disjunction, there wasn't a single vote for me in that audience. And then there wasn't a single vote against me. The lesson: a Sime has to zlin things for himself. We're going to lose this chance at Unity and our funding if we don't get you out on tour."

"We'll take Tansy with us," said Shanlun, glancing at Mairis.

The World Controller said, "Of course you can go."

"You see?" said Shanlun to Laneff. "That way you can be sure we'll be back for Mairis's transfer, and then you can get to work."

She glanced from one to the other, sensing conspiracy, but there was nothing else she could do. Mairis would give her transfer—and Shanlun's selyn—even if he had to chase them around the world to do it.

There are no certainties in life. There never have been. There never will be.

She wasn't sure she was going to like her new life, but it was better than anything she'd ever dreamed; a good reflection of her current self.

In the not-too-distant future . . . the human race begins to mutate. Generally unnoticed, some normal-appearing adolescents start to produce extra quantities of selyn, a biologic energy—becoming Gens. Then others, upon reaching puberty, suddenly sicken, change, and become Simes. They possess an extreme empathy and the ability to sense or zlin nagers, the fields generated by selyn in motion. Simes *need* the selyn to live—and at changeover, and once a month thereafter,

DATES	STORIES	PREVAILING SIME/GEN RELATIONS
−700		Period of warlike coexistence. For several centuries, since Gens developed gunpowder, world has been partitioned into many setteled Sime and Gen Territories. Neither half of the mutation sees the other as human. In Sime T., drugged Gens are raised in pens and on Genfarms; all Simes are junct (Gen-killers), and believe no other way is possible. Fear is rampant; no one knows until puberty if they are Sime or Gen. Sime T. children who become Gens are sold for the kill unless they escape to Gen T. Children of Gens who become Simes kill a relative or neighbor when berserk with First Need—whereupon the Gens hunt and murder the new Sime. Sime and Gen governments remain isolated from each other.
−500	FIRST CHANNEL*	
	CHANNEL'S DESTINY*	
	(COMPANIONS**)	
−450	(THE FARRIS CHANNEL)	
−20	AMBROV KEON**	Beginning of cooperation. Sime T.s merging; in most, all Simes outside Houses are junct. Though illegal, some people cooperate across borders. Growing Sime population approaches Zelerod's Doom, point when all Gens have been killed and Simes die of selyn attrition. Weather factors precipitate crisis. Massive group of displaced Simes raid both Sime and Gen T.; Zeor's Sectuib Klyd Farris takes over his T. government, initiates negotiations with nearby Gen. govt; they cooperate to eliminate raiders. First Contract signed; Modern Tecton promises Gens it will never allow ren-Simes to be driven by need, giving them channel transfer. New calendar established.
−15	HOUSE OF ZEOR	
	ZELEROD'S DOOM***	
YR ONE	(SHEN THE TECTON***)	

(. . .) BOOKS NOT YET WRITTEN, titles subject to change.

*by Jean Lorrah and Jacqueline Lichtenberg
**by Jean Lorrah

SIME/GEN UNIVERSE

they will find a Gen (any Gen) and take it. The Gens, terrified, die with their nerves burned out. Chaos follows, as civilization collapses, and the original humans disappear. Man is reduced to a nomadic existence; but, hidden here and there, isolated communities maintain certain bodies of the Ancients' knowledge. At least a thousand years pass . . .

CHANNELS AND HOUSEHOLDINGS // THE OTHERS

[CHANNELS & HOUSEHOLDINGS] Rimon Farris discovers he is a channel, a Sime able to take selyn from Gens without killing and transfer it to ordinary Simes (renSimes). Able also to promote healing and otherwise manipulate selyn fields. Takes a Gen wife (!); they discover that Gens *can* transfer their selyn directly to Simes and love it—the key is total fearlessness and a deep need to give. She becomes the first Companion (Donor). Only new Simes can switch from killing to transfer, going through agonizing process called disjunction. After several fatal experiments with Gens, renSimes in the community restricted to channel transfer. Zeth Farris discovers anti-kill conditioning for channels to further protect Gens. Zeth's son Del Rimon founds Zeor, the first Householding, Sime/Gen living unit sworn to one virtue, following a trade that shows the virtue to the world, bound together by vows to the Sectuib, best channel in the House. Farris submutation of extremely sensitive Simes and Gens is identified and labeled—they upset all generalizations.

[OTHERS] Gen Church of the Purity calls Simes demons to be destroyed. Sime raiders capture Gen T. people for the kill. Retaliatory Gen raiders murder in Sime T. Gypsies travel peacefully everywhere, making wickerwork and hiring themselves out for odd jobs; secretly, some are channels.
Rathor, hidden Sime/Gen community surviving since Ancient times, preserves and practices esoteric arts. Some members (the Company) travel with gypsies to influence history and to maintain Ways of the Starred Cross, escape routes from Sime T. for new Gens. Rathorites help give Zeor its protected, spiritual base of power to be handed down the centuries.

[C & H] Householdings proliferate, spread to other Sime T.s, spurring technological redevelopment. In Gulf T., Risa Tigue builds Keon as a business, involving juncts commercially and educating their children. First Tecton, barely legal organization of Houses. Juncts stage pogroms against these "perverts" in some places. Two things make Modern Tecton possible: materialistic force of Keon meeting spiritual power of Zeor, and discovery of Third Order channels.

[OTHERS] Hugh Valleroy, Klyd's Donor, gets to know Zeor but founds House of Rior. Foresees depersonalization of channels and Donors, objects to notion that Simes must protect Gens; supports right to direct Gen transfer for all. Starts Distect in oposition to Modern Tecton; most Houses, including Keon, join Tecton.

***by Jacqueline Lichtenbert and Jean   Chronology by Katie Filipowicz.
Lorrah.
All others by Jacqueline Lichtenberg.

Transition to nonjunct (never-having-killed) society in Sime T. For a while, pens retained. As older Simes die, only those who kill accidentally must disjunct. Gens become citizens. Tecton, civil govt and and selyn delivery system, spreads; first World Controller in 110. Most channels, Donors, and renSimes non-Householders. Gen T.s retain own govts, merge. Allow in Simes wearing retainers confining their tentacles. Sime Centers collect selyn, provide first transfer; new Simes then sent to Sime T. Acceptance is slow.

132	UNTO ZEOR, FOREVER	
152	MAHOGANY TRINROSE	
	(SILENT REPROACH)	

Peaceful coexistence and cooperation. Some cities straddle borders; inter-T phone calls; first student exchanges. Gens now fear losing jobs to physically "superior" Simes; prejudice still strong. Because of growing Sime population, last time when decision might be made to switch to direct transfer for all without precipitating new Ages of Chaos. Digen Farris, knowing Gen transfer is healthier, locks in the safer (for Gens) Tecton way for 1000 years.

224	"Operation High Time"	
232	RENSIME	
	(SIME FROM GEN DIVIDED)	

Beginnings of Unity. Digen's Gen T. PR campaigns create sympathy for Simes; Gens accept Simes wearing attenuators, devices to reduce effect of surrounding nagers, instead of retainers. Greater interchange of people; small combined-law zones; first common legal tender. Laneff Farris develops 85% reliable test to determine Sime from Gen before birth; no Gen rush to abort Sime fetuses. Gradual dissolution of Territory borders.

c. 1200	"The Channel's Exemption"	
c. 1400		

Interstellar travel; various groups, including Keon, emigrate. Meet races who have not differentiated as Man has, and one species which has. Tecton interstellar govt. On a faraway planet Yone Farris, not of Zeor, leads band of crash survivors in founding new way of life. Some centuries later, Klairon Farris, Sectuib in Zeor, discovers Yone's World, brings it into Tecton Worlds.

SIME/GEN UNIVERSE

[C & H] Schools for channels, Donors, renSimes founded; Rialite is first and best. Houses become non-localized corporations; living units broken up, member services spread out. Householding channels and Donors lose special privileges, become cogs in Tecton wheel. Tecton workers as interchangeable as possible, rotating assignments to avoid close relationships between Sime and Gen.

[OTHERS] Malcontents continue to blame the mutation on many causes, including biological experimentation, throwing suspicion on current medical profession. After Hugh Valleroy's death, Distect/Rior flees to mountains, rebels and is defeated at Leander Field, then goes into hiding.

[C & H] Intense training stretches channels to limit; development of 4+'s, channels and Donors of extreme capacity and sensitivity. High-level Donor shortage begins to destroy best channels; new machine-based training techniques alleviate problem at last minute.
Digen's daughter Ercy becomes first fully Endowed channel able to do psychokinesis and other "power functionals." It remains the Channel's Secret, that a few 4+ channels are so Endowed; though this is true evolutionary purpose of channel mutation, Gen T. not ready to accept such powerful Simes.

[OTHERS] Distect, still in hiding, places sole responsibility during transfer on Gens, leading to Sime irresponsibility; despise channels utterly. Turn terrorist under temporary Sime Head of House, seek to destroy Tecton; purposely blown up by own Gen Head, Ilyana Dumas. Mutation now blamed on Ancients' use of magic. Anti-witchcraft riots, legal execution of gypsies in Gen T. Rathor guards secret of kerduvon, drug which allows disjunction, and awaits Fully Endowed. Ercy, denounced as a witch, forsakes Zeor for Rathor. Later returns to give Zeor an heir. Rathor decentralizes, moving out into world from mountain retreat.

[C & H] Endowment remains a secret. Third Order channels and Donors common, sometimes allowed by Tecton to pursue other work.

[OTHERS] Diet, reactionary Gen terrorist group, fears further steps toward Unity. Conservative Sime opinion agrees things moving too fast. New resurrected Distect, heavily Gen, now works for Unity through ties to Establishment. Channels used as special physicians and judges of proper transfer matches between members. Sophisticated underground HQ. Decimated in private war with Diet.
Rathor maintains school and library in P'ris; keeps unofficial ties with Zeor's Sectuib. Kerduvon becomes known to the public.

[C & H] Endowed channels use abilities openly. Office of Sectuib purely symbolic. When Yone's way of life is accepted, Zeor disbands, its spiritual binding and protecting force no longer required by humanity.

[OTHERS] Simephobes still exist, some clustered on own planets. Distect active again, still illegal and members exiled if caught; a small group survive with Yone and contribute to the new way.

DAW

DAW BRINGS YOU THESE BESTSELLERS BY
MARION ZIMMER BRADLEY

☐ DARKOVER LANDFALL   UE1906—$2.50
☐ THE SPELL SWORD   UE1891—$2.25
☐ THE HERITAGE OF HASTUR   UE1967—$3.50
☐ THE SHATTERED CHAIN   UE1961—$3.50
☐ THE FORBIDDEN TOWER   UE1894—$3.50
☐ STORMQUEEN!   UE1951—$3.50
☐ TWO TO CONQUER   UE1876—$2.95
☐ SHARRA'S EXILE   UE1988—$3.95
☐ HAWKMISTRESS   UE1958—$3.50
☐ THENDARA HOUSE   UE1857—$3.50
☐ HUNTERS OF THE RED MOON   UE1968—$2.50
☐ THE SURVIVORS   UE1861—$2.95

Anthologies

☐ THE KEEPER'S PRICE   UE1931—$2.50
☐ SWORD OF CHAOS   UE1722—$2.95
☐ SWORD AND SORCERESS   UE1928—$2.95
